LEILA'S LEGACY

MADELINE MARTIN

All rights reserved.

No part of this publication may be sold, copied, distributed, reproduced or transmitted in any form or by any means, mechanical or digital, including photocopying and recording or by any information storage and retrieval system without the prior written permission of both the publisher, Oliver Heber Books and the author, Madeline Martin, except in the case of brief quotations embodied in critical articles and reviews.

PUBLISHER'S NOTE: This is a work of fiction. Names, characters, places, and incidents either are the product of the author's imagination or are used fictitiously. Any resemblance to actual persons, living or dead, business establishments, events, or locales is entirely coincidental.

Copyright Madeline Martin

Published by Oliver-Heber Books

0 9 8 7 6 5 4 3 2 1

CHAPTER 1
JANUARY 1349, BRAMPTON, ENGLAND

The great pestilence had come.

Lady Leila Barrington, youngest daughter to the Earl of Werrick, had seen it in her visions for as long as she could remember. Lingering on the horizon like a patient beast stalking its prey, growing hungrier, stronger, and more desperate.

She'd told no one of the things she'd seen in her mind. Not when the visions were so horrible, not when she'd hoped so fervently that time might cause them to change.

But the future had not altered. It had pressed upon Leila throughout her life until the visions came daily, and she knew the beast was about to pounce upon the unsuspecting people of Christendom.

And it did.

Leila tied the handkerchief filled with herbs around her face. The sage, lavender and mint crinkled as she secured the handkerchief, the dried bits of leaves and stems poking at her cheeks. Once the combination of such scents had reminded her of all things clean; now, the scent recalled illness and death. Isla, the healer at Werrick Castle, had wanted to soak it all in heifer's piss for good measure, but Leila had refused.

The older woman waited for her presently by the entrance to the castle with a similar handkerchief tied to her withered face, and a basket slung over either arm. She handed one to Leila as she approached, her sharp amber eyes narrowing from over the top of her makeshift mask.

"Are ye certain ye want to venture out today?" Isla asked.

It was the same question she asked every day.

Leila took the basket and replied as she always did. "There are people in need."

The basket tipped precariously, but Leila quickly steadied it. The flagon of water weighted one side more heavily, but it was by far the most important of the items they carried with them. Through all of Isla's and Leila's knowledge of healing, neither had found a way to heal the illness. No one had.

There was no cure for the great pestilence.

Outside of the people who sustained a random injury or non-pestilence illness, Isla and Leila had become little more than easers of suffering, bringing water and comfort to the dying.

"Ye shouldna be going out there." Even as she offered the protest, Isla turned toward the doorway to lead the way to the village. "Ye're lady of the castle."

"All the more reason to be there for my people." Leila followed her outside where the otherwise sunny sky was hazy with brown-gray smoke. It stung at her eyes and its acrid odor penetrated the sweetness of the herbs about her face. Ash floated in the air like light snow and sifted silently around them.

The ground was sodden, the dirt churned into a sludge that was as slippery as it was thick. Even with conditions such as these, they left the horses safe in their stalls. It was more than the fear of them falling ill that encouraged the ladies to keep them stabled. It was the very real concern that a villager so eager to try to escape the grasp of the pestilence would steal their lord's horse.

Sadly, a large number of people left their families. Wives were abandoned by husbands, aging parents were deserted by their grown children, mothers fled their sick children. The latter was the most difficult to happen upon. Dirty-faced children whose eyes were bright with fever, screaming in pain and fear, with no one to care for them. Those were the ones that most broke Leila's heart.

Such was the terror of the great pestilence: it overtook even a mother's love for her children. Extreme measures of escape, however, had been for naught, for the great mortality lay its shroud over the whole of Christendom.

There was no escape.

They neared the village with smoke rising from within, where pyres had been lit to burn the dead and their belongings.

"I dinna like ye doing this," Isla muttered from beneath her mask of herbs.

Many did not like Leila going out into the danger of the pestilence to aid others. They did not understand what it meant to her, how it helped heal the hurt within.

For all of her life, she had felt very much outside her family. It was not only her looks that set her apart from her sisters, her dark hair or the narrowness of her face. The sense of not belonging even went beyond her visions.

She had never felt as though she was worthy of the love her family offered. How could she, when she knew the truth? She was not a child of Lord Werrick's loins, but that of a marauding Graham reiver. The attack had nearly killed Lady Werrick, but it was Leila's birth that finally snuffed out her life.

It was why Leila had turned to healing. In giving others life, she was repaying the one she had taken. It gave her purpose; an action she could perform in a situation she was otherwise helpless to change. As though her support for others might put the violence of her making to peace.

"You put yourself at risk every day too," Leila reminded the old healer.

Isla snorted. "Death wants nothing to do with me, or I'd have been dead several dozen times over."

"Death will not come for me." There was confidence behind Leila's words, the same as there had been when she finally made the declaration of the incoming arrival of the pestilence to her family. "Not until I meet the Lion."

Isla slid her a wary look. The older woman didn't like when Leila brought up her visions of him. For it would not be the pestilence that took Leila's life, but the man with golden hair, bronzed skin and hazel eyes. A man who was as ferocious as he was beautiful. A man who would first steal her heart, then her life.

It was preposterous, the idea that she would love a man she knew would kill her. But was it not equally as preposterous that illness would consume the population of the world as readily as a spark set to dry tinder?

Leila shuddered as they stepped into the empty village. Under normal circumstances, it would have been a market day. But now where once there had been the bustle of people, there was emptiness; save for several bodies strewn out for collection. Where once people called out to bring shoppers to their wares, now cries of anguish and mourning pitched through the chilly air.

A woman moved on the ground as they passed, lifting her hand to them. "Water," she groaned.

It was not an uncommon sight, seeing those who dragged themselves to the filthy streets in search of water as Death reached for them. Before Leila could bring the flagon to her, Isla was at her side crouching with knees that popped in protest.

The woman's breath huffed in white puffs in the icy air. Her skeletal fingers clutched the flagon to her lips, drinking greedily then releasing it with a gasping breath.

"Thank you." The woman struggled to sit up. "My neighbors. We must go to them."

Isla assisted her so that her back rested against the wall of the hut they stood near. "Is it the swelling?"

From what Leila and Isla had gleaned from tales of travelers, there were two sorts of pestilence. One which caused swelling in the form of knobs of darkened skin that rose at the neck, armpit or groin, and one which covered the sufferer in a rash and made them vomit blood. Of the two, the latter was almost always fatal.

"'Tis the swelling." The woman brushed aside her tangled red hair and touched the side of her neck where the skin remained flushed with infection beneath a bump that appeared to be diminishing.

Leila breathed a sigh of relief. Thus far, they had only seen the swelling in the village. At least it was possible to survive that, even if the chances were higher for death.

"Ye shouldna be outside," Isla chastised gently. "'Tis colder than a witch's soul."

The woman's cheeks were sunken from her illness, and her pale blue eyes were bright with the effects of her fever. She had not been outside long for if she had been, she would not have survived. Not in the bitterness of the winter.

"There are children nearby." She pushed up as though she intended to walk. "I could hear them crying." She gazed out desperately to the small home beside hers. "I was trying to go to them."

That was all Leila needed to hear. She left Isla and the woman behind and hastened into the small cottage. The putrid odor of sickness within was like a slap, even with the facecloth of herbs covering her nose. Two skinny children lay side-by-side on the cot, their hands clasped together. Their wails did not cease as she entered, but instead continued even as they stared up at her with large, dry eyes.

They were emaciated, filthy, and obviously had gone too long without water if they were devoid of even tears. Leila rushed to them with her flagon of water. Fleas darted over the bedding, but she ignored them as she settled beside the children.

She called out to Isla and bent to offer the children water. They parted their cracked lips and drank with a thirst that hurt Leila's heart.

Isla appeared immediately and together they were able to get the woman, a widow named Rose, as well as the children, to the large hut that had been erected to assist those who had fallen ill with the plague. It was a way of containing the illness, not that it had done much good. But also, it was a means of having all assembled to offer the most care.

While the swelling pestilence had some survivors, there was an alarming number of people who entered the structure and did not emerge alive. Rose, who had insisted on walking without help, appeared to be in the healing stage of the illness and would doubtless be one of those who lived.

Once she and the children were tucked into pallets near one another within the pestilence hut, Leila and Isla returned to the village in search of more souls to aid. Every day it seemed there were more in need. As well as more stacks of dead.

An old woman scurried by them, her haste indicative of good health. "They're here," she hissed. "Hide yourselves."

Leila met Isla's gaze, but the old healer merely shrugged with equal confusion. The villager stopped and glared irritably at them. "Reivers." And with that, she was gone.

A hot wind of anger blasted through Leila. In this time of death and suffering, when all were losing so many souls, the marauders still thought only to take what belonged to others. She handed her basket to Isla and slid a pair of daggers from her belt. This was why she wore trews, instead of a kirtle, when she attended the ill, and why she was never without her weapons.

Whoever sought to take advantage of those within the village would not leave unscathed.

NIALL DOUGLAS CURSED the day the Keeper of Liddesdale made him his deputy. Granted, it was a position Niall had coveted, but he hadn't thought his duties would someday include stomping through a pestilence-ridden village in search of a witch.

And it had been a witch responsible for the illness, of that Niall was certain. There was no better explanation for the disease that had ravaged their land. He brought only five men with him, men who joined him at the risk of death and disease solely because of his reputation.

The Lion. Fierce and brave, honest and loyal, all things Niall had spent his adult life working toward. And it had led him to this stinking lot of land outside the opulence of Werrick Castle. The massive structure stood safe behind its protective curtain wall where the English West March Border Warden lived without fear of illness, with his witch of a daughter who nine years before had cursed the Armstrongs.

Niall put his arm to his nose to prevent the foul-smelling miasmas from transferring contagion to him. He had no dried herbs with him, or even a sponge of vinegar to protect himself from inhaling the illness. He would ensure he had at least that much next time. If there was a next time. If he survived this fool's errand for information.

He pushed his nose into the crook of his gambeson sleeve

and breathed in the musty smells of worn leather and dirt. The five men following did likewise. Mayhap it would save them.

He stepped around a body with a painful looking lump thrusting out from the skin of their neck and shuddered. Mayhap it would not.

There was naught within the village but death. Prior to their arrival, he'd been so certain of his purpose: seek out information on the dark-haired daughter of the Earl of Werrick. There would be many dark-haired lasses in the village.

"Water." A croaking voice pulled Niall's attention to an old man sagging on a bench, wavering forward.

Good sense told Niall to keep walking, but there was a deeper part of him, a thread of genuine kindness from his father that stilled his steps. He pulled the stopper of his flagon free. "'Tis ale."

The man's thin lips curled into a smile under the wispy strands of his beard. "All the better."

Niall handed the skin to the man who accepted it and drank in great gulping swallows. The villager sighed in satisfaction and held it out to Niall with a shaking hand.

"Ye can keep it." Niall stepped back from the flagon and the man, both likely contaminated with pestilence now. But he did not leave. Not when the villager might be good for information.

The five reivers with Niall held back, fear passing between them in side glances.

Niall wouldn't be cowed thus. Instead, he regarded the villager. "I hear ye had warning of the plague. Is it true?"

The man's gaze turned suspicious. "Ye want to steal our food stores?" He tightened his grasp on the ale.

Niall shook his head. "Nay, we've plenty of food. We're searching for the reason why the pestilence has swept upon us." And they did have plenty of food. For the first time in decades, no one complained of an empty belly. There was more food than they could possibly consume, for there were too many people dying.

"Tell me about the warden's daughter," Niall said. "Yer lord."

The villager blinked slowly, as though on the edge of sleep. "He's got several daughters."

"Ye know which one I mean." Niall spoke loudly this time in an effort to wake the villager.

The man's eyes blinked open. "Lady Leila."

"The one with dark hair?"

The villager nodded slowly.

Leila. Such a benign name for one who had sent the pestilence streaking through Scotland. But Niall knew better than to trust benign.

"'Tis rumored that she warned the castle, as well as the rest of her family, of the pestilence before anyone fell ill," Niall said. "'Tis said she knew it all, for she brought it. Is she a witch?"

The man's mouth curled up in a smile, revealing yellow teeth. A low whimper sounded in his chest and grew into a chuckle.

Niall folded his arms over his chest. "Ye think I jest?"

The man tipped the flagon to his mouth and drained the ale as he slowly dipped to the side of the bench.

Niall took a cautious step back, lest the man fall forward and touch him. Something flew in front of Niall's face. Exactly where his head had been. It slammed into the wall at his right with a hollow thunk.

A dagger jutted from the white-washed surface. A *dagger*?

Niall darted behind a cottage and pulled his dagger free. His body acted before his mind fully wrapped around the idea that someone in this death-ridden village was healthy enough to fight them. He peered out in the direction the dagger had come from. A tingle at the back of his neck alerted him to danger, and he jerked back as the next blade sailed past him.

He nodded to his men, motioning for them to go around the opposite side of the building. They would be a distraction while he moved closer. No villager would throw daggers at his head and live to laugh over it later.

He dashed forward, ducking behind buildings and abandoned carts as his men obeyed his orders. The clash of steel told him his men had arrived. No longer needing to mind his back, he ran toward the hut and charged toward the whoreson seeking to attack.

Except it was no bedraggled man fighting off all five of his warriors.

It was a woman.

A bonny woman at that, with streaming black hair and long, lean legs encased in red leather trews with a belt fastened over a loose leine. She kicked a lean leg high into the air and caught one of Niall's men in the side of his head. The man dropped like a sack of grain.

"Stop." Niall spoke the word with booming authority.

Everyone went still. Or rather, his soldiers did. The woman spun around to face him; twin daggers gripped in her hands.

The fierce set to her face dissolved for a moment, letting him glimpse the softened expression beneath. Delicate muscles stood out at her neck and her bright blue eyes widened.

"'Tis you," she whispered.

He lifted his eyebrow. While he wouldn't mind knowing the lass for a bit of bedsport, he'd never met her before.

He stepped closer and her face hardened.

"Be gone from here." There was a huskiness to her proper accent. English, of course.

"We're no' here for theft," he said.

Niall's injured man rolled to his side on the ground and slowly staggered to standing.

She didn't bother looking at Niall's reiver. Instead she

dragged her gaze over Niall as though sizing him up. "What are you here for?"

"To find the warden's daughter." He crossed his arms over his chest in an attempt to appear at ease.

The smirk of her rosy lips indicated she saw through the guise. "He has several."

She stalked closer to Niall with those daggers poised in her hands. Several more lined her belt; perfect for throwing, no doubt. Her hips swayed in a decidedly feminine manner as she stepped one foot in front of the other in his direction.

His men tensed, but he shook his head. He would not be intimidated by this woman. "She is called Lady Leila." His gaze remained trained on her to see if she reacted to the name. Mayhap she knew her. Mayhap she *was* her.

After all, he'd heard the warden's daughters were skilled in weaponry. But would the warden really send her to the pestilence-ridden village? With no guard?

If the woman recognized the name, she did not show it. She came to a stop and stared boldly at him. There was a sweet, fresh scent about her, like herbs. Sage and mint and lavender, or something of the sort. A handkerchief was tied about her neck, no doubt filled with herbs, presumably pulled down when she'd launched her attack. "Leave."

Niall squared his shoulders. "We want information."

"Are you not afraid?" She slid her daggers into her belt. "The contagion carries on the air. It's breathed in as an odor. Do you not smell it?"

Unbidden, Niall's thoughts wandered to the man he'd left on the bench. The villager had smelled terrible, of illness and rot.

"The man you spoke with is already dead." Her cold stare held his, ice-blue and veiled with thick, black lashes, slightly tilted at the corners like a cat. "Do you know how the pestilence strikes?"

Niall held his ground, as any warrior worth his merit should.

"As it works its way into your humors, it will heat your blood and carry a fever." The woman tilted her head in a pitying manner. "'Tis quite uncomfortable. I wouldn't be surprised if you were already growing warm…"

Niall gritted his back teeth against her words. His body had begun to heat after speaking with the man. His pulse raced with intensity.

"Your heart will bang in your chest like a drum." She curled her hand into a small fist and bumped it over her own heart. "*Dum*," she intoned. "*Dum. Dum. Dum.*"

The pounding was in his head now, thrumming an unmistakable rhythm of fear.

"An aching head comes next." She kept her ice-blue stare on him and pressed her slender fingers to her temples. "Roaring in your ears until you can scarcely hear."

He said nothing as her husky voice wound around him like a spell, saying aloud every symptom as he felt them.

"If you leave, you might still be safe." She turned on her heel and Niall's men's eyes went wide. "Otherwise, you will all soon be dead. Go." She tossed a glance over her shoulder at Niall. "Now."

He jerked his head toward the direction they'd come from, and his men immediately scrambled to obey his silent order to retreat.

"How do ye know me?" Niall asked.

The woman said nothing.

"Do I know ye?" he demanded.

She smirked at him. "Stay, then." She turned, putting her well-formed backside toward him, and strode casually away. "'Tis your death."

Damn her. And damn the whole bloody mission he'd had to accept in coming to the village.

He spat out a curse and went after his men. If they weren't on English soil right then, he would have hauled the woman off with him. For he knew without a shadow of a doubt in his mind that this woman was Lady Leila. Just as he knew with certainty that she was indeed a witch.

CHAPTER 2

Leila fought to keep her easy stride as she walked away, a feat difficult to do when her knees were soft with fear. She turned around the corner of a nearby hut and leaned her back on the wall while her heart galloped in great slamming beats.

The Lion.

That man had been the Lion. She gasped around the tightness in her chest. Remembering the contagion all around her, she hastily brought up the kerchief around her face to filter the air through the herbs. Her breath blew hot and humid behind the dry, prickling leaves and stems, but she scarcely noticed.

He had seen her. Talked to her. She pressed her hand to her chest, but the thrumming continued with wild abandon.

Was he there still?

Her body tensed with what she must do. The villager on the bench was most likely not dead as she had claimed, but he would be soon if she did not hurry to his side. Steeling herself beyond her fear, she carefully peeked around the building. No one remained, save the man still laying where he fell. Her legs almost buckled with relief.

The Lion was gone.

She slid her daggers free and cautiously made her way to the villager.

"They're gone?" he asked from his prone position, his words muffled.

Leila glanced around the surrounding area and saw no movement save for the billows of smoke and floating ash. The stink of it all hung in the foul air despite the mask she wore.

"Aye." She slipped her daggers into her belt and helped the man sit upright.

"They were asking about ye." The man wobbled and righted himself, the flagon still locked in his hands.

She'd seen the Lion give it to him. But why? No doubt to put the man at ease, to get him to talk. Leila assessed the man in front of her, his back hunched, his grizzled face lined in pain. "Let's get you to the hut where you can be properly cared for."

Leila was able to assist the older man to the pestilence hut, where Isla rushed about distributing teas to aid cool fevers and poultices to help with the pain of the swollen contagion. The woman they'd found earlier, Rose, refused to lay still and instead hovered over the children, whose names Leila had learned were Joan and John.

Once the man was settled into an unoccupied bed, Leila set to work assisting Isla and showing Rose how to care for the children.

It was late afternoon by the time Leila and Isla began the walk back to the castle. They changed in a spare room in the guard house, scrubbed their exposed skin and put their dirty clothes in boiling water to prevent bringing illness into the castle.

"'Tis getting worse," Isla said as they walked through the bailey. "Can ye see if it will get better soon?"

"My visions don't tell me." Leila scratched at an itchy red

welt on her wrist. There were two more on the back of her hand and several on her forearm.

"Aye, I know. I just hoped..." Isla drew back Leila's sleeve and tsked. "Ye're covered in flea bites. Come, I'll give ye an ointment to take out the itch."

"Nettle juice and calendula." Leila pulled her sleeve over the itchy bumps on her arm. "I have some in my room that I made the other day for this very reason."

"Ye'll be taking my position at the castle as healer soon, my lady." But the rebuke was given with a gleam of pride in the older woman's eyes.

"You're as much as a part of this castle as the stone. We would never get rid of you."

"I'm almost as old too." Isla's good-natured expression faded to one of concern. "I dinna like ye going to the village."

"You put yourself at risk too," Leila said, playing her part of their usual conversation.

Isla stopped and took Leila's hand in her cool, dry one. "Ye're a lady and ye're covered in flea bites, venturing into a village that has scores of dead lying about underfoot as ye tend to the dying."

"I'll be fine," Leila protested.

The healer narrowed her eyes and shook her head, saying nothing further.

"I'll be fine," Leila repeated the words again with certainty in an effort to offer reassurance.

And she *was* fine.

Four days later, however, she was not. She awoke to a slight stiffness to her joints and a mild discomfort under her right arm. By the time she dressed for the day, the stiffness had become an ache. Exhaustion pulled at her, drawing her back to her unmade bed, which she lay upon fully clothed. She had meant to be there only a moment when a knock came at the door and startled her awake.

Leila sat up to answer and a wave of nausea overtook her in a grip so firm, it was impossible to fight. She was sick upon the floor beside her bed, gasping for air from the violence of her retching.

"Do not come in," she cried out to the person on the other side of the door. "I…" Chills rippled over her skin with the words she knew she needed to say to protect those around her. "I have the pestilence."

The door flew open despite Leila's warning and Isla rushed in. "Nay, my lady." She ran to Leila's side and immediately pressed a hand to Leila's brow. The older woman hissed and drew her hand back as though she had been burned.

"My arm…" Leila shifted to allow Isla to pull back the shoulder of her kirtle and examine the pain in her armpit.

Isla gingerly pressed her cold fingers around the lump. Even such small proximity brought enough pain to steal Leila's breath.

"It is the pestilence, is it not?" she asked weakly.

But in truth, she did not need to ask. The answer was already in Isla's glossy eyes, in the way she pressed her fists to her chest as though the ache within was too great to bear.

Fatigue pulled at Leila, making her mind hazy and her limbs heavy. "You needn't worry." She spoke even as her eyes drifted closed. "I'll survive. You know why. Because of him."

"The Lion," Isla murmured from somewhere that sounded distant to Leila's ears.

The Lion.

His name repeated in Leila's mind, echoing in a chasm of pain and suffering that came in flashes of altered awareness. Isla had been there with her dry hands and the sweet scent of herbs. There had been another woman as well, one with hair as red as the flames licking at Leila's body. The woman was not fire, though. She was soothing; her hands cool like water, her voice a beautiful caress through the ugliness of pain.

They were not the only ones to attend Leila.

Death hovered near her, salivating like a dog gone too long without a meal, his breath snarling and ragged, huffing against her skin like ice. Leila stared into Death's vacant eyes and saw herself reflected in those milky depths. Death came closer and the frigid fog around his body left her skin prickling. Still, she was not afraid.

She had seen her true death far too many times to fear this one. An end by the pestilence was preferable to the one she had seen; the death she knew she would endure. At least her demise through illness would come without her suffering the raw hurt of love betrayed.

The Lion.

Water welled around her, so cold it froze the breath in her lungs. Panic splashed through her veins. She knew this vision and did not want it. Death could have her soul now. Not later. Not with the Lion.

Strong arms held her down, his face distorted by the churning water above her, roiling with the force of her struggle. She didn't need to see him when she knew so well what he looked like: the straight nose, those almond shaped hazel eyes, wavy blond hair falling to his broad shoulders, a strong jaw that bristled with golden whiskers.

Leila's heart caught in her chest in a tangle of horror and hate. And love.

The Lion.

The water cleared from her throat and Death breathed in her fear, feasting on her fragile mortality. He reached for her with a skeletal hand, moon-white in the darkness. His fingers caught at her shoulder, lingering before all at once, he slithered away like a serpentine night terror.

Pain replaced Death's presence, brilliant in its agony.

"Is it your shoulder?" a soft voice asked.

The question rattled through Leila's awareness. Was it her shoulder? Even as she wondered at it, she found herself nodding through gritted teeth.

A gentle hand brushed her shoulder. The discomfort began to ebb.

Leila blinked her eyes open in an attempt to see what had caused such horrible agony. A woman with red hair tilted her head and pulled aside Leila's nightrail to examine the blazing area. *Rose*. The name lifted in Leila's memory. She was the woman they had helped in the village.

The woman lifted her attention to Leila and a smile lit her face. "Isla will be pleased to know you have awoken. She has been so worried." Sadness touched Rose's pale blue eyes. "We all have been."

"What is on my shoulder?" Leila twisted her arm to better see what Rose was looking at.

The woman sat back. "Strange marks. It isn't from the swelling."

It was then Leila noted the lump under her arm, demonstrating the signs of recovery. The darkened knot had begun to lighten. She glanced to her shoulder and found five white dots, each about the size of a fingertip where Death had touched her.

Fear prickled a cold sweat on her brow. It was a message. A constant reminder.

The Lion was coming for her.

THE PRIEST HAD PISSED HIMSELF. Niall slid his gaze away from where liquid dribbled over the chair and soaked into the man's robe.

Alban Armstrong, son to the Keeper of Liddesdale, released the fistful of the cloth where he held the priest and gave an exclamation of disgust. The stench of the priest's urine mingled with the coppery odor of his fear and left the air in the narrow dungeon rank.

"Looks like ye finally found a use for yer prick, eh?" Alban drew his fist back and the priest scrunched his face in anticipation of the impact.

"Enough," Niall said. They'd had the priest in the dungeon for a full night already. Men of God were used to discomfort, aye, but not violence. No doubt the bald man had spent the time after the Armstrong reivers found him wondering if he was to be killed.

Alban narrowed his dark eyes at Niall's orders and shook his red hair from his eyes. "This bastard—"

"Enough." This time Niall said the word with a ring of authority. He wouldn't be challenged. Not even by Lord Armstrong's son. The whelp needed to learn his place in the order of things. Alban was not Keeper yet.

And when he was, Niall would sooner abandon the position of deputy than work for him.

Alban lowered his arm and gave a sulky scowl which Niall pointedly ignored.

"What's yer name?" Niall asked of the priest.

"Bernard." The priest did not relax from his tensed position, as though still waiting to be struck.

Niall kept his distance from the man in an effort to put him more at ease. "Where are ye from?"

"Oxford, where my father was a lord. If you kill me, it will be a declaration of war on England. My brothers all know how to fight. I never did. My mother—"

"Our kings dinna meddle in affairs on the border," Niall said, putting a stop to the nervous rambling. "Ye're a long way from Oxford, Priest. What are ye doing in Liddesdale?"

Bernard shivered and glanced around with fearful eyes. "Please don't hurt me."

"We'll do what we want with ye." Alban leaned menacingly over the priest, mindful to avoid the puddle of urine. "And ye best be telling the truth."

Niall lifted the Bible from the stool it'd been set upon when they brought the priest in from the nearby village. He handed it to Bernard, who accepted it with eager hands and hugged it to his chest as though it were a shield.

"Swear on it that yer answers will be honest." Niall nodded toward the Bible. "If ye do that, we willna need to hurt ye for answers." He cast a hard look at Alban.

Bernard nodded and clutched the Bible more tightly.

"Where are ye from?" Niall asked again. "No' Oxford, but where ye currently reside."

"Werrick Castle. I'm priest there."

Niall's shoulders relaxed somewhat. This is what he had been hoping for. When a scout told him that the priest had been wandering about the outskirts of Liddesdale, claiming to be from Werrick Castle, he had thought it too good to be true.

It was the first opportunity he'd had to speak with someone from the Castle since the day they ventured to its nearby village. Niall and his men hadn't returned, not since the witch cast a spell on them convincing them they were becoming ill with the plague.

They'd felt immediately better once they fled the village, after her power over them had dissipated.

'Tis you.

What had she meant by that? The question had circled in his mind as much as the lady herself. Those long legs in red trews, her glossy dark hair, the depth to her blue eyes. He clenched his fist. Even now she infiltrated his thoughts. Distracting him. Mayhap he was bewitched.

"Why are ye in Liddesdale?" Niall asked Bernard to take his mind from Lady Leila.

"I did not know I was so far north. Many priests have fled their villages to escape the pestilence and the ones who remained have all died." He released the Bible long enough to make the sign of the cross with a shaking hand. "I had been hearing confessions and delivering last rites to the dead. There are so many English and Scottish on both sides of the border that I did not know I had gone so far north."

Niall stared incredulously at the man trembling behind his Bible. A man he had thought to be a coward. "Ye put yerself at risk for Scotsmen?"

"All are souls in need of absolution regardless of their land of birth." Bernard lifted his head up a notch, showing an unmistakable bravery Niall would not have credited him with moments ago. The priest knowingly put himself in danger to help others.

Alban began to pace the room with a bored expression.

Niall ignored him. "We were told ye had warning the plague was coming. Is that correct?"

Bernard hesitated. Niall said nothing and let silence pressure the priest into speaking.

"Aye," Bernard answered at last.

Alban met Niall's eye. It was answer enough for Alban, who was ready to find Lady Leila and put her on trial. Niall, however, held himself to a higher standard of honor and wanted firm proof before he arrested someone on the charge of witchcraft.

A priest's word, especially the priest of the castle where she lived, would be ideal.

"Was it Lady Leila who gave ye warning?" Niall pressed.

Bernard shifted in his seat and Niall tried not to think of the discomfort of the man's wet clothing beneath him in the chilly dungeon.

"She's ill," Bernard said eventually. "With the pestilence. She goes to the village often to help others, to heal them. We feared her being around the contagion, but she insisted. We don't think..." He swallowed. "We don't believe she will survive."

"It'd be fitting if she didn't," Alban spat. "Considering she cast it upon us with her magic. She made it obvious by cursing the Armstrongs first. Families of the very men who took her several years—"

"Enough." Niall's voice echoed off the stone walls.

In truth, it did not surprise Niall to hear she had the pestilence. What better way to appear innocent than to suffer from the same affliction she had cast with her spell? That her own people had become ill as well had troubled him initially, but her determination to aid them brought it all to light.

No doubt her own spell had grown beyond her control, spreading out to hurt her own countrymen over the whole of England.

Witches had great power, more than even they surely realized. However, Niall knew well the impact of their craft. As did his father, Renault the Honorable, God rest his soul.

"Is Lady Leila Barrington a witch?" Niall asked abruptly.

The priest's eyes went wide. "I b...beg your p...pardon?" he stammered.

"Do ye think Lady Leila Barrington is a witch?" Niall repeated slowly.

Bernard's chest rose and fell quickly from behind the Bible, making it move with each frenzied breath. "She's different from her sisters," he answered carefully. "I was different from my brothers too. Markedly so. Like her. She feels alone, cast out from them, despite their attempts to make her feel loved and wanted. It is hard to be different. So, so very hard to be different."

The tirade had yielded nothing of use. If the man didn't hold a Bible in his hands, Niall would have assumed he was lying to get out of the questioning. The woman he met in the village outside of Werrick Castle did not appear to care if she was unloved or unwanted.

Niall crossed his arms over his chest. "Do ye believe Lady Leila to be a witch? Aye or nay."

Sweat glistened on Bernard's brow and he huffed in frenzied pants.

Alban stepped closer to him. "If he willna talk, I'll make him."

Niall held out a hand to stay the younger man. Bernard was still a priest, one who had put himself in harm's way to aid their people. He deserved their respect.

"I'll ask ye one more time, Priest," he said levelly. "Do ye think Lady Leila is a witch?"

Bernard swallowed and met Niall's gaze. "Nay."

Niall narrowed his eyes at the twitchy little priest, who shrank behind his Bible. Slowly, Niall moved back to allow access to the open door. It hadn't been necessary to close it. If the priest even tried to run, Alban would have killed him before he got to the entryway. Lord Armstrong's son was fast, Niall would give him that.

"Ye can go." Niall nodded toward the door.

The priest did not move.

"Now. Before I change my mind."

Bernard scurried from the room, his wet robe clinging to his flat bottom.

Alban stared after the man with contempt in his eyes.

"Why'd ye let him go?"

"We have all we needed." Niall left the room. The priest was nowhere in sight, having already fled.

Alban exited the dungeon and fell into step beside Niall. "He'll go back and tell them we're seeking the witch. We should have killed the coward."

Niall stopped and stared down at the younger man. "That 'coward,' as ye put it, was the only man brave enough to offer last rites to yer people when yer own priests were too frightened to stay. And ye'd kill him for having made the effort?"

Alban brushed aside a lock of red hair from his eyes, not bothering to reply.

Niall had enough. He climbed the stairs, eager to be done with the whole mess. It didn't matter if Lord Werrick knew they were asking about his daughter. If she was out tending to her people, Niall would see her again. They would have a scout watch the village and once she was seen again, they would find a way to lure her from the village and trap her.

Once she'd recovered from the pestilence. And she *would* recover; of that, he was certain. He was also certain of another truth: that even as the priest held his beloved Bible, he had lied.

Niall would notify Lord Armstrong, who would summon Father Gerard from Edinburgh, the famed priest who had sent many a witch to her death. The earl had held off as Niall did his own investigation to be able to say with absolute confidence that Leila Barrington was indeed a witch.

Now, with Bernard's lie souring in Niall's gut, he would stop at nothing to see her brought to justice.

CHAPTER 3

After a day and night of laying abed, Leila could not stand it a moment longer. Her back had begun to ache and every part of her was restless. If nothing else, she could at least help Isla sort items to make teas, or grind up herbs, or mayhap even work on the book of remedies she had been writing. Anything but this inertia.

She sat up slowly, her muscles weak after over a sennight of inactivity while she'd been ill. Rose was there in an instant.

"I must get out of this room." Leila pulled her feet to the side of the bed. "Please help me dress."

"Where do you intend to go?" Rose was already aiding her, despite her apparent concern.

"To assist Isla." Leila put up a hand before the woman could protest. "Not to the village, but to the small room she keeps in the castle. To assist with preparing what she'll need on the morrow for the village, as well as organizing other herbal remedies."

Rose's slender face had filled out some now that she was fully recovered from the pestilence. There was a lovely rosiness about her cheeks and her hair shone like copper with threads of white running through. She was a lovely woman, Leila realized for the first time, with pink apple cheeks and a kind smile.

She helped Leila first by running a cool, damp linen over her skin to clean her thoroughly, and then helping her into a blue wool kirtle with a red surcoat. The belt at Leila's waist needed to be linked more tightly to compensate for how the fashionable attire hung on her frame after the weight she'd lost during her illness. Over the gown, Rose had insisted on putting a thick fur mantle.

While Leila had protested initially, she was grateful for Rose's persistence once she was in the hall. The winter chill permeated the stone and left the halls icy cold. She kept a brisk pace, eager for the fragrant warmth of Isla's small room, where the woman usually had a small fire in the hearth to keep a pot of water set to boiling. The door to the room, however, was closed.

Leila leaned her back against the opposite wall while she waited and caught her breath. The journey down to Isla's healing room had been more laborious than Leila had expected. Not that she would ever admit such a thing.

The door opened, and Bernard stepped out.

Leila straightened in an effort to appear as though she had not been panting from overexerting herself. Bernard glanced at her, then immediately lowered his head and mumbled something she could not make out. With that, he quickly strode down the hall with an awkward gait.

A tsking sound turned Leila's attention back to the open doorway where Isla regarded her with a frown. "Ye shouldna be out of bed."

"I couldn't stand to lay there a second longer." Leila stepped past Isla and into the room.

"Ye and yer sisters are a heap of mischief. Ye know that, aye?" But Isla was not looking at Leila when she spoke. Instead, she stared off after Bernard, her face pinched into a map of wrinkles.

"Is Bernard unwell?" Leila popped her head out of the room to peer at the priest's departing form. It was strange to see him meeting with Isla of his own volition. He'd always been cautious of the healer, assuming her to be a witch, or figment of evil or something of the like. Every time she was near, he crossed himself and muttered a quick prayer. Isla had found it a great source of entertainment and took joy in goading him.

She was not smiling now though as she led Leila into the room. "The reivers took him. Armstrongs." She spit into the fire, where it sizzled amid the flames.

"Bernard?" Leila asked in horror. The poor man had always been deathly afraid of reivers.

"Poor bastard pissed himself." Isla shook her head, looking as regretful as she sounded. "Those robes of his chaffed his arse the whole ride back to Werrick Castle. I gave him a balm to ease the discomfort, but there's only so much I could do." She cast another sad stare back toward the empty doorway from where he'd waddled off. "'Tis his soul that weighs most heavily on him."

Leila covered her mouth. The poor priest; frightened to the point of making a mess of himself in front of the people who scared him most.

"He lied on the Bible, he said," Isla continued. "Fears his soul belongs with the devil now." She scoffed. "If every holy man who lied ended up in hell, there wouldna be room for the rest of us. Bernard is one of the few good ones, I tell ye."

Isla must truly feel bad for the priest if she was saying such kind things for a man she'd always reveled in tormenting. Leila discreetly lowered herself to a stool to ease the burden of her body weight on her tired legs. "What did he lie about?"

"Ye." Isla turned to Leila. "They asked him if he thought ye were a witch, and he said on the Bible that he dinna."

Upon hearing such news, Leila was glad she was sitting. "He thinks me a witch?"

"Bah, he thinks I'm one too." Isla waved without concern. "But they werena asking about me. They were asking about ye." She lifted an empty basket to the tabletop. "I dinna want ye going to the village anymore. No' even when ye're fully well, and even then, it would be best no' to go. There are mad men about, my lady."

Leila's hands went to work stuffing herbs into linen bags. "When I'm fully well, it will be the best time for me to go. I cannot get the pestilence again. We've never heard of a second bout."

"I'm no' talking about the illness," Isla said. "I'm talking about the man asking about ye. Bernard said the Armstrongs pulled him from the bedside of a dying man and put him in the dungeon to be questioned. They dinna even let the man get his last rites. Bernard shouted them as they dragged him off but worried it hadna been heard. The poor bastard."

Leila didn't know which man Isla referred to as "poor bastard" but didn't bother to ask. Not when it seemed quite applicable to both men.

"Bernard was questioned," Isla's voice was soft in the way people did when they wanted to be heard, "by a man called the Lion."

Leila sucked in a breath. The weakness she'd experienced earlier buzzed in her mind and made her suddenly dizzy.

"Ye shouldna be out of yer bed." Isla's strong grip caught Leila's shoulder, keeping her upright. "And I shouldna have told ye."

Her hand on Leila blazed in icy pain. The mark of Death on Leila's skin flew into her thoughts, as well as his message. The Lion was coming.

She would do well to keep from the village. And she did, for at least a fortnight. She remained within the castle where it was safe. But there were only so many times she could walk past the walls she was so familiar with. She remained within them until they started to close in on her and squeeze at her awareness, until thoughts of the villagers and their suffering pressed at her heart.

Isla and Rose still went out every day to the village to tend the scores of ill. Leila wanted to be there with them. *Needed* to be there with them. To be an extra set of capable hands, to prevent the likelihood of Isla getting ill. Especially when most likely, both Leila and Rose could not get sick again.

Bernard, who now did not ever wander past the village, had remained busy comforting and administering last rites. It was through his bravery that Leila found herself out at the pestilence hut once more, caring for the dying.

It was there, on the fifth day, she met a small girl who wore little more than a scrap of cloth in protection against the frigid winds.

"Are ye the healer?" the girl asked.

Leila crouched to be on the child's level. Her dark brown eyes were nearly hidden beneath a fur cap far too large for her.

"Aye, I'm a healer," Leila replied. "Are you in need of one?"

"'Tis no' me, but my mum. Will ye help her?"

"Of course." Leila straightened and prepared to follow the girl. "What is your name?"

"Ainslie." She took Leila's hand and led her, not into the village, but away from it.

Leila hesitated. "I cannot go this way," she protested.

"Please," she girl pleaded. "My mum is delivering a babe and there are no' any healers to aid her."

"How far is your home from here?" Leila asked.

"It isna far on a horse." The girl pointed to a beast tied to a tree at a nearby forest line.

"Where did you—?"

"Dinna tell anyone, please." Ainslie twisted her bare hands together. Her fingers were red chapped from the cold. "I happened upon it wandering around the fields and no one was about. I took it. To help find someone to save my mum."

Leila relaxed. It was not uncommon to find animals roaming with no master. The number of abandoned beasts had been so great, in fact, that many lords were foregoing heriot, their tenant's family's gifts of an animal to the lord when a laborer died.

Ainslie led Leila to a nag, most likely an animal left to fend for itself after the family owning it died of the pestilence. "'Tis over the border," the girl said sheepishly.

A knot of unease twisted in Leila's stomach.

The girl's large brown eyes went liquid with fear. "Please dinna say ye've changed yer mind."

Leila gazed out to the sprawling landscape before them, where winter had turned the grass to straw and sifted a fine dusting of snow over it all.

"She keeps screaming." The girl whimpered. "I canna help her. Please."

Leila set her shoulders. "I will go."

They climbed onto the horse's bony back and the girl led the way to the small hut on the outskirts of the debatable lands. Her immaculate sense of direction was not surprising. Most likely the child had been on at least one raid with her father at some point to the English side of the border.

Leila leapt from the horse, following Ainslie's eager steps as the girl pointed toward the hut. That disconcerting sense of uncertainty pitched to a scream of alarm. Leila shook her head in silent apology and clambered back onto the nag's back.

"Where are ye going?" Ainslie cried. "Please! My mum!"

If she said anything else, Leila did not hear. She was running the knobby-kneed nag as fast as its hooves would carry her. Only it wasn't nearly fast enough.

A prickle of fear tingled at the back of her neck. She chanced a glance behind her and found a band of reivers chasing her at full tilt, far faster on their stocky-legged horses than she was on the skinny nag.

A frantic glance to find a place to hide returned nothing but straw-like wheat-colored grass covering swells of hills. No forests, no trees, not even any large bushes to crouch behind. She was vulnerable on this landscape; exposed.

Her options would be to try to outrun them, which was impossible. Let them catch her, which surely held an unsavory outcome, or she could turn and fight. After all, she had been well-trained with her sisters. She would not go down easily.

She pulled on the reins to stop the aging horse and turned to face the men. Icy winds stung at her cheeks and made her eyes water, but she threw off her cloak anyway. The bulk of the garment would slow her down and could cost her life. Warmth was not worth the risk. She slipped the first set of her daggers free from her belt and tensed for battle.

If they were going to capture her, she would at least put up a fight.

NIALL WASN'T AT ALL surprised when the witch stopped to face them. He turned to the ten Armstrong clansmen with him and looked pointedly at Alban. "We're taking her alive."

The reivers following Niall nodded while Alban simply stared forward.

Niall returned his attention to the road in time to catch her drawing her arm back. The low afternoon sun flashed on a blade.

"Mind her weapons," Niall called out.

She launched her first dagger, sending it flying in Niall's direction. Except he was still riding; a moving target was much more difficult to hit, especially with a thrown blade. He leaned hard to the right, avoiding a direct hit. Regardless, the blade glanced off his left arm. Only a nick.

Not that it mattered. They were nearly to her now. "Prepare the ropes," he cried out above the galloping of their horse's hooves.

Niall and his band of men approached quickly, ropes ready to sling around her, weapons drawn for protection. She didn't cower. Instead she reached for another one of her blades and launched it in Alban's direction. He tried to move, but the dagger slammed into his left shoulder. He jerked back with the impact as he howled in outrage and drew his sword.

Niall's men were near enough to toss their ropes at Leila. The first one missed. The second one, thrown by Niall's most trusted guard, Brodie, landed perfectly around her torso. Before she could tug it off, the rope yanked taut and she was pulled from her horse. She grunted at the impact and struggled, flailing on the ground.

Nay, not struggling. The lass was working her dagger at the length of rope with frenzy in an attempt to free herself. Alban charged his horse directly at her.

Niall edged closer to the lord's son with his attention fixed. "I order ye to let her be."

Alban didn't slow. He continued toward Lady Leila where she lay on the ground trying to free herself from the rope. Once he was nearly upon her, he pulled back his sword and swung it toward her.

"I said to stop." Niall arced his sword to block the blow that was meant to kill the English witch. "Ye will listen to me when I give ye an order."

Alban's horse came to an abrupt halt and Alban jumped to the ground, undeterred. The witch was furiously sawing at the rope with her dagger.

"Get another rope around her, now!" Niall said to his men.

They rushed to do his bidding, looping another rope about her even as she writhed to free herself of the first. As they worked, Niall approached Alban. "She will have a trial where they will determine if she is guilty. Then she will be punished accordingly. Ye are no' to judge her."

Alban's eyes blazed with bloodlust, the hilt of Leila's weapon still jutting out from his left shoulder. "She threw a dagger at me."

Niall moved to stand protectively in front of her. "She is to live so she can have a trial."

Already, Alban had too much say in how the capture had taken place. It had been his decision to use the little girl to lure Leila to them, an idea that Niall had adamantly protested. He didn't like the child being exposed to the village with the pestilence. It had been too dangerous for the girl, who did it only for a bit more coin in her pocket.

But Alban had gone to Lord Armstrong with the idea and the earl had issued the final say in the matter. Lord Armstrong was not here now, and Alban had to obey Niall's orders, whether he liked it or not.

One of the men exclaimed in alarm. Niall spun around in time to tense as Leila launched herself at him, her daggers locked in both fists. She slammed into him, knocking him to the ground. She lifted her daggers and brought them down with the intent to kill. Niall pushed his hips up in an attempt to throw her from him. She stayed in place, but her aim went astray, and the dagger slammed into the frost-covered grass directly beside his face.

The guards were on her immediately, grabbing her arms and

pulling her off him. She fought like a warrior. Nay, like a hell cat. Her legs kicked out in those fitted red trews, catching Niall's men wherever she could: in the face, the neck, the stomach, wherever she could reach. She was disarmed quickly before she could do any real damage and the blades fell uselessly to the wheat-like grass, no longer a threat. Even then, she used her fists, pummeling and striking until one man bellowed in pain and blood gushed from his nose.

He held his hand over his face and stepped back from the fray. "The witch broke my nose."

"Still think 'tis a good idea for her to go to trial first?" Alban stopped prodding at the blade in his shoulder long enough to give Niall a smug smile.

Irritation spiked through Niall. Not only at the bastard's snide attitude, but at this woman who had complicated what should have been an easy capture.

The witch still struggled with the remaining men struggling to hold her in place. She threw a punch at one of the shorter reivers, a man closer to her own height than the rest. Niall shot forward with the speed of a striking snake and caught her wrist. "Stop."

She fixed her attention on Niall and drew back her free hand. He caught that arm as well and held her thus, clasping her wrists. They were delicate against his large fingers, slender, dainty things that did not appear capable of the fight she put up. He held her as firmly as he dared, fearing accidentally injuring her.

She glared up at him with brilliant blue eyes, her cheeks flushed with the exertion of her battle. Her breath puffed in front of her in frozen clouds.

"I'm Niall Douglas, Deputy to the Keeper of Liddesdale." He was forced to tighten his hands as she attempted to twist away from him. "Ye're being arrested on the accusation of being a witch. We outnumber ye, and yer horse is too slow to escape. If ye dinna come with us, we will have to use aggressive force and may hurt ye. We dinna want that." And he truly did not want to see her hurt.

Justice would be served, and she would get what she deserved then.

Though the lass could fight with the strength of a beast, she did not appear as strong as she was. He should think of her as a witch, a prisoner awaiting execution, but how could he when she was an earl's daughter worthy of respect? Especially when she was so slender, so beautiful. Aside from the men's attire, she looked every bit the part of a lady. One more in need of saving than arresting. It all triggered in him the desire to protect.

Lady Leila's face hardened. "I'm no witch." She tilted her pointed chin higher and met his eyes. There was no fear there, only determination. "How dare you charge me with such a crime?"

How dare they? Niall scoffed at her impertinence. "Ye had the sickness and ye survived. The Armstrongs were the first to get sick here, many of whom are now dead. I assume that isna a coincidence."

"It is indeed," she ground out.

He indicated her to his men. "Bind her."

Alban stepped forward with a cold grin. The bastard knew Niall couldn't deny his assistance without looking sympathetic to the witch. Niall was forced to hold Lady Leila's arms straight despite her many attempts to draw them away while Alban wrapped the rope around her slender wrists with such force even with his one good arm that the skin beneath turned white.

Niall gritted his teeth until it was done. Never once did Leila's face register the discomfort of what was no doubt quite painful. When Alban finished the task, he had one of his clansmen secure it with a solid knot.

They had officially arrested the Witch of Werrick Castle, the one that they had tirelessly sought for more than a fortnight. But before Niall could bring the witch up to his horse, there was something that must be done.

He dragged Lady Leila with him to his horse, passing Alban as he did so. With a sure hand, Niall grasped the hilt jutting from the lord's son's shoulder and yanked it free.

CHAPTER 4

Leila tried to breathe through the panic snapping in her heart, making it race, leaving her dizzy with fear. She had been captured. By the Lion.

This was it, then. The way she would die.

She had thought there would be more time. Mayhap an opportunity to bid farewell to Lord Werrick who had loved her as his own daughter, to her sisters who had always sought to protect and love her, to Isla who had become a mentor and a friend. The old healer didn't even know Leila had gone off to help the girl, that Leila had been so stupid as to fall for the trap.

She'd been so foolish. Too trusting. And now she would pay the ultimate price for that mistake. She ground her back teeth together to keep the tears at bay. Not that anyone was paying her any mind.

The younger clansman, with a head of straight red hair and finer clothes than the others, continued to cry out though the dagger had been ripped out some minutes before. His attempts to staunch his pain through closed teeth left him sounding like a dying animal, hissing, huffing and grunting. The Lion still held her dagger that he'd pulled from the younger man's shoulder.

He wiped the blade on the snow-covered ground, leaving the snow pink with blood, and stuck it into his own belt. Leila's palms ached with want of the weapon, a chance to defend herself from these men who meant her harm. Or mayhap, her hands were simply tingling at the tension of the ropes at her wrists. Already, her hands were beginning to take on a purplish tinge. She'd tried to wriggle at the bindings to loosen them, but they only cut more into her skin.

The Lion approached her once again, his face set with determination. "Dinna do anything foolish or I'll set him on ye." He flicked a glance to the red-haired man with the dagger wound in his shoulder. "Alban would have no qualms about killing ye."

"And you would?" Leila demanded.

His hazel eyes met hers, light brown with notes of amber and flecks of black and green. Striking. "I've no desire to hurt ye."

If only he knew how ridiculous a statement that was.

He glanced down at her hands. His lashes were tipped with blond, the same wheat-gold color as his shoulder-length wavy hair. He put his hands over hers, too quickly and with too sure a grip for her to pull free.

"Hold still," he said in a low voice. His fingers moved swiftly, unknotting the rope, loosening the painful binding and then securing it once more. His actions were deft and done with such speed, no one paid him any mind.

Pain prickled through her hands and the purplish discoloration immediately lightened with the flow of blood to her fingers. She moved her wrists at the newfound freedom, ignoring the abrasions that remained.

He lifted his gaze to her eyes. "Better?"

Leila nodded slowly, uncertain. Was this kindness a trap?

"I can look at his wound if you like." She glanced toward the man she'd hit with her dagger. The one still in the Lion's belt, mere inches from her bound hands.

The Lion smirked. "Let him suffer." His fingers brushed light as a feather over the reddened mark on her wrists where some of the skin had torn in her initial attempts to loosen the bonds. "He deserves it."

He swept her cloak off the ground and put it around her shoulders. The thick fur lining within blocked the wind and warmed her body instantly.

Leila studied the man who was supposed to kill her. The man she was destined to love. Aye, he was kind, but it would never absolve him of the sin of murder. How could she ever love a man who was so dangerous?

He put his hand to her back and nudged her forward. "Walk. Lord Armstrong is expecting ye."

Leila stubbornly held her ground, but the Lion applied pressure to his hand at her back, enough that her body staggered forward. She caught herself and he used her momentum to force her onward toward his horse.

"Cease yer whimpers, Alban." He tossed an irritated look at the younger man. "One of the other guards will see to ye when we arrive."

Alban glared at Leila, his dark eyes glittering with hate. She let her own gaze clash with his, rising to the challenge. After all, it was not Alban who concerned her.

The Lion lifted her easily onto the back of the horse. Before she had time to clap her heels against the beast's sides and gallop away, the Lion had swung up behind her. She froze at having a man's body pressed against her own. His arms squeezed around her on either side as he lifted the reins, keeping her tucked snugly in his grasp. She sat forward in an attempt not to allow any part of herself to touch him, a nearly impossible feat when they were in such close proximity.

He was like an unyielding wall at her back, strong and warm. She begrudgingly admitted the latter part. For he was warm, the heat of his body welcome against the unforgiving wind that sent chips of ice stinging painfully in their faces.

"Dinna even think about trying to escape." He spoke into her ear, his breath hot on her neck. "There is nowhere ye can go that I willna find ye."

A shiver wound its way down Leila's spine. This time, however, only part of it was due to fear.

They rode for the better part of an hour before a castle loomed in front them, the stonework dark gray from years of weathering. It sat like a hulking monster against the dingy winter sky with smoke and ash belching behind it from where the villagers were no doubt burning the effects of the dead.

They were passing the outer walls when she was informed Lord Armstrong wished to see her. While her harbored fears were primarily for the Lion, thoughts of Lord Armstrong filled her with a wary dread.

Some years back, she and her brother-in-law's sister, Lark, had been taken by the Armstrong clan and held for ransom. The sum had been exorbitant, and the demand given in an attempt to bring down the powerful Lord Werrick.

As much as her family always loved her, there had been a part of Leila then that had worried Lord Werrick would let her remain with the Armstrongs. After all, why relinquish one's fortune for a child that was not even of his own loins?

In the end it had not mattered. Her sister, Ella, and her husband, Bronson, crossed into the debatable lands and had seen both Leila and Lark to safety. But not before cutting down their fair share of Armstrong clansmen in their attempt to flee.

Upon her return home, however, she had found that Father was indeed in the process of raising the funds to pay the extraordinary ransom. For her.

Now she would meet Lord Armstrong, a man who thought her responsible for the pestilence. Or so she gathered. Worse still, he thought she had targeted the Armstrong family specifically.

They did not ride through the village to the castle, but instead made their way around the great side before arriving at the portcullis. Once she was inside the castle, escape would be nearly impossible, and yet there was no opportunity to flee now.

Nay, she had no choice but to be led in like a lamb to the slaughter and face the full force of Lord Armstrong's wrath.

~

Upon their arrival inside Liddesdale Castle's curtain walls, Niall gratefully slid from his horse and guided Lady Leila to the ground. Though she had tried to keep a stiff-backed space between them, her red-clad bottom had been pressed to his groin for the better part of the journey. Every step of the horse made her sway against him, grinding her arse against his cock and dredging up lustful thoughts he did not need to have about a prisoner.

But he hadn't been able to stop his mind from wandering as he imagined himself capturing her hips in his palms and driving into her from behind, then flipping her over and thrusting hard into her while her breasts gave eager little bounces as they moved together, sweat-slick and panting.

Enough.

Niall adjusted his gambeson to ensure it covered any evidence of his thoughts. He breathed in the cool air, allowing the chill to tamp down the heat of his blood.

Lord Armstrong's page, a boy of about ten with a tangle of blond hair, approached them. "Lord Armstrong has been waiting on ye."

"We're here." Niall smirked. "Though we may need one of the barbers."

Several months prior, a healer would have attended to the lord's son, but they'd all been run out of the village by the pestilence or had succumbed themselves. Now all they had to see to the people were the men who did various battlefield patches. Men who were often rough and unqualified, but better than nothing.

Alban glowered and did not reply.

"After we've seen Lord Armstrong," Niall added.

Alban opened his mouth to protest, but the page nodded in agreement and set about leading the way to the great hall.

If Leila was frightened, she did not show it. Her steps were confident, her shoulders set proudly back, and her head tipped with just the right amount of arrogance for an earl's daughter. She did not look like a prisoner. She looked like the lady of the castle, ready to take what was hers.

Lord Armstrong sat in an ornately carved chair with a mug of ale gripped in his hand. His hair was the same fox red as his son's, though frosted with age. A hard-lived life had left his face lined with the serious expression that made him appear unobjectionably stern.

"What is this?" He indicated Leila. "I thought ye told me ye'd be bringing a lady of noble birth forward as the accused. This woman dressed as a mercenary looks more like a slattern at play than a lady."

Lady Leila's back stiffened.

"I assure ye, she is the woman we were sent to find, my lord." Niall inclined his head respectfully.

"The bitch put a dagger into my shoulder." Alban's tone took a piteous note with his father that made Niall want to plunge the dagger back into the young man. "Then Niall ripped it out."

Lord Armstrong stared at his petulant son for a long

moment before lifting his hand in a nonchalant gesture. "It had to come out at some point, aye?" The Keeper of Liddesdale shrugged without sympathy. "It looks like little more than a flesh wound. The barber can see to it when we're done. For the time being, ye willna die while I deal with her."

He turned his attention back to Leila and waved her forward. She did not move. Niall stepped forward and nudged her lower back. *Walk*, he demanded silently. He did not wish to shove her across the floor.

She strode forward with not a whisper of fear evident on her.

"Too bad ye're no' a slattern," the older man said appreciatively as she approached. "I might hire ye myself." He got to his feet, pushed the cloak from her shoulders and walked slowly about her. He paused for a lengthy amount of time behind her and tilted his head appreciatively in admiration of her arse.

Heat effused Niall, blazing through him with a rage that came on as sudden as his desire for the witch. The Keeper of Liddesdale leaned toward her and the murmur of his voice floated toward Niall.

While his words were indecipherable, Niall could not ignore how Lady Leila's shoulders tensed.

Lord Armstrong completed his assessment and stood before her, towering over her slight height. "Are ye a witch?"

"Nay," Leila said ferociously. "These charges are—"

"Do ye deny then that ye're a witch?" Lord Armstrong pressed.

Lady Leila gave a little growl of frustration. "Aye, of course I deny the accusation when it isn't true."

Lord Armstrong nodded slowly. "As I expected." He folded his arms over his chest. "We've called upon Father Gerard from the north. He'll be the one to decide what ye are and what ye're no'. He's devoted his life to the study of sinners engaging in witchcraft and devil worship."

"Then he'll find me innocent," Leila said sharply.

"Take her to the dungeon." The Keeper of Liddesdale summoned a nearby servant. "Give the lass a kirtle to wear. I'll no' have her presented to the village looking anything less than the lady I promised them, aye?"

The servant rushed off to comply with the earl's bidding even as several clansmen came forward to take her to the dungeon. She did not protest or fight them off. Instead, she went of her own volition, without needing to be held as she was led from the room.

"God's bones, lad, get yerself to the barber and stop bleeding all over the rushes." Lord Armstrong rolled his eyes heavenward. "We've just had them replaced nigh on six months ago."

Alban didn't wait to be told again and hastened from the room to see to his needs.

Lord Armstrong waved Niall over. "It's easy to see why they call ye the Lion. Ye're determined, lad. 'Tis the reason I tasked ye with finding the witch. And ye did." He nodded in approval.

Niall inclined his head in gratitude. "My men were flawless in their execution of the plan today as well, my lord."

"Aye, yer men are always good too. Loyal, like ye." Lord Armstrong drank from his mug. "All that loyalty will be necessary until the mess of this is handled."

A pretty blonde servant entered with a length of blue cloth draped in her arms. She paused before Lord Armstrong and held it out for his inspection. He snatched it up and grunted. "'Tis fine enough, I suppose."

The woman curtseyed and departed.

The Keeper of Liddesdale tossed the bundle to Niall. "Ye need to get the witch into this kirtle, aye? I'll no' send the Earl of Werrick's daughter down the streets looking like a strumpet. Nay, she needs to look like the lady she is, so they all know I willna shy even from punishing nobility if they are in the wrong."

The dress was made of quality wool, much softer than the tunic Niall wore under his gambeson. He hung it from his arm discreetly to ensure it did not wrinkle before Lady Leila could be asked to wear it. If she was to appear as the nobility she was, it would not do for the fabric to be crinkled.

"Ye mean to send her down the streets?" Niall lifted his brows, uncertain what the lord meant by such words.

"Aye, let the people see the witch for who she is." Lord Armstrong shrugged. "She'll be held at the prison at the village center. I want everyone to have a go at her as she passes them, to throw about their rotten food and the like. Give the people what they want, and the people will be good to ye." He winked as though imparting a good bit of advice.

"Nay."

The skin around Lord Armstrong's eyes tightened. "Eh, lad? What'd ye say?"

"Nay, my lord." Niall maintained his soldier's stance with his legs spread wide and obdurate. "I'll no' take a lady down to the village for them to demean her when she's no' been condemned as yet. She's no' even had her trial."

"She'll have her trial," the lord assured him. "But the people will get their revenge as well, aye?"

"Nay," Niall repeated. "Ye like me working with ye for my honor and I tell ye now: what ye ask me to do is unjust."

"I'll do it, Father." Alban entered the room with his arm bound in a sling and his shoulder bandaged with a swath a linen. "I'll drag that whore in front of the crowd and let them do anything they want to her."

Lord Armstrong smiled at his son. "Verra well." He lifted a brow at Niall. "Shall I have Alban help the lady dress as well?"

Niall bit back a growl. He knew how Alban would get the

lass from her clothes before ensuring the dress was on her. Witch or no, there wasn't a woman alive who ought to endure such abuse.

"I'll see to it, my lord." Niall bent to retrieve her discarded cloak. A lady would certainly not be in such weather without the heavy garment.

With that, the Earl of Armstrong dismissed them both. Niall made his way to the dungeon with the damn kirtle tucked carefully over his arm, dreading ordering her to change into the garment. With the exception of Alban, Niall had never encountered issues with being obeyed. The clansmen had always respected him and listened without question.

But lasses...he knew little about lasses, especially ones with a feisty spirit like Lady Leila. And while he hoped she would be easy and compliant, he suspected she'd be anything but.

CHAPTER 5

Leila paced the narrow dungeon cell. The chill in the damp air sank through her trews and linen shirt, though she hardly felt it amid the torrent of her thoughts and emotions. What did they mean to do with her? Would they leave her to rot until the Lion came and finished her off?

She looked down at her wrists. The ropes were still there, holding her hands with enough tension to keep her from freeing herself, but loose enough they did not hurt. Why had he done that?

Footsteps sounded in the distance, the grit of stones beneath the wooden-soled shoes of a warrior echoing around her. Getting closer. She pressed herself to the wall, behind where the door opened. If she could take down the captor coming to see her, she could use his weapon to cut loose her bindings and flee.

She hid and tried to keep her breathing smooth and even so it wouldn't echo off the stone. Better for the person to think she was not there, to be momentarily confused so she could surprise them and attack.

The footsteps stopped in front of her cell. *Breathe in. Breathe out. Remain focused.*

Keys jangled together before one clinked in the lock. The door swung open, the ancient hinges squealing in protest. Leila tensed.

A golden light filled her cell. A candle. He was inside.

The door closed. Leila ran forward, slinging her elbow toward the man's face, an awkward strike when her hands were bound, but far more powerful than a simple punch. The impact of it turned the Lion's head. But the blow did not knock him down and he stood before the only means of escape.

He rolled his jaw and regarded her with a flat expression. She flexed her muscles in preparation for being hit.

"I'd prefer no' to strike a woman," he said in a smooth, nonchalant tone.

Leila stepped back, uncertain what to do with such words. Were they a threat? He remained by the entryway and brought a stool into the room, where he set the candle down. He opened the door, careful to not put his back to her, and brought in another stool with cloth piled atop it. Once the items were settled in the cell, he pushed the door closed and locked it from a ring of keys at his waist.

Leila regarded the folded cloth, something difficult to discern in the candlelight. The cloak beneath it, however, she recognized as her own.

"I thought ye might be cold." The Lion shrugged indifferently.

Leila fought down a shiver, though due to the cold or fear, she did not know. She was trapped within a dungeon with the Lion. He stepped toward her and she had to steel every nerve in her body to keep from backing away from him.

"Let me see yer hands." His voice held a note of authority, even when softly spoken as it was now.

Heart drumming hard in her chest, she lifted her bound hands. He settled his fingers over the knot and worked it loose.

With great care, he unwrapped the rope from her wrists, then pulled something from a pouch at his side.

Leila immediately recognized the stone jar as her own, the one with a healing balm in it.

"It was from the basket ye dropped." He lifted the top off and the sweet scent of herbs filled the dank dungeon cell. "I assume it is for healing."

Leila nodded.

He dipped his fingers into the balm and smoothed it over the abrasions on her wrist. His hands were nearly twice the size of her own, and yet his touch was impossibly gentle. When he was done, he sealed the top on the pot and put it back into his pouch.

"I canna have ye breaking it and killing a guard." He lifted his shoulder in a casual shrug.

"Thank you," Leila said. "For this kindness. For my cloak." Her gaze slid to the heavy garment. The wet cold had settled so deep into her bones that her whole body ached with it. She craved the weight of the cloak over her shoulders, blanketing her in warmth.

"I have a kirtle for ye as well." He indicated the blue garment folded on top of the cloak.

She regarded what looked to be wool, then turned her wary gaze on him.

He gestured to the kirtle again, the move awkward. It was not common to see a man who carried himself with such a commanding demeanor appear so uncomfortable. "Ye need to put it on." He tilted his head. "To look like a lady."

Leila lifted her brow and crossed her arms over her chest.

"No' that ye're no' a lady." His jaw clenched and he ran a hand through his long hair. "Put on the damn kirtle."

"I haven't a lady's maid to assist me." In truth, her lady's maid at Werrick Castle was a former laundress, Freya, who was also wife to the Master of the Horse. Leila needed no exceptional adornments or care outside having her hair scrubbed with Freya's wonderfully soothing touch and having the laces done up on her gowns.

A muscle in the Lion's cheek twitched. "I can aid ye."

"You're skilled with lady's clothing then?"

His brows furrowed. "Get on with it."

"Why?"

"Because ye've been told to don it."

"Why am I wearing it at all?"

Something flashed in his eyes, something he hid quickly behind a blank stare.

Leila took a step closer to him, so she was directly in front of him. She let her stare wander from the center of his chest up to his face. "Why do they want me to dress as a lady?"

His hazel eyes were dark in the dim light, all those wonderful flecks of color muted into shadow. He studied her with a shielded expression before finally answering. "They wish to walk ye through the village to the prison at its center."

Lord Armstrong's intent did not come as a surprise to Leila. Humiliation was exactly the kind of thing a man like him would afford a prisoner. The Lion's honesty, however, did surprise her. He could have threatened to send Alban down to do the earl's bidding. Instead, he had trusted her enough to tell her the truth.

Leila reached for the carefully folded garment.

"Ye'll wear it?" he asked.

She drew the kirtle toward her. The wool between her fingers was fine, tightly woven yet soft. It would be warm, especially beneath her cloak. "I've never been one for threats and lies."

The corner of his lip lifted. Or mayhap it was only her imagination, for as soon as she thought she'd seen it, his mouth was set in a firm line once more and he had turned his back to her.

She rested her hands on the ties of her trews. "You trust me enough to put your back toward me for a length of time?"

"I can care well enough for myself, lass." The confidence was back in his tone, sure and unmistakable.

She took advantage of the moment to let her eyes trail down him, to take in all of this man she would love; the man who would betray her. His shoulders were broad with muscle, his waist trim. The edge of his golden hair fell to his shoulder blades, imprinted with a slight wave.

Leila pulled at the first fastening of her trews and realized she was trembling. This time, however, she knew for certain it had little to do with the cold and everything to do with the man.

∽

NIALL FOUND himself grateful for the chill in the air as Leila undressed behind him. Though he kept his back to her, he could imagine well enough what she looked like.

And with her wearing men's attire, clothing he was intimately familiar with, it was all too easy to imagine exactly what she was taking off. The drag and pop of the ties of trews slipping free. Three so far.

Shhhk...pop.

Make that four.

Niall shifted his weight. The thick rustle of leather being peeled away from skin filled the small cell.

Her legs, long and lean, were now bare. That pert arse of hers no doubt peeking from beneath the hem of her oversized leine. Niall gritted his teeth and tried to force the image away. Not that it worked. He'd have a better time swallowing a mouthful of Murdock's dark hearty bread without a bit of ale than he did shoving those lusty thoughts aside.

The cloth that followed was quieter, a whisper of temptation as the leine was lifted over her head and discarded. His heart pumped loudly in his ears, nearly drowning out the sound he shouldn't have been straining to hear. She was naked behind him. Without a stitch of clothing on.

Were her breasts bound?

Surely, they were beneath the loose leine, or he'd have seen the pink of her nipples showing through the fabric. He had the sudden desire to cup her breasts in his hands and close his mouth over the cloth covering her nipples, to lick and tease until they pebbled beneath the wet fabric. Hard. For him.

Like he was for her.

Damn it.

He adjusted his trews. This woman was a witch.

The reminder was a douse of icy water to his lust. A witch like the one who had cursed his father. That wretched old woman had taken a life of a good man; the best man in all of England, Scotland...the whole world for that matter.

A witch. He repeated it to himself again and balled his hands into fists.

A witch. A witch. A witch.

It was so difficult to separate Lady Leila, daughter to an English earl—a lady, despite what she wore—from a creature he knew he must hate. It was all the more difficult when she was so petite, so slender...

"You may turn now." Her voice interrupted his thoughts.

He spun around with rage and loathing coursing through his veins, fully prepared to detest this woman.

She held a hand to her chest and cast a modest glance up at him. "Do you truly mean to act as my lady's maid?"

He hesitated, ready to demand what she meant when she put her back to him and lifted her glossy dark hair off her neck.

Niall's mouth went dry.

Merciful Heaven.

The fabric gaped open on either side, revealing the smooth, delicate skin of her back. Her shoulder blades were fragile lines against her skin, framing the dip of her spine that led to the sensual curve of her lower back. Except the kirtle was secured further still. There, amid a crisscross of lacings partially done, was the swell of her finely formed arse. Dear God, help him.

She glanced over her shoulder at him. "'Tis rather cold."

True to her word, small bumps, like those of a plucked goose, rose over her fair skin.

Niall shook himself from his stupor and took the thin lacings in his hand. They were dainty things in his large clumsy hands. He managed to thread them through the first three loops. In his haste to dress her, to seal away the vision of her partially undressed form before him, his hand brushed her back.

She jerked from his touch. Her shoulders snapped back and evidence of her strength showed in the flex of her lean muscle. Her body was slender, mayhap too much so. Most likely from her bout with the great illness. But her skin had been warm to the touch; warm and soft.

He wanted to take the pad of his middle finger and slide it down that sweet center of her back, to unravel the silky lacings as he went, to part the fabric. Would she shiver for him as she'd done with the cold?

She glanced at him over her shoulder once more but said nothing. She didn't need to. He was taking too long; he already knew as much.

His gaze fixed on the loops set within the blue wool garment and concentrated on the lacing sliding through. He couldn't keep staring at the loveliness of her naked back or he might end up taking the kirtle off. When finally he was done, he secured the gown with a knot.

"Done," he said gruffly and backed away.

"Will you do my hair for me as well?" Leila turned around as she released her hold on her hair. The glossy dark tresses slid down like silk over her shoulders.

Her breasts had been bound. The swell of her bosom was unmistakable against the fitted kirtle and generous enough to have shown in the simple leine she'd worn.

She glanced down at herself and he realized he'd been staring for too long.

"I like yer hair how it is." He didn't know why he said such a foolish thing. Mayhap because she was a lady, used to flattery. Mayhap to set her at ease. Mayhap because he couldn't get the image of her naked with that beautiful hair spilling down her fair shoulders from his mind.

She was disconcerting, this woman of noble birth who was rumored to be a witch. Everything in Niall told him to respect her for the lady she was, even as everything told him to hate her for the witch she was. Or rather, the witch she was accused of being. Father Gerard from Edinburgh had already been sent for and her trial would occur upon his arrival, most likely in the next sennight.

But the feelings she produced within Niall—the need to protect, mingled with his disgust of her accused crime and the blood-searing desire—left him addled in a way he did not enjoy.

He shifted her neatly folded clothing on the bench to get her cloak for her. The warmth of her body lingered on the leather trews and heated his palm. A sweet scent of herbs rose from the garments. He grasped the cloak in his free hand and passed it to her.

She did not accept the cloak from him. "I will wait until I arrive at the prison, if I may."

He set her clothing aside. "I need yer hands."

She set her jaw and slowly lifted her wrists to him. The ointment he'd applied glistened against her skin over the chaffing caused by her prior binding. He was careful as he wrapped the rope around once more and secured it. With that, he led her from the cell with specific instructions for one of his men to bring her clothing to the prison later.

Four guards followed Niall and Lady Leila from the dungeon, up through the castle and into the courtyard. People had already gathered in great numbers, or as great of numbers as one could expect in such times. Many had left their sick and risked their own good health to come see the witch who had cast such a curse upon them.

Their faces were settled in scowls and their eyes glittered with hatred. A crowd of such rage was capable of many things. Including murder.

"Good people of Liddesdale," Lord Armstrong announced. "I give ye the witch of Werrick Castle."

Insults hissed from the crowd to where Leila stood behind Lord Armstrong and the clansmen surrounding her. They would not be near her soon and she would be at the mercy of the mob.

Niall left Leila's side to approach Lord Armstrong. "I ask that ye reconsider making her walk to the prison this way," Niall said.

The Keeper of Liddesdale smirked. "Need I remind ye how yer own da perished at the hands of a witch?" His gaze was cold. "She walks on her own. And mind ye dinna get the same soft-heartedness yer da did, aye? I need soldiers, no' mums."

Niall gritted his teeth but said nothing. What could he say when faced with a mass of angry people and a leader who called his logic soft-hearted? It was the first mention of his father being as much, however. It made him want to question Lord Armstrong further. But now was not the time.

One of the castle's minstrels thumped a drum, the rhythm that of a wildly beating heart. What was Lady Leila's heart beating like now? Niall glanced at her and found her face calm, her expression serene.

This was wrong. No matter how much Niall detested witches, no matter the wrong done to the people of Liddesdale, this woman had not been yet judged by Father Gerard and still Armstrong would see her punished regardless. It went against everything in him to allow this treatment of a woman. Especially one of noble birth. Especially one that looked so delicate.

Damn it. This was wrong.

And he was powerless to stop it.

CHAPTER 6

Leila stood before a beast uglier than any she had ever known. The people had congealed into a mass, crowding one another to get a better look at her, heedless of being in such proximity to those who might be spreading the contagion. Sweat prickled at her armpits and palms despite the frigid air and left her skin clammy.

She didn't want to face these people. She didn't want to be here. All her life, she had known moments like these would happen, and all her life she had dreaded them. It was why she stayed within the familiar walls of Werrick Castle. Now, she was thrust from its safety and living her greatest terror, one that would not be over until she was slain by the Lion.

Lord Armstrong turned to her with a smile curving his lips. His gaze passed over her in obvious approval of the wool kirtle. It was loose around her waist and the sleeves and hem were too long, most likely a garment belonging to Lady Armstrong or a daughter, if they had one.

Leila turned her attention to the Lion where he stood at Lord Armstrong's side. Better to see him this way, in a stance of complacency rather than with the gentle kindness he had exhibited in the dungeon.

"Walk among the people, witch," Lord Armstrong commanded. "Let them see ye for what ye are."

Hard hands shoved at Leila's lower back, sending her sprawling forward. By some miracle, she managed to keep upright without tripping over her overlong hem. Next time she might not be so lucky.

If she would be presented to the masses with such degradation, she would maintain her dignity in any way she could. The way Lord Werrick had raised her. She grasped her skirt in her bound hands and tried to lift the hem as daintily as possible as she walked out into the waiting crowd.

Threatening hisses rose around her like demons in a nightmare as the people pressed closer to her. A woman spit at her, the action coarse and intentionally vulgar. But Leila had known this would happen. She had seen this in a vision once, or at least part of it, with people rallying against her. It had been confusing at the time, lost in a place with no reference. She understood it now, as well as the poignancy. Except there had been a shadow descending on her in the vision.

She turned her face to the gray sky. Would the clouds fall over the sun to cast such a shadow? And what would happen then?

Something smacked her neck, hard and wet where it struck. She staggered in that moment, taken aback by the iciness that still clung to her skin. Her toe caught on her hem and she stumbled, managing to catch herself at the last minute. The scent of earth was strong in her nostrils. Mud. They were throwing mud at her.

"Go back to hell, ye slattern." An older woman sent a head of cabbage hurtling toward her.

Leila maintained her dignity as much as was possible and

turned her head to avoid the hurled vegetable. It hit the ground where it lay intact. In that one moment, she had a ridiculous thought that the people were not so bad off if they were throwing perfectly edible vegetables when in the last year, the rains had wiped out enough crops to keep the people of Scotland and England hungry.

A hurled spray of mud splashed over Leila's skirt. One man stepped forward and shoved her. She might have been able to keep her footing, were it not for the long hem. The tips of her shoes pinned her skirt to the ground, drawing it tight and preventing her from stepping properly forward to keep her balance. She crashed into the soupy earth as cheers rose up all around her.

A foot in front of her lifted to stomp down on her, but she scrambled to her feet. A peasant with his few remaining teeth bared tried to push her to the ground once more, but she edged away from him in time to avoid another spill.

"Dinna kill her before she can be tried," Lord Armstrong called out in a bored droll.

"Then she shouldna have brought on the pestilence," someone cried out.

A balding man sent his fist rushing toward Leila. She threw her bound hands up in front of her face, blocking the hit as she ducked away.

A glance toward the center of the village revealed the large stone prison. Too far away. Her heart pounded with such a frenzy, it left her head light and spinning. She knew the Lion would be the one to take her life, aye—but it didn't mean all the bones in her body wouldn't be broken by the villagers first.

Would this hell have no end?

Thoughts of her family crowded into her mind. How she would never be able to tell them she truly loved them; how appreciative she was for the way they had loved her when she had always been so undeserving. A knot of tension clenched at the back of her throat, but she swallowed hard to clear it. She would not give these people the satisfaction of seeing her tears.

They pressed into her path, crowding close enough that she could smell foul breath and sweat and the lingering sickly sweetness of illness. It would be impossible to fend them all off at once. Especially now, as people were pelting her with food, shoving at her, spitting at her.

Her ears were filled with their vile hate; her body assaulted from where rough hands shoved at her. The kirtle was soaked through from her fall and clung icy and wet to her body and while she tried to be stronger than the cold, she could not help but shiver.

A parsnip flew through the air, flying toward her.

Leila tensed in preparation for it to hit when the shadow fell over her. Another attacker. She held her ground, prepared to fight. Except the person did not hit or shove or even shout.

A glance upward revealed a targe held aloft in the air by someone with a leather cloak hanging like a curtain of protection. Bits of refuse bounced off the wooden shield and the cloak rippled under the assault, but still the man did not move. He held his ground, targe lifted with a solid body, his back straight and proud, daring any mortal to challenge him. She knew him before she looked higher to his face.

There he was, strong jaw clenched, hazel eyes narrowed and facing forward as he shielded her from the villagers' wrath. The Lion.

Leila wanted nothing more than to sink back against his large chest, to give into the trembling weakness of her legs and the clawing fear scrabbling within her. But she was raised as a daughter of Lord Werrick. She was above fear, above simpering.

"You needn't do this." Leila notched her chin higher.

He tilted his head. "I disagree."

"'Tis not their fault."

He continued to hold the shield, pausing only to shove a man back with it. "They want to kill ye."

"They're scared." The truth of it worked itself through her mind, even as she spoke. If nothing else, having the Lion at her side helped her thoroughly rationalize the situation. "Everyone is dying: friends, neighbors, children. They're frightened and they have been told I am the one who caused it."

"And is it true?" He did not lower his shield even as he asked.

"It is not," she said. "But they do not know that, and neither do you."

"Ye've no' been declared a witch yet. I'll no' let them kill ye until ye have been." He nodded. "For now, ye'll be locked in the prison to await Father Gerard. When he arrives from Edinburgh, he'll pass his judgment."

Bile rose in Leila's throat. She had heard of the ways they found witches guilty, with trials no person could possibly survive.

The prison loomed before them and a wall of guards pushed the crowd back as Leila was led to the massive iron door. The Lion unlocked it with a key from the ring at his belt and led her in while the crowd roared in protest behind them.

At least behind the locked gates of the prison, she would be safe.

For now.

∼

NIALL HAD ALWAYS PUT a considerable amount of trust into the strength of the well-built prison at the village's center. At least before a hoard of frenzied villagers tugged at the bars at its front gate.

They wanted Lady Leila. Noble birth or not, they wanted her dead.

He had unbound her hands and locked her in her cell but remained outside the iron bars in the event the villagers broke through. She was a pathetic sight, especially for an earl's daughter. Mud spattered her face and neck; the blue gown was no longer so fine as it hung heavy and wet with filth. However, never once did she complain or rail against her containment or the people who put her there.

Nay, she remained in the center of the whitewashed room with her arms folded firmly across her chest.

He hated that her bravery tugged at a deep place within his heart, that even filthy and sodden, she was still beautiful.

The crowd had settled after an hour or so, but still Niall did not relinquish his post.

"You needn't wait here with me," Lady Leila said softly in that lovely throaty voice of hers.

"They may come for ye still." Niall shrugged as if his attention to a prisoner was not atypical. "Especially if I leave."

"You didn't have to protect me when I was walked through the village." She shivered and hugged herself tighter, though he didn't know if it was from the perceptive chill in the room or the memory of what Lord Armstrong had made her do. "I thank you."

"They may have killed ye and ye've no' stood trial yet." Niall pushed himself out of his chair beside the cell as Brodie appeared with Leila's clothing.

He pushed the dark hair from his eyes and handed Niall Leila's clothing from the dungeon. "I made certain Lord Armstrong dinna see me."

Niall nodded in understanding and appreciation. Lord Armstrong's displeasure at what he'd done for Leila had been palpable. The Keeper of Liddesdale had let his gaze linger on

Niall before he'd left, the almost imperceptible narrowing indicative of a stern discussion at a later date.

Not that it would have altered Niall's decision to protect Lady Leila from the crowd's wrath.

He took the bundle, as well as the sack of food Brodie had brought, and turned to Lady Leila. Her gaze fell on her clothing.

Brodie's footsteps fell away in the distance and a quiet settled over the prison once more. Niall hesitated outside Lady Leila's cell. "What did ye mean when ye said 'tis ye'?"

Her wide blue-eyed stare slowly lifted to study him before sliding away. Doubtless, she thought he intended to hold her clothes ransom for the answer to his question. It was in the back of his mind to do so. But he found himself dreading the answer.

A shiver went down his spine this time. Not with the cold, but with the knowing. She *was* a witch. And yet, he wanted her to be otherwise.

"We were told ye warned yer people of the upcoming pestilence," Niall continued. "Is that true?"

Her silence answered him once more and a hard ball of ice tightened in Niall's gut. He thrust her clothing through the iron bars, extending his hand toward her.

She started and slowly reached for her clothes, as though she thought he might pull them away. Only when she had them in her possession did she offer a soft word of thanks.

Niall pushed a bowl of water and linen through the small opening meant for food. "Clean up." He turned to go, to give her some privacy in the barred cell. "I'll give ye some time."

"Wait."

He paused.

"I need you to please undo this kirtle." Her voice was gentle, timid. As if she did not wish to ask for his assistance in her changing of clothing again. Only this time, rather than putting her gown on, he would be assisting her in taking it off.

Heart pounding, blood racing, he returned to the small cell and reached through the bars at the lacings she'd put toward him. With shaking hands, he slid the silky ties free, revealing her flawless back one precious inch at a time.

Once the twin dimples at the base of her spine were visible, he spun away and quit the room abruptly. He did not stop until he was at the prison's center. Even there, guilt nipped at him. A hollow sensation in his gut told him she was a witch despite her claims she was not. Why else would she remain silent? Why would she not answer his questions?

The plinking of water echoed off the cold stone walls of the prison and Niall went still as another trickling sound teased at his senses. Lady Leila was washing herself, or at least as best one could in a prison cell with an ewer of cold water.

His cheeks burned at the thought of her naked within that cell, imagining what went past that slender, smooth back. He closed his eyes and leaned his head back against the wall as another splash of water came from the rear of the prison. Mayhap she was pouring it over herself, letting it sluice down her naked body, her skin prickled with gooseflesh against the cold, her nipples hard, pink points. How he would love to draw one between his lips and warm them with his tongue and mouth.

His cock swelled with the enticing idea and dragged his mind further into the fantasy. He could run his hands up the insides of her slender thighs to where they met, where she would be slick with desire.

Nay.

Niall snapped his eyes open and stared hard at the bare white-washed walls in front of him. His breathing came hard and his body burned with the aftereffects of his imagination. He pressed the flat of his palms to the cold wall and tried to calm his racing blood. Why did this woman have such a strong effect on him?

He waited for his lust to ebb before returning to her cell. She had changed into her trews once more and had her cloak wrapped snuggly around her. The blue kirtle had been neatly folded beside a pile of wet rushes near the back of her cell where she had apparently dressed. Her skin was rosy from scrubbing where she could and even her hair was wet as though she'd attempted to wash it as well.

"Yer hair willna dry quickly." He handed her a crust of bread and bit of cheese.

She accepted the food with a nod of thanks. "Why do they call you the Lion?" she asked before taking a small bite of the bread.

Niall settled in his chair beside her cell once more. "I'm as fierce as I am loyal. A lion guarding his pride, his land from all threats."

She considered him for a long moment with her lips pressed to one another, as though holding back a thought. He lifted a brow.

"Were you always so loyal?" she asked the question carefully.

"Nay." He watched her carefully. "But ye already knew that, dinna ye?"

She turned her attention to her food and did not reply to his question. Aye, she knew it already.

"I used to be wild," he admitted. "I reived from lands on both sides of the border. I was dishonest and held loyalty to no man."

She broke off a piece of bread and slowly brought it to her mouth without looking at him. Oh, aye, she knew all this already.

He continued regardless. "My da was an honest man and always tried to make me realize the wrongs of my actions. I dinna care. One day, I held a Scotsman for ransom for a bit of coin. And my da was furious with me."

More than furious. He'd been disappointed. Niall could recall all too well the heaviness to his father's expression, the sadness in his eyes. It had wounded Niall to the core to see his da look upon him with such displeasure. But he didn't tell Lady Leila that now. He would never tell any soul of how he'd felt that day.

"He died that afternoon." Niall kept his tone flat to keep from letting his emotions show.

"How did he die?" Lady Leila asked. Again, her words came with slow care, as though she already knew the answer.

"He was cursed by the wife of the man I was holding for ransom." Anger and hatred loosed from a walled-up dam and swept over Niall. "She was a witch who cast a spell on him. He was dead by noon. Two things changed for me that day. The first being that I stopped my foolish, youthful ways of lying and stealing. I became honest, like him." Someone Niall's da would be proud of.

Niall looked pointedly at Lady Leila, although he was reminding himself as much as he was informing her. "The second being my hatred for witches."

CHAPTER 7

The dim glow of early dawn limned the shutters and woke Niall. His body was cramped by the cold where he sat against the heavy iron bars of Lady Leila's prison cell. He stretched out his legs with stiff knees and slowly got to his feet. His back popped in protest, even as he tried to stretch away the knots in his body.

A glance at the cell behind him confirmed Lady Leila was still sleeping. She lay in the rushes with her cloak tucked around her on both sides like a blanket. Niall used to do the same when he'd been a boy, stuffing the blanket under the weight of his body to keep any currents of cold air from seeping into the warmth of his bed.

The muted light coming into the room was enough to see her face, relaxed in slumber and beautiful. She looked fragile, innocent.

That last word tugged at his senses, pulling his gaze from her. He detested the confusion warring within him about her, how her noble birth and bonny face and bravery made him soft to a woman he would otherwise hate. A woman he *should* hate.

The journey for the priest to come from Edinburgh would

take only a few more days. Niall was eager for his arrival, to hear the declaration from the man known for his ability to identify a witch. Then Niall would have his answer. Then there would be no confusion as to his feelings toward Lady Leila.

Niall strode away from the cell and caught the distinct sound of the keys clattering in the main prison door. He quickened his pace. No doubt it was one of his guards. But what if it was not?

The heavy iron-banded wooden door opened, and Brodie stepped in.

"I thought ye might have stayed." Brodie grinned with his usual affability. Other clansmen and warriors thought less of him for his jovial nature, until they sparred with him. He was mayhap the only warrior faster than Alban. Mayhap the most dexterous warrior Niall had ever seen. So, he wore his smiles without care or concern for what any man thought of him. Niall had always respected him for that.

Niall lifted his shoulders. "I thought the villagers might try to get in."

"Not on yer watch." Brodie winked. "I came to relieve ye so ye can prepare for yer discussion with Lord Armstrong."

Niall cast a dark look at the taller man. "Did he already request to see me?"

Brodie shook his head. "Nay, but he had that look about him. Ye know the one. The scowl like he's had a bit of pottage gone bad."

Niall's mouth lifted at the corner at that. He knew exactly the look Brodie was talking about, where the lord's whole face sagged down in a frown of extreme displeasure. Aye, there'd be a discussion later to be sure.

Niall had enough time to clean himself, don a fresh set of clothes and break his fast before Lord Armstrong summoned him. The earl was not sitting in the grandly carved chair at the dais when Niall entered the great hall, however. He was in front of the long head table, pacing with apparent agitation.

Niall squared his shoulders for a fight. He knew Lord Armstrong would be displeased but had not suspected it would be to this extent. The earl spun on Niall as he approached. "How dare ye disobey my orders?"

"I dinna disobey orders," Niall replied casually. "Ye said for her to walk to the prison. She did."

"Aye, with yer protection." Lord Armstrong grasped the back of a wooden chair nearest him and hurled it to the ground, where it landed with a sharp crack. "Are ye sympathetic to witches now? Need I remind ye what a witch did to yer da?"

Niall had been prepared for the earl to throw this question, and yet it still knocked painfully at his chest. "She hasna been declared a witch by Father Gerard yet."

"It doesna matter," Lord Armstrong roared. The rage in his voice filled the great hall and echoed around them. "We only do that for the people, so they dinna rally like they did when we killed Lady Elliot."

Niall didn't even flinch. Something else was amiss with the Keeper of Liddesdale to inspire such wrath. "Ye value my judgment," Niall said with confidence. "It's why ye came to me—"

"I am still yer lord and will be obeyed."

Niall folded his hands behind his back, unfazed. "Then I will offer an apology once she has been officially deemed a witch." He was prodding the bear, but he could not allow Lady Leila to be put to death. Not without a final judgment. And even though Niall suspected Lady Leila of witchcraft, there was a part of him hoping she truly was not guilty.

Lord Armstrong sputtered and went a subtle shade of purple. "If ye believe her to be innocent, then I hold ye personally responsible for her and her well-being. That includes meeting with the Earl of Werrick."

Niall drew up short. Suddenly Lord Armstrong's displeasure made sense. "The Earl of Werrick is here?"

"Aye," Lord Armstrong said sourly. "He's demanding the release of his daughter."

Niall ran a hand through his hair. This complicated matters. If nothing else, he assumed Lord Werrick would have sent a missive to demand a meeting with Lord Armstrong. But to come in person? Such an audience was not easily put off.

"He's outside the castle gates." Lord Armstrong nodded toward the door to the great hall in apparent dismissal.

Niall said nothing more and made his way from the great hall, through the bailey and to the castle gates. Lord Werrick sat on horseback with several of his guards surrounding him. Certainly not enough to attempt to sack the castle. The man had arrived to talk.

Niall ordered the portcullis raised and went out to meet the English earl. Lord Werrick dismounted from his steed and met Niall halfway. The older man's face was lined with worry, his bright eyes sharp and assessing. "My daughter...?"

"She is safe at present," Niall assured him.

"I want her released," Lord Werrick said with the boom of authority. "I demand it."

"Ye've no authority here."

Pain shone in the older earl's eyes. He knew well the limits of his power in Scotland.

"What is it you want?" Lord Werrick's brows furrowed. "Ransom? If it's prisoners released, know that we have none."

Niall shook his head. "Nay. She's being tried for witchcraft, for causing the spread of this pestilence."

"That is the most fool logic I've ever heard." Even as Lord Werrick said it, he did not appear surprised by the accusation. "Let me speak with Lord Armstrong."

"Ye're better off speaking to me." Niall folded his arms over his chest.

"He won't see me, will he?" Lord Werrick turned his bright blue eyes to the castle behind the curtain wall. "The coward."

Niall did not reply to the slight against his lord. Especially because he agreed with Lord Werrick. The Keeper of Liddesdale was indeed a coward for not going to meet the English earl.

"We will stop at nothing to ensure her safety," Lord Werrick vowed.

"I have been doing all I can to see to her comfort." Niall spoke the words gently in an effort to put the older man at ease.

The Earl of Werrick studied Niall for a long moment, as though seeing him for the first time. "Who are you?"

"I am Deputy to the Keeper of Liddesdale," Niall replied. "Niall Douglas, oft referred to as the Lion."

"The Lion," the earl whispered through lips that did not move and crossed himself. "Where is my daughter?"

Niall considered the man warily. "What is it ye've heard of me?"

"Where is my daughter?" the earl repeated.

While he had only a handful of guards with him, it would still be enough to overwhelm Brodie and the few clansmen at the prison. Niall crossed his arms over his chest. "I canna tell ye where she's being held."

"Please," Lord Werrick said, a powerful man with a newly frail voice. "Do you have a child?"

Niall gave a subtle shake of his head.

"Then you do not know of the power of parental love." The earl took a step toward him, his back straight, his lean body tall, his brows furrowed with the agony of his words. "I beg of you, let me see her. To know that she..." He swallowed. "To see for myself that she is safe."

Niall thought of Lady Leila, of how delicate she seemed. If

she had roused such a protective instinct in him—who had fought her, who knew firsthand how deceptive her appearance—how must her father feel?

It was far too easy to recall the depth of his own affection for his father, as well as the sharp regret of how it felt to have never said goodbye. Niall sensed in his gut how Lady Leila's trial would go and was well aware this might be a father's last chance to see his daughter. And how he hated the twinge in his stomach for his role in her demise.

"If I concede to allow ye to see her, I bring only ye," Niall answered in a low voice. "And it will be done with the knowledge that she will be moved afterward. Ye willna find her in the same place again, aye?" Regardless of if the earl was taken to see Leila or not, she would need to be relocated into the castle. The prison was not sufficient to hold Lord Werrick's army if he stormed Liddesdale for Leila, something Niall would not put past a father who clearly loved his daughter.

The earl nodded.

"If yer men follow us, or if ye try to attack, we'll kill her and we'll kill ye, aye?" Niall knew he could easily take down the older man. Doubtless, Lord Werrick knew as well.

"I understand," he replied solemnly. "You have my word that I will not attack. Please. My daughter."

Niall didn't trust Englishmen, but he did put weight on reputation and the Earl of Werrick's was pristine; a man who did right. With the seal of an honest man's word, Niall led Lord Werrick to the prison to see his daughter. Most likely for the last time.

∽

LEILA HAD WOKEN to the extreme cold, her body stiff and her mind confused at the surrounding whitewashed walls and iron bars. It took only a moment for her to realize where she was and what had happened. Understanding what would soon come to be, however, was the hardest to come to terms with. Especially when she'd spent a lifetime knowing.

There was nothing to do now behind the iron-barred door but wait for her destiny.

She leaned her back to the cold wall, tucked her knees to her chest and let her mind drift from one painful thought to another. About her sisters, about her father, about the Lion. She wished he would not show her kindness, that he would be as cruel as Alban.

She rested her forehead on her bent knees. Her visions had always been so frustrating. Showing who but not how—or how but not when—or any other combination of the three. She always had pieces that never fit into anything whole, especially when it came to her own future. To where she was now.

"Ye're awake." A masculine voice sounded from the barred door.

Not the Lion. Leila made the assessment before she even lifted her head. This man's voice was not as deep and lacked the authoritative edge. She looked up to find a reiver with wavy dark hair standing outside her cell. He crouched and slid a plate through the gap in the bars near the floor. The space was not large enough to climb through, but wide enough to properly deliver food and a bit of ale.

A spear of light streaking through the shutters cast its light over the plate, revealing a heel of brown bread and a knob of cheese. Her stomach knotted at the idea of eating, but still she thanked the man who had brought it to her. He continued to watch her through the bars.

"Are ye a witch?" he asked.

"I'm not," Leila replied honestly.

"But ye are a healer?"

"I've been trained in the art of healing and know much about herbs." Leila got to her feet to better look at the man who stood several feet away.

"My sister's been sick more than a sennight." He glanced behind him, as though he feared someone catching him speaking to her. "No one will see to her. All the healers are dead and anyone who could help willna for fear she's ill with the pestilence. 'Tis no' the pestilence, but I canna get anyone to listen."

"Does she have swelling at her armpits, neck or groin?" Leila asked.

The reiver shook his head.

"Is she coughing up bloody sputum or vomiting blood?" Leila tensed. Heaven help them if that illness descended up on them.

He shook his head again and her body relaxed.

"Can ye help her?" The reiver asked. "Even if ye are a witch, if ye can cast a spell—"

"I'm no witch, but I have herbs that can help. In the basket I dropped, there are several small linen bags with herbs in them. They are to cool a fever and ease body aches. If it is simply a fever, it will aid her. If it is something more than a fever, I would need to see her to offer better guidance."

He lowered his head in gratitude and opened his mouth to say something more. A clattering came from the front of the prison and sent him jumping back from her cell as though the bars had burned him. Someone was coming.

Leila's heart slammed hard in her chest. She straightened from her position against the wall to peer into the hall, to glimpse who had arrived.

Mayhap it was the villagers come to break her bones. Mayhap it was the Lion with his kindness and gentle hands.

"Leila." The voice echoing down the long hall was all too familiar and filled with desperation.

Leila's heart crumpled with recognition.

He was perhaps the one person who could destroy her control. Already, the stoic reserve around her had started to crack.

"Papa." Leila whispered his name from lips that did not move.

She had not called him that in years. Not since she was old enough to realize the ugly truth of her birth, that her true father had been a marauder, a murderer, a thief and a rapist. She could not say Papa after that, not when she was so undeserving. Yet, neither could she bring herself to so formally refer to him as Lord Werrick.

She pressed herself to the icy bars of her cell. They stank of old iron, a dirty, metallic odor that she tried to ignore. "Father?" Her voice broke and echoed back at her from those cold white-washed walls.

The clipped footsteps coming toward her fell faster and suddenly, he was there. Lord Werrick, the man who had always loved her as a father, stood before her cell in his regal doublet and mantle. He sucked in a pained breath as he regarded her, his eyes filled with such hurt that another crack splintered through Leila's composure.

"Leila." He said her name in a thick voice. Exhaustion lined his face and created shadowed hollows beneath his eyes.

"Father." The word quavered in the thin air and she had to swallow before speaking again. "You should not have come. The pestilence—it's too dangerous—"

"God himself would not be able to keep me from coming for you." He rushed to the iron barred door and grasped her fingers in his warm, warm hand.

She wanted to curl her entire being against him to revel in

that heat, the way she'd done as a girl when she sat on his lap, his chest rumbling at her back as he spoke, telling tales of wandering knights and defeated dragons. She was no little girl now though, and this was no story. He could not stay. It was far too dangerous.

"You're freezing." Her father cast a hard look over his shoulder to the Lion. "She is a noblewoman and should be treated thus. Your treatment of my daughter is reprehensible."

"She's been arrested on the crime of witchcraft." The Lion's face revealed no emotion. "She will be tried by Father Gerard, who is coming in from Edinburgh to judge her for her sins. I will personally ensure she remains safe until then."

"And then what?" Father growled. "You let her die if some self-important man deems her a witch?"

The Lion did not flinch. "Ye've seen yer daughter."

Lord Werrick's warm hand tightened on Leila's as though he could keep from letting go. "What can I do to free her?"

"There isna anything ye can do." The Lion pushed himself off the wall he'd been leaning against. "She'll be tried and judged in due time."

"Nay." Father shook his head. "I can pay you. Exorbitant sums. I can give you land. A castle upon it, even." He was pleading, his voice trembling.

It cut through Leila's composure and heat prickled in her eyes with the threat of tears. "Please, Papa. You cannot stay here. It is too dangerous."

He turned to her abruptly, his own eyes brimming with tears. "Papa?" He blinked. "You haven't called me that in so many years, my sweet daughter."

A sob choked from Leila. "I know…" She tried to force back her tears. "I also know you are not my father."

He shook his head as though he meant to stop her, but she rushed on. "You are not my father. I know the man who sired me nearly killed my mother and I finished what he started with my birth. You and my sisters have given me a love I have never deserved. I cannot repay that kindness now by putting you at risk. I already killed my mother; I will not now be the cause of your death as well."

"Leila," Lord Werrick said sharply. "Nay." He reached through the bars and touched her cheek tenderly, the way he'd always done when she was a child. "You are one of us: a Barrington. You may not be my daughter by blood, but you are a daughter of my heart." He frowned hard and his chin trembled in an obvious attempt to hold back his tears. "You are my daughter and I love you." He gave a sharp sob. "I will always love you and I will never stop fighting for you." He met her eyes, fierce with determination. "Never," he vowed.

"It is time." The Lion appeared beside the cell. "Please, Lord Werrick."

Father leaned into the bars as though he could go through them to be in the cell with Leila, to protect her the way he always had.

Tears streamed hot down Leila's face. "I love you too, Papa. I always will." She kissed the warm hand holding hers with all the reverence of a daughter who truly did love her father. But it was the next act that was more wrought by love than any other, for she stepped back and pulled her hand from the warm comfort of his. To allow him to leave, to get him from this place of death and chaos, so he could return to the safety of Werrick Castle where the contagion could not touch him.

Her father reached for her, but she shook her head. "You must go."

"Lord Werrick." The Lion's tone was soft as he silently indicated the hall.

Father hesitated, staring at Leila as though he would rather cut out his heart than leave.

"Please, Lord Werrick," the Lion said.

Her father's face crumpled in pain. "I will not rest until you are free." With a harsh intake of breath, he turned away from her and strode down the hall.

Leila stepped back toward the iron bars and pressed her face to them as he left. The agony in her chest was exquisite. It tore her heart in every direction like a savage beast wild with blood lust and left her wounded and ragged. "Goodbye, Papa," she whispered at the departing footsteps.

For she knew deep in her heart, it was the last time she would see her father before her death.

CHAPTER 8

Niall took his time walking through the muddy streets on his way back to the prison. He hadn't meant to listen to the conversation between Lord Werrick and Lady Leila, but it had been impossible given their proximity. Leaving would have been equally as impossible. The second his back was turned, the earl could have slipped Lady Leila a dagger and Niall knew all too well what the lady could do with weapons.

He stopped before the banded gaol door and dragged out the process of selecting the door's key from the wide ring on his belt. Lady Leila was not the true blood daughter of Lord Werrick, though it was clear that he cared for her as if she was his.

Niall slipped the key into the lock and paused, clenching his back teeth against the stirring in his chest. He was well-acquainted with the pain of feeling undeserving of love and how deep it could furrow into one's soul.

His own father had given him love and understanding, no matter how often Niall in his youth had floundered on the right path. But rather than encouraging him to be good, to make his father proud, it had twisted into his gut and left him agitated with guilt.

It appeared Lady Leila, despite the pride she wore like a crown, the possession of her powerful confidence and the control she held over her person—she was just like him. She felt guilty for a love she did not deem herself worthy of receiving.

Niall unlocked the door to the prison, slipped inside and locked it behind him once more. Brodie stood in the small guard room and nodded in greeting. Even his usual grin had faded in light of what he had most likely overheard of the conversation between father and daughter.

"Get a gambeson and helm for Lady Leila," Niall instructed. "We need to move her and I'll no' have the village people recognizing her."

Brodie immediately set to the task without question, as had the staff within the castle as they went about clearing out one of the rooms to make way for Lady Leila. Lord Armstrong had not been in the castle to consult and the matter of moving Lady Leila was most urgent. With Lord Werrick now possessing the knowledge of where his daughter was located, they had to remove her with haste.

Niall strode down the prison hall and into the room containing Lady Leila's cell. She appeared to have recovered from her broken composure, her face no longer red from her tears and her back once more straight and proud. Her unfocused stare at the ground, however, bespoke of her despair.

"Lady Leila." He spoke softly, but she started at the sound. "We must move ye to the castle."

She tensed, no doubt anticipating she would be led through the village again.

"I'm having one of my men bring a gambeson and helm," he explained. "It will mask yer identity. Then ye'll walk to the castle with me, aye?"

Her brows drew together with the understanding she would not be put on display before the villagers once more.

"If ye try to run from me, or attack me in any way," he cautioned, "I will kill ye."

Her mouth lifted in a small smile that teetered on amusement. "I do not doubt that."

Brodie appeared at that moment with the items Niall had requested. "I tried to find the smallest ones I could." The dark-haired reiver hesitated before leaving and slid a worried glance at Lady Leila. Apparently, Niall was not the only one concerned for her.

Why could the witch of Werrick Castle not be a crone? Someone toughened by age and made bitter by a hard life, an old hag who spat and cursed at them. Why did the witch have to be a petite woman who had grown up as an earl's daughter? Why did she have to arouse this fierce need to protect her?

Niall handed the gambeson to Lady Leila through the bars. "Put it on."

She stepped closer to accept the offering and took it with her long, graceful fingers. But she did not immediately step back and don it. Instead, she looked up at him, hitting him with the full force of those lovely blue eyes, in which an entire world of depth and mystery was held. "Why are you so kind to me?"

"I was just asking myself the same thing." He smirked.

"You needn't be." She hadn't said it with malice. Nay, the words came out gently, more like a plea than hurled in spite.

He shouldn't be, he amended in his own mind.

She pulled the gambeson to her and proceeded to remove her cloak to put it on over her shirt. While she did this, Niall opened the door to her cell and handed her the helm. The band of metal running down its center to protect the nose of the wearer would aid in hiding her identity.

She accepted it from him, but this time did not meet his

gaze. Her brows pinched, her look pained for only a second and was gone, replaced by her lifted chin and her usual show of strength.

But it had been there, that crack, that glimpse of her hurt.

"This way." He led her from the cell. She followed without protest.

Before they exited the building, Niall instructed Brodie to reclaim the ruined kirtle from Lady Leila's cell and have it sent to the castle. If nothing else, it would be one less thing Lord Armstrong would be displeased about in this whole mess. Mayhap the thing could be laundered clean once more.

Niall pushed open the heavily banded door to the village prison and strode out. Except this time, Lady Leila hesitated before following.

"Guards dinna pause in doorways," he whispered in reminder.

Lady Leila, unrecognizable from the woman who had donned the fine kirtle, now appeared a youth in a gambeson inherited from his father. She stepped outside and tilted her face to a narrow patch of sunlight where it gleamed down on her.

"They dinna revel in sunshine either," he murmured.

She lowered her head and strode forward with the confident gait of a warrior. Soon they would be at the castle and she would be locked within a chamber where she would be safer. Mayhap then he could stop thinking of her, worrying after her—this woman he should hate.

The walk to the castle was uneventful until they passed through the heavy stone curtain walls and into the bailey. A familiar figure stalked toward them. Niall tensed in preparation for the last person he wanted to encounter with Lady Leila out in the open and vulnerable. For as soon as Alban turned in their direction, he headed straight for them.

~

Leila's limbs were soft, and a tang of fear tickled at the back of her throat. She'd tried to swallow it down—to no avail. With each villager who passed them, she had waited with trepidation for their wrath. Their rage had haunted her in her cell, colder than even the chill in those whitewashed walls, and penetrating far deeper within her.

There had been madness in their eyes, a wild desperation, as though the spilling of her blood could douse the contagion and end the great mortality.

Now though, the people were not unlike those of the village outside of Werrick Castle—sagging under the duress of illness, withered by the sapping of life.

The Lion tensed at her side. Leila followed his gaze and the waning energy of her body roared to life once more.

Alban was heading straight for them, his eyes narrowed with spite. "I heard ye had to handle Lord Werrick."

The Lion ignored him.

"Who's this ye've got with ye?" Alban nodded toward Leila.

She resisted the urge to tuck her head lower, hoping that the helm would be sufficient to mask her identity.

"Is Lord Armstrong within?" the Lion asked curtly. "I need to speak with him."

"Why've ye got yer helmets on?" Alban interjected.

"'Tis a matter for me to discuss with yer da," the Lion said in an unflinching tone. "No' ye."

Alban sneered and strode around them as if he meant to leave. Before he could go past them, however, he swept his hand up and struck the bottom of Leila's helm. It had fit her loosely from the start and popped off with ease. Leila sucked in a gasp and shot a glance toward the open portcullis where the villagers might still recognize her.

"Her?" Alban growled. "I thought that witch was in the prison, rotting where she belongs."

"I need to speak with Lord Armstrong posthaste." The Lion grabbed Leila's arm and dragged her toward him, taking the position of captor with his prisoner once more.

Though his hold on her was firm, it was not painful. As with all things, he took care to ensure he did not hurt her. She was close enough to catch his scent, the unmistakable warmth of masculinity mingled with leather and the slightest hint of cedar. It was a pleasing smell, though she conceded that as grudgingly as she admitted to his kindness.

"If ye wish to speak with me, I'm right here." The cool voice of Lord Armstrong sent prickles of gooseflesh rising over Leila's arms.

"My Lord." The Lion turned around, bringing her with him.

Lord Armstrong settled his small eyes on Leila. "Is this our prisoner? What is she doing here? Why is she wearing the armor of one of our reivers?"

"Her father demanded she receive the proper housing of an earl's daughter while she is held," the Lion said. "He wouldna leave if I dinna grant it. I've already had a room cleared out for her."

"And ye sneaked her through the village rather than making her walk?" Lord Armstrong settled his gaze on Leila and her unease turned to revulsion as he sampled her with his eyes. "Where did her kirtle go?"

"Too damn wet to wear and no' die in the prison." The Lion widened his stance, a subtle show of his determination to stand by his decisions. Mayhap this was why he had earned his epithet. He did not back down from a challenge but stood his ground and defended it as he even now defended her.

"More's the pity if she were to die." Lord Armstrong scoffed. "Get that gambeson off her."

"She's no' been found guilty by Father Gerard yet," the Lion countered.

The Scottish earl's face folded down into a frown, an obvious reflection of his displeasure with the Lion's defiance. "Give the witch to Alban. I want ye to come with me."

The Lion tightened his grip on Leila. "That isna necessary."

Lord Armstrong's frown deepened, scoring the lines on his face deeper. "Ye would do well to remember yerself. Lion or no, ye work for me. Mind yerself with this lass, or I'll think ye bewitched." He shifted his attention to Alban. "Take the witch to her room and get a kirtle upon her."

"I'll see it done." Alban's insinuation slicked over his words the way oil did over water. He grasped Leila's wrist, directly over the torn skin from her bindings, and squeezed painfully before tugging her. The Lion's hold on her slipped and Leila plunged toward Alban, all but crashing into his chest. While her gambeson had held the musty remnants of someone's sweat, the one Alban wore was sour with it.

She did her best to hold her breath as he unfastened the gambeson from her torso before spinning her around to jerk it from her back and pin her hands together.

"She's to be put in the left front tower." The Lion issued the one simple order before turning his back to Leila and walking away with Lord Armstrong.

It wasn't until he was gone, until she was at Alban's mercy, that she realized she missed the Lion's quiet stoicism at her side. He had kept her from having to walk through town with the villagers, he had not mentioned what had passed between Leila and her father, and he had even now tried to ensure her safety.

"Walk," Alban commanded. "Or I'll have to make ye." His fingers dug into her wrists.

Leila bit back a cry of pain and walked forward. While the silence between her and the Lion had been somewhat companionable in coming to the castle, the quiet between her and Alban stretched on like an unspoken threat. He had been commanded to get her back into a kirtle. She was not so naive as to wonder at his intent once she was disrobed and at his mercy. Nor was she so weak that she would not fight.

Even as they walked, she considered what she'd seen when he approached them. Had he worn a sword at his belt? Surely, he had. Mayhap a dagger? Possibly. But which side?

Her head ached from trying to probe at the image, but she could not resurrect the necessary information in her mind.

He shoved her into the yawning entrance of the castle where the shadows swallowed them, leaving the world dark and cold. A chill raked its way down her spine.

"Are ye scared, witch?" Alban's grip loosened on one wrist long enough for him to drag a finger over the goosebumped flesh of her forearm. "If no', ye should be."

She clenched her jaw and said nothing. She wouldn't give him the satisfaction of knowing how much his words truly did frighten her. Her mind darted around for something else to think on and immediately went to her father.

Only, that wouldn't do. Not when seeing him had nearly shattered her composure. It had been good of the Lion to not mention the conversation he'd no doubt overheard. The one where he must realize Leila was not Lord Werrick's daughter, where she had bared her soul, unearthed her unworthiness of all she had. Yet he had not spoken of it. Nor had he regarded her with pity or scorn. It was as though he truly had not heard it. And as that was impossible given his nearness to them, she was all the more grateful for the courtesy. Just as she had been grateful for the way he'd guarded her in the prison to ensure her safety, and how he'd provided her with warm, dry clothing.

It was only when Alban had begun to push Leila up the stairs that she realized the comforting thought she had been clinging to as they made their way through the castle. It was not of her father, but of the Lion. Her heart shrank in her chest. Was this how it happened then? How she fell in love with the man who would kill her? Was she so foolish?

Alban pushed the door open, startling a maid who was dragging a trunk across the floor. The red-haired woman looked at Alban with wide eyes.

"Leave," Alban stated.

The woman's gaze slipped to Leila and pity flashed there before she scuttled from the room.

"Bring a kirtle." Alban called his order after the woman, though it was said with a lack of concern, as though he didn't care whether Leila had the garment or not.

Leila stared forward at the room with Alban still holding her hands behind her. The room had been stripped bare of most of its furnishings, save for the trunk left in the middle of the floor and a simple carved bed set in the corner. No doubt everything else had been removed to ensure she did not devise a way to escape.

Alban released Leila and shoved her hard into the room, so she sprawled forward awkwardly. She would have caught her balance were it not for the sharp-edged trunk her shins hit, sending her sailing over it. She crashed to the floor as the door to the room slammed shut and the key clicked the lock into place.

She leapt to her feet as Alban approached, his face revealing a smug smile of victory. "Take off yer clothes."

CHAPTER 9

Leila glared at Alban, refusing to even deign to respond to his command that she remove her clothing. He had no sword at his belt. She'd at least been able to determine that.

He took a slow, menacing step toward her and let his shoes thunk heavily onto the wooden floorboard. It was evident he was trying to intimidate her. Mayhap he expected her to run, to give chase around the room until he finally caught her and gained the upper hand.

Leila stood her ground. If he was going to advance on her, the attack would begin on her terms, not his. She would have the element of surprise on her side.

"I told ye to take off yer clothes." He reached out and pinched at her shirt. "I want to see ye—"

Leila's fist slammed into his face. He stumbled backwards, the fool. He'd underestimated her once before, and clearly was doing so again. She swept her leg toward the back of his knees, so they buckled and sent him falling toward the floor. He hit the ground with all the grace of a sack of rotten vegetables and issued forth a satisfying *oof*. A dagger was affixed to the side of his belt.

In that split second, she had to make a decision: to either snatch up the dagger or kick him in the head. The latter would no doubt kill him, a crime that would guarantee a lifetime of being hunted down. A crime that would have vengeance exacted on her entire family until not one remained alive.

She grabbed for the dagger. Unfortunately, he anticipated that would be her move. He grasped her wrist as she reached for the weapon and tugged with the weight of his body, dragging her to the floor with him. She rolled forward in an attempt to lessen the impact of her fall.

A strong arm knocked her to the side and something hard and sharp slammed into the side of her head. She reeled for a moment, addled by the force of the blow. It was all Alban needed. He was on her in an instant, pressing her with the weight of his body.

"I told ye to take off yer clothes." He peered at her chest, angling his neck to better see down her shirt.

Pain radiated from her head where she'd been struck so sharply and brutally that she was certain she was bleeding. From the corner of her eye, she made out the trunk that had been abandoned in the middle of the room. First it had tripped her; now it had given Alban the upper hand.

A knock came from the door. "My lord, I have the kirtle ye requested."

"Leave it," Alban barked, casting a mist of spittle. He ground his teeth into a grin, then grasped the neckline of Leila's shirt with his good arm and tugged.

The fabric gave with a savage rending that yanked painfully at the back of Leila's neck. The ruined pieces fluttered on either side of her torso.

"Binding?" Alban bemoaned his discovery bitterly and sat up on her higher to better work at it with both his hands.

"Please," Leila said in a weak voice, intentionally not fighting back. Intentionally acting as though the blow to her head had been enough to defeat her. "Stop. Please."

"Ye bewitched me," Alban said through gritted teeth. "Ye make me lust for ye when all I wanted to do before was kill ye."

He did not release her. As she had anticipated. She thrust her hips up as she rolled hard to the side, propelling him from her. He fell, splayed on the ground and floundering in his surprise.

Leila fell on him without mercy and drove her knee into his groin. His eyes nearly bulged from his head and his face colored to a purple-pink heather-like shade. So intense was his injury, he issued no protest as she dug into the pouch at his belt and pulled free the key as well as the dagger.

Having all she needed, she raced for the door. With shaking hands, she worked the key into the lock. Alban grunted and rolled over to the side, where he remained. Leila forced her breath to come out slow and even, to quell the tremble of her anxious fingers. Finally, the lock clicked, and she opened the door to her freedom. A pile of wool lay on the stone platform before the door. Most likely the kirtle the maid brought back for Alban.

Standing two steps down from it, however, was truly a cause for concern. An Armstrong clansman glared up at her, his eyes bright where they fell on her split shirt. "If he's done with ye, I'll be taking my turn with ye, lass."

She pulled back her dagger and began to throw it forward when someone crashed into her. Her aim was knocked aside, and the dagger clattered uselessly down the stairs.

"There willna be anything left of her when I'm done," Alban growled. Sweat dotted his pale brow. He yanked her back and slammed the door shut.

"Give me the key." He held out a shaking palm.

Leila hadn't even realized she'd drawn it out from the door

when she'd run. She gripped it harder, the metal now hot from where she held tight to it.

His face flushed to a deep shade of red and began twitching. "Give me the Goddamn key before I have every man in the castle come in and have a go at ye," he bellowed.

Fear spiked Leila at that. With one guard below, mayhap another at the foot of the stairs, and many more barring her exit from the castle walls, her chances of escape were slim. Contrarily, the likelihood of Alban making good on his oath were high. Frighteningly so.

She threw the key on the ground.

He picked it up with a sneer and let his gaze slither down her body. "Ye havena bested me, ye witch."

She wished the dagger was back in her hand so she could plunge it into his heart. Blood feud be damned. She wanted him dead. So great was her wish that she clenched her fingers around her empty palm as though gripping an imaginary dagger.

"Once my cock isna aching, I'll be back." Alban's upper lip curled up, revealing his sharp, white teeth. "It may be while ye sleep. It may be while ye are idly passing the time in this empty room. It may while ye're curled in fear in the corner awaiting my arrival, but I will come back for ye. And I mean to have ye again, and again, and again."

He opened the door and flung the kirtle to the ground. "Get dressed before I order the men to cut yer clothes off ye and leave ye naked." He spat upon the wool, leaving a puddle of bubbled spit on the costly fabric.

The door slammed shut behind him and the click of the lock sliding into place told her he was gone. For now. Leila waited for the thumping of his feet to descend down the stairs before she gave way to the weakness of her knees and let herself slowly sink to the floor beside the kirtle.

Eager for a distraction, she ran her fingertips along the soft crimson wool. She used the hem of her ruined shirt to wipe away his spittle and took the kirtle to the far corner of the room to dress with hands that would not cease their shaking. He would be back, of course. He had promised he would be, and she knew it to be so.

Daylight faded to dusk and then to night and still Alban did not come for her. The maid who had been in her room before arrived with a meal and eyed her like some horrible monster. Regardless, the girl had done up her kirtle in the back, scant protection from Alban that it was.

Through the day and on into the night, Leila's gaze continued to drive toward the door in anticipation of the springing of the lock, the groaning of the hinges. She hated the weakness of her fear and how very much she dreaded his arrival. For she knew she would not always be so lucky to escape.

∽

BEWITCHED. The word echoed in Niall's head throughout the day and well into the night. He had kept from Lady Leila's room of confinement to prove to himself he was not indeed bewitched.

Except he might truly be.

His mind wandered back to her often, conjuring up images of her, sampling memories of her, teasing himself with fantasies of her. By the time he'd retired to his room, his body was hard and aching for a release that was not fully sated with the grip of his palm. He'd gone to bed with his thoughts firmly settled on Lady Leila, first in admiration and then as the heat of his body rose, once more in lust.

The door to his chamber opened. A shadow in his doorway revealed a feminine shape with a slender waist and long, shapely legs.

His mouth went dry. He knew that figure. He meant to ask how she'd escaped from the tower, how she'd known which room was his, what she meant to do...but all questions slipped away like wisps of smoke as she sauntered into his room. Her hips swayed with sensuality; her intent proclaimed.

He swallowed as she approached his bed, now naked—beautifully, gloriously naked—and crawled across the length of the mattress to him. Her sweet, clean scent of dried herbs swirled around him like a spell. She put a hand to his chest and drew one naked leg over his hips, cradling his arousal with the cleft between her thighs. She was wet and warm where she pressed herself against his shaft. He wanted to grab her hips, shift himself into her and thrust until they were both crying out with passion.

As if reading his thoughts, she shook her head and leaned forward to press her lips to his. Their tongues met and she left the sweetness of honey where she licked inside his mouth. His fingers skimmed over her body, warm and silky. He groaned aloud, a sound which grated in his own ears and made the image shimmer.

He shook his head and groaned once more, louder this time. The image shattered and left him panting in the darkness, alone and reeling from the dream. What devilry was this? Was her bewitchment now entering his dreams as well? Haunting his night as she had haunted his day?

He whipped the blankets off and pushed up from the bed, spurred on by the flare of rage. The cold winter chill of the room greeted his blazing blood but did not cool it. This bewitchment would end tonight.

He pulled on clothing, a mantle and soft leather shoes, and left his chamber, his pace quick as though she might anticipate him coming. As surely as he had only recently imagined her naked over him, he now pictured her muttering incantations under her breath to send him such fevered dreams. His fingers worked through the keys as he walked, plucking their icy stems for the correct one to her chamber.

The two guards standing before the stairs leading to her room cast him side glances as he passed them but did not move to stop him. His leather soles were silent upon the stone stairs. Silent as the sin in the witch's heart, he slid the key in the lock, opened the door and froze.

Lady Leila was bundled beneath the covers, her face turned toward the door, lit by the moonlight seeping in through the shutters. Her expression was relaxed with sleep, serene and exquisitely beautiful.

He watched her form and noted the rise and fall of her breathing from beneath the furs bundled over the top of her. The rhythm was not slow and deep as one sleeps but quickened. She was awake, mayhap hiding her misdeeds under the pretense of slumber.

She would not enter his dreams again. She would torture him no longer.

He locked the door behind him as silently as was possible and strode across the room to her bed. He opened his mouth in preparation to speak, but never got a single word out. For before he had the chance, she flew out of the bed like a banshee and lunged at him. He reeled back in surprise, but her hand came down, fisted over something sharp and wicked.

The thing hit his chest, puncturing slightly before it splintered apart and her hand jerked to the side awkwardly. She growled in a savage show of frustration, tensing to strike at him again, this time with her fists. He grasped her wrists in his hands to still her movements, though it did little good.

She writhed in his grasp, her legs flailing, torso wriggling, arms churning back and forth in a feral attempt to free herself. Her foot came up and kicked at his thigh, the blow powerful with intent. He winced but held tight to her.

"Don't touch me," she snarled.

"Cease this at once," Niall said.

She ignored his order and slammed a shoulder backward, so it smacked into his chest like a punch. "I'll kill you." With that, she redoubled her efforts to escape, as wild as the wind before a squall and just as hard to trap on one's hands.

"Leila." He said her name firmly and without her formal address. "'Tis me, Niall. The Lion."

She went still in his arms. "Release me."

"Will ye continue to attack me?" Even as he asked the question, he eased his grip on her.

"Nay," she said weakly.

He released her as asked. She turned and regarded him, her brows pinched with confusion. "Why have you come here at such an hour?"

Heat flooded Niall's face. "To catch ye chanting a spell while ye bewitch me."

Those pinched brows lifted now. "I've bewitched you?"

The dream flooded back to him, hot with lust. "Ye lodged yerself in my mind. I know it. Ye sent me dreams…"

She was looking at him as if he was mad. "What fools you Scotsmen are." She spoke in a low, quiet tone that was absent malice, and yet cold as ice. "You confuse your own lusts for bewitchment and set the blame at my feet when I never asked for your attention or that of any other."

Niall frowned. "Any other? Has someone else claimed ye've bewitched them as well?"

"Alban," she replied, as if disgust roiled in her stomach. "I thought you were better than him. It appears you are not." Her shoulders fell and she sounded suddenly very tired. "Please leave me."

"Alban was here?" he demanded.

She sucked in a hard breath. "Leave me." She put her back to him and hugged her slender body.

What had Alban done to her? Niall ground his teeth, assuming the worst and most probable scenario.

"Did he touch ye?" Niall asked.

"Leave me," Leila repeated. "I'll not have you presuming I only seek to further bewitch you this eve."

Niall approached slowly. "Lady Leila. Forgive me."

She lifted her eyes to him, large and luminous in the muted moonlight. "I have not bewitched you," she whispered. "I swear it on my love of my family."

And in that one moment, Niall realized the truth of her words, as well as the power of his own longing and care for this seemingly frail woman. God, he was a fool.

"I know," he said quietly. He wanted to reach a hand up to her face, to stroke the creaminess of her skin in the fragile light, but he tamped down the longing. "Did Alban come to ye?"

She nodded and his stomach dropped.

"Did he...?" Niall could not force the question out. It was his own cowardice that stayed his tongue. He had been avoiding Leila for fear of her having bewitched him. He had not been there to protect her.

"He tried." Leila folded her arms over her chest. "He will try again."

"Ye thought I was him."

Leila nodded. "I peeled a bit of wood from the trunk because nothing on the bed would give way. It was only a sliver, but I'd hoped it would be enough. Apparently, it was not."

He glanced down at his chest and found flecks of splintered wood remaining. It had not even pierced his leine. "Alban willna bother ye again," he vowed.

She nodded but did not appear convinced. Not nearly as much as Niall. For when he was done with Alban, the man would never think of laying a hand on another woman again.

CHAPTER 10

The following morning, Niall arrived early to the practice field. He'd spent the remainder of the night biding his time, planning out exactly how he would handle the matter of Alban. He couldn't kill him, of course. Not with him being Lord Armstrong's son.

But Niall could best him on the practice field. It wouldn't resolve the issue, but it would ease the rage searing through him. Afterward, Niall would take up the matter with Lord Armstrong.

Niall paced the well-worn earth to burn the energy racing through his veins as the sun stained the sky red with its ascent. The men slowly trickled into the area of the castle they used for practice, with Alban being one of the last to arrive. Niall ran through the basic moves with them to ease the stiffness from their joints and get their bodies warm on the cold morning.

It had been torment to bide his time when he was hot and ready for battle. He paired himself with Alban and stood across from the younger man.

"I heard ye attacked the prisoner," he spoke casually as he circled his opponent.

"She's a witch." Alban spit on the ground between them.

"She's also a noble's daughter." Niall lunged, bringing his practice sword down.

Alban was fast, aye, but not when faced with the magnitude of Niall's rage. The blade struck Alban hard on his injured shoulder. His grunted exhale gave proof of the hit's accuracy, as did the narrowing of his eyes.

"It doesna matter," Alban growled. "She'll be dead once Father Gerard judges her. How can she be anything but when the Armstrongs were the first to fall to this illness? 'Tis a miracle my da, me and my sister havena fallen ill."

Niall wouldn't call it a miracle. He ducked to avoid being struck by Alban's blade. The wind of its passing brushed by Niall's cheek. Too close. He shoved his torso against Alban, catching him off guard, and brought his own sword up hard, disarming his opponent. Here, he could have put the tip of his dulled sword to Alban's neck to signify victory.

But that was not enough. He wanted Alban to feel some of the pain and terror Lady Leila had felt when he'd attacked her.

"Would ye have someone treat yer sister thus?" Niall rushed Alban, gripping his shoulders and swiping his legs out from beneath him so he crashed to the ground.

The Keeper's son ground out a harsh exhale. "My sister isna a witch."

"Lady Leila may no' be one either."

Alban threw his fist at Niall. It glanced off his jaw without much impact but opened the door for Niall to retaliate. And retaliate he did. With fists and feet and all the pent-up rage he had radiating inside him.

He and Alban rolled about on the ground like youths in a village brawl, tearing at each other's gambesons to get a better grip on one another, to strike harder. Niall was hit several times, but not nearly as often as he delivered blows.

His final one was to Alban's nose. There had been a fleshy crack beneath Niall's fist and an immediate eruption of blood. Alban let out a gurgling howl of pain and the fight was over.

"Leave Lady Leila be," Niall warned. "She's a prisoner, and an earl's daughter at that."

Alban held his face and glowered from beneath the mess of his ruddy hair. "My da will hear of this."

Niall didn't bother to reply to the petty threat. He had anticipated Alban would go to his father to complain. In fact, Niall had been counting on it.

The summons to see Lord Armstrong came almost immediately after practice, implying Alban had made good on his threat as soon as the Armstrong guards had been released. The Keeper of Liddesdale was waiting for Niall impatiently with Alban at his side.

"Ye broke my son's nose," Lord Armstrong said dryly.

Niall bit the inside of his cheek to keep from smirking. "'Tis what happens on the practice field."

Lord Armstrong cast an irritable side glance at his son, as though in agreement with what Niall had said. The Scottish earl was a notable warrior himself, one who never backed down from battle. One who would never go to his father to complain of a broken nose.

"Alban suspects ye're bewitched by the prisoner." Lord Armstrong made the accusation in a bored tone, clearly placating his son.

"If protecting the purity of an earl's daughter is bewitchment, then mayhap I am." Niall folded his arms over his chest. "We've already arrested Lord Werrick's daughter and are holding her to be tried for witchcraft. We dinna need to insult the man by also raping his daughter."

"She bewitched me," Alban hissed. "She made me lust after—"

"Cease yer whining." Lord Armstrong's voice rang out against the cold gray stone. He glared at his son. "Ye're a man, no' a child. Cease yer prattling at once. And if ye are indeed bewitched, ye best be as far from the chit as possible. See to the scouting party. Lord Werrick hasna taken his daughter's arrest well and I dinna doubt he will attack us to save her."

Alban opened his mouth to protest, but Lord Armstrong cast him an icy stare that stayed his son's tongue.

"Niall, handle the witch." Lord Armstrong rubbed his brow, as one does when their patience is sorely tried. "Already there has been too much squabbling about this lass. I grow weary of it and pray the priest arrives posthaste."

Alban huffed. "Da, I—"

Lord Armstrong's face went with red. "Silence! I havena skirts for ye to hide behind, so dinna act like a spoilt bairn. On the morrow, ye'll depart to join the scouting party."

He issued forth a heavy sigh and sank wearily into the great wooden seat of power. "Leave me now. I've other matters to tend to and dinna wish to be vexed by ye further."

Alban stormed from the room, his footfalls thundering over the rushes. Niall inclined his head respectfully and took his leave. He too had matters to tend to. But before he began any of them, he needed to secure Brodie to act as guard before the tower room stairs where Lady Leila was being held. Next, he wished to see to her himself and offer warning.

After all, Alban was not leaving until the following morning, which meant he still posed a very viable threat to Lady Leila.

∼

THE WAITING WAS ENDLESS. Leila glanced toward the closed door to the chamber she'd been locked within. It had opened only once since the Lion had left, when the young maid had brought in a fresh ewer of water as well as some oatcakes and ale for Leila to break her fast.

The Lion had said he would see to Alban, but what if he could not? She had overheard some of the men speaking when she'd been in prison. Alban was no normal reiver. He was the only son to the Keeper of Liddesdale, heir to the Armstrong earldom. Powerful men were dangerous.

Especially great men who had been humiliated. As he had been by her. She had prepared for his arrival in case the Lion had been unable to stop his advances. Or worse, if the Lion's efforts incited him further.

A sliver of wood from the side of her bed was tucked within the sleeve of her kirtle. It was firmer than the one she'd peeled from the trunk before and hard-won. She was relatively certain it would not crumble apart as the last one had. Mayhap it would even prove to be fatal.

She'd torn her nails digging it free. Her fingertips ached with a raw, angry heat that pulsed with her heartbeat despite the cold air of the room. Her nerves were just as jagged.

She paced the room, trying not to count the steps lest the ten she was able to take could become too confining with no way out. She'd been trapped thus before. When the Armstrongs had taken her and Lark.

Somehow Leila had been able to sense Ella coming to their rescue that day. The connection had been fast and immediate, as all-encompassing as a mantle on a cold day.

But she had been seeking aid then, as a young woman trapped with another who had been terrified. That fear had been contagious, feeding off the dark uncertainty within them.

But Leila was no longer that girl and there was no one else with her to protect. She would not allow her family to sacrifice themselves for her. This time, she did not seek to be rescued.

She knew well her fate. Her shoulder throbbed with a sharp, crystalline pain where Death's fingers had marked her. Life was running short and he was waiting for her.

Footsteps sounded on the stairs leading up to her chamber. She stopped mid-pace and let the wooden spike slide from her sleeve into her waiting hand. Armed and ready, she pressed herself against the wall to hide behind the door, the same as she'd done in the dungeon before with the Lion. The key rattled in the lock and the door groaned open with a squeal of protest.

There was a moment's pause, with no further steps into the room. Leila tensed.

"I'm no' falling prey to that trick again." The Lion's familiar voice eased the knots from Leila's stomach.

The door slowly closed to reveal the Lion's powerful frame and a note of humor glinting in his hazel eyes. His mouth quirked to the side in a relaxed grin as he took her in where she stood behind the door with her stake lifted in preparation to attack.

He crossed his arms over his chest and the muscles of his arms bunched beneath his sleeves. "Ye've used that one before."

"Only on you." She quickly slid the stake up her sleeve. He did not comment on the weapon or demand she relinquish it. She could not be in such a place with no weapon at her side. Especially with a man like Alban nearby.

"I've spoken to Lord Armstrong. Alban willna be bothering ye. He's being sent off with a scouting party and my most trusted guard, Brodie, will be watching ye to ensure yer safety." He watched her with his steady hazel eyes that were almost golden in the wash of late morning sunlight. "I'll ensure no one harms ye."

"Why are you being so kind to me?" Leila asked. "I'm your prisoner, a woman you suspect of being a witch."

A muscle in his jaw flexed at the last word. "Ye've no' been judged yet."

His back was straight with confidence and a righteous justice emanated from him. He commanded a room simply by being in it and the power of his presence was intoxicating.

She stepped forward before she could stop herself, so she stood directly before him, the tips of their shoes almost touching. Her hands lightly came up to rest on his fingers. They were large and warm and callused with strength.

It was then she noted her own ravaged nails and quickly withdrew her grasp. "Thank you for your kindness."

He didn't reply at first, his gaze fixed intently on her. Up close, she could make out more green than hazel in his beautiful eyes. He had shaved earlier and his cheeks were now absent the golden whiskers she'd seen on prior occasions. His jaw looked smooth and she was left with the ridiculous urge to run her fingertips over the skin there.

Her attention swept over his mouth. He had fine lips, another thing she could not appreciate until she was closer. They were fuller than she had realized, as they were usually set in a hard line of authority. They were not now, however, and she couldn't help but wonder if they were as soft as they looked.

The Lion lifted his hand and gently swept it down her cheek. She drew in a quiet breath and her pulse spiked. Her eyes fell closed as she reveled in the tender caress. She wanted to sway against him, to feel the power of his body against her own.

All at once, the touch was not there and the glorious heat radiating off him had eased away. Her eyes opened and she found him standing a solid step away, his forehead crinkled. "I'm no' like Alban." He nodded. "Good morrow."

Then, as soon and sudden as he'd arrived, he was gone. Leila exhaled and sagged against the wall behind her.

Never in her life had she kissed a man, and never had she wanted to. Her mind swirled in frustrating circles, pulled in every direction by the crush of lustful thoughts and the resonating logic. After all, how could she truly love a man who was meant to kill her?

CHAPTER 11

Niall cursed himself the better part of the day. He didn't know what had possessed him to reach out and stroke Lady Leila's cheek. Even now, hours later, his fingertips hummed with the whispered memory of the connection between them.

He curled the offending hand into a fist and squeezed. She was a prisoner. Mayhap a witch.

He'd been so blinded by her beauty and strength that he had conveniently set aside what he knew to be true in his heart. Lady Leila had warned the castle of the arrival of the pestilence based on what others had said, and her own priest had lied when he'd said he didn't believe she was a witch.

The condemnation ringing within Niall, however, was hollow. He knew the truth of his incensed thoughts and it had everything to do with how he had treated Lady Leila. She was locked in that room with nowhere to go, and he had touched her.

Truth be told, he had almost kissed her.

Her blue gaze had lowered to his mouth, unintentionally teasing, an innocent gesture that tempted him in the most carnal way possible. She was a lady, and quite possibly a witch, so either she was out of his realm of consideration as a lover, or she would be drowned for her heresy.

But witch or not, the fact remained that she was a lady and he would not leave her to Alban's wrath. Niall carried the tray of food with him through the torch-lit halls. Brodie stood at the base of the curving staircase leading to Lady Leila's tower chamber and broke into a smile as Niall approached.

"Yer relief is coming soon," Niall promised.

Brodie lifted his shoulders in a good-natured shrug. "I'm happy to guard the lass. After all, 'tis because of her that Bonnie's fever has quelled."

Niall lifted an eyebrow in silent question. He hadn't been aware Brodie's sister was unwell. But then, in times of such pestilence, it was scarcely news when someone fell ill. "I'm pleased to hear she's recovered."

Brodie's blue eyes crinkled with as much concern as Niall had ever seen in them. "There wasna anyone to aid her. I told Lady Leila what ailed her, and she told me to use one of the bags of herbs." He leaned closer to Niall. "It wasna a spell or charm. I looked through it before I made the tea. Just bits of flowers and stems." His gaze flicked up to the stairs that twisted into darkness. "I dinna think she's a witch. If she was, wouldna she fly out of here?"

Flying out of the castle seemed a bit far-fetched. However, if she truly did have the powers of a witch, she wouldn't be hiding behind tower room doors with bits of her trunk broken off to use as a weapon. The image of her fingers flashed in his mind, her nails torn, the cuticles still stained with blood. "That isna for us to decide."

"I'll speak for her at the trial with Father Gerard," Brodie said earnestly. "If we're able. I'll do it for her."

Niall was uncertain how such things worked. He'd only witnessed the trial of one witch before, the one who had killed his father. It had been hastily done in the course of a morning and Lady Elliot was dead by that afternoon. She'd been much loved by the people of the village and they had protested their outrage at her death. It was why Lord Armstrong now went to such lengths to ensure Lady Leila was properly declared a witch, especially as Lady Leila was an English earl's daughter. Regardless, Niall nodded at Brodie's generous offer before ascending the stairs to Lady Leila's locked chamber.

"Put yer stake away, woman." He held the food with one hand and unlocked the door with the other.

He found her standing in the middle of the room, no doubt pacing. All prisoners paced. It was a way of passing time, of assuaging some of the pent-up tension.

"I've come to bring our food." He set the tray atop the abandoned trunk that had never been moved. While a table could be easily disassembled for a wooden club, which Leila would no doubt try to use, the trunk was too flimsy to be of any real threat but held food quite nicely.

"Our food?" She stepped closer and eyed the roasted venison. Thus far, all she'd been fed were heels of bread and wee bits of cheese.

"I intend to stay with ye until morn." He sat on the floor on one side of the trunk and took a small hunk of bread to dredge through the savory sauce. It was a rich brown sauce, spiced with saffron and various herbs he couldn't name. It was damn delicious—that was all he knew and cared about.

"I'll be outside the door, of course." He gestured to the opposite side of the trunk for her to sit. "But I figured first ye might like a bit of real food." He popped the morsel into his mouth.

Lady Leila joined him where he'd indicated and gracefully tore off a bit of her own bread. "Thank you," she said softly.

They used their fingers to eat, something that would never be permitted at the lord's table. But lacking their eating daggers, they were left with little choice. Especially when Niall knew exactly what Leila could do with a blade. While she was compliant and respectful, she was still a prisoner and every prisoner would do anything to get free.

They talked while they ate, with her sharing stories of her life growing up with her four sisters at Werrick Castle, and with him telling her of some of the more amusing misdeeds of his youth. Like the time he'd put a lizard in his ma's favorite pot and various other innocent pranks of a boy with too much time on his hands.

He didn't delve into the later crimes that were far more egregious, far less forgivable. The stolen cattle and food, the fights with rival clans, the man he'd tried to ransom, which ended with his own father getting killed.

Leila's stories were far more fascinating, and her eyes lit up with a quiet joy as she spoke. While her previous conversation with her father was proof that she did not feel she deserved the love of her family, affection for them still glowed within her.

The tray sat between Niall and Leila; the decadent food now gone as well as the last of the wine in the skin he'd brought. The light in the window was beginning to wane, but still Niall did not wish to leave. Not when the time they'd spent speaking had been so enjoyable.

The wistful smile on Leila's mouth wilted somewhat. "You never said anything about what was said during my father's visit, yet I'm sure you heard it all."

Niall nodded once.

Leila's gaze slid away. "Then you know I don't deserve the treatment you're giving me. I don't deserve the fine food, or the protection and kindness. I'm not the daughter of an earl, I'm—"

"Ye're loved by Lord Werrick and he's claimed ye as his daughter. That is all that matters."

She chewed her lip. "You know the truth of it, though. What

my true father did. What *I* did." Her brows pursed. "I never told them how sorry I was. I was..." She swallowed. "I was too much of a coward." Her voice broke on the last word.

"If ye're a coward, I dinna know what name to possibly assign to a man like Alban." Niall scooted closer to where Leila sat.

She looked up, and though her eyes were bright with unshed tears, the corners of her mouth lifted in a ghost of a smile.

"Ye're brave and from what I've known of ye and seen of ye, ye're considerate of others." Niall ran his thumb over the back of Leila's slender forefinger where the fingertip was pink and raw. "Ye deserve better than ye're getting here. In fact, ye dinna deserve to be here at all."

Leila shot him a questioning look. But she did not pull her hand away from his touch. Her hand was cool under his, but not cold as before.

"Brodie told me what ye did for his sister," Niall explained. "Even when captured and held in prison, ye sought only to assist others. Even the man guarding ye."

"Most people with knowledge of healing would have aided her." Leila's thumb rose slightly, a scant bit of movement that was just enough to whisper over his. "I pray she is recovered."

Niall's mouth went dry at the delicate connection forming between them. "Aye," he said softly. "Thanks to ye."

"Brodie steeped the tea and tended to her." She gazed up at Niall, her blue eyes wide and innocent and beautiful.

"Ye're too good to be here." Niall lifted his hand to carefully touch the smooth line of her jaw. She was smooth and warm against his palm. It made him ache to caress all of her thus.

Her lashes swept over her cheeks as she closed her eyes and nuzzled into his touch. She was a bonny lass, with fair skin, and plump, pink lips that begged to be tasted. Not that he ought to be tasting them.

Even as he thought as much, he found himself leaning toward her to capture that mouth in a tender, eager kiss.

⁓

Leila had been expecting the Lion's kiss. She had not, however, expected the softness of his lips nor the intensity of need that scorched through her veins. His mouth moved over hers carefully, as though he was afraid of frightening her.

She leaned her head up farther to let him know she welcomed the kiss. Though God knew she should not. Not with this man who would kill her.

Yet everything in her drew her to him. His scent of cedar and leather, the slight rasp of the whiskers on his chin, the heat radiating from his body.

His large hand slid up to cup the back of her head, cradling its weight. The tip of his tongue brushed the seam of her mouth and something innate within her parted her lips for him. He tasted her then with a sweep of his tongue, and she gave a small whimpering sound in the back of her throat.

His mouth slanted over hers as his tongue teased against hers again and again. Everything within her burned with a lustful craving unlike anything she'd ever experienced. It pulsed hot and insistent between her legs and prickled at her nipples, so her breasts felt heavy and overly sensitive. In fact, all of her felt overly sensitive, and in tune to every movement of the Lion. Every smell, every taste, every sense was totally and completely enraptured with him.

Her breath came faster; her heart beat harder. She wanted more of this. Her tongue met his on the next stroke, tentative at first, then with a keenness that made her want more and more and more.

The Lion gave a low growl that sent tingles of pleasure skimming over Leila's body. She reached out a hesitant hand and put it to the solid wall of his chest. His groan rumbled beneath her palm, encouraging her exploration of his body.

She let her fingers roam over him, learning the strength of his torso beneath from atop his doublet and shirt. In doing this, she eased up onto her knees from where they sat to better smooth her fingers over his powerful shoulders.

He lightly cupped her bottom, rounding his touch to fit over her perfectly as he raised himself to his knees as well. Her skin practically sizzled at the contact. She shifted closer to him and her kisses took on a passion she could not control; a passion she did not want to control. Her tongue tangled with his, their lips meeting and caressing against one another.

His hands ran up the sides of her waist and higher still to her breasts, where he cupped her against his palm and swept a thumb over her nipple. The highly sensitive bud needled with pleasure. She cried out in delight.

The Lion drew her closer, so she was fitted against him. A hardness strained between them. Though she was an innocent, she knew well what such a reaction from a man meant. A moan slipped unbidden from her lips and was muffled by their kisses.

His arms curled around her, solid with muscle and strength as he drew their bodies together. The length of his manhood pressed even more firmly against her. It was sinful of her, but she wanted it lower, near the source of her lust where she thrummed with hot abandon. She rubbed against him, panting with need at the hint of friction.

He propped one of his legs up, bracing her weight with his muscular thigh. She straddled his leg and immediately noted the delicious pressure against her intimate place. His mouth ran down her throat as his hands guided her hips to move over his thigh.

Leila blinked in surprise at the rush of pleasure as she

ground herself against him. She arched her head back to give him better access to her neck and panted at the incredible sensation wrought by arching against him. Her fingers worked free the top few buttons of his doublet and explored his strong chest beneath. His skin was lightly dusted with wiry, golden hair and lines of hard muscle teased at her touch.

It made her want to see all of him, explore all of him. She gave a frustrated whimper she had not intended and began to work free several more buttons.

The Lion broke from their kiss with a ragged groan. "Nay. We shouldna be doing this. I never should have..." The longing on his face did not match the regret of his words, especially when his gaze dipped to her mouth.

Leila tucked her lower lip into her mouth, savoring the sweet memory of the feel of his mouth on it. "Kissed me?"

His reply was a mere grunt. He had not pulled her from where she straddled his leg still.

"I liked it." Leila slowly reached out and slid free another button of his doublet.

It was foolish to do, to encourage him further when he was ready to stop, to know that every kiss, every moment of longing brought her closer to loving him and thus closer to her own demise. But she could not stop, even if she wanted to. And she did not.

He gave a short groan and caught her face in his hands, kissing her once more. This time, the first meeting of their lips was explosive with lust. Their mouths moved frantically, tongues tasting, licking, stroking. His hands were all over her body, sending ripples of delight through her.

She moaned as she rocked her hips against him. He lowered his leg and pulled her into his lap, so she straddled his body. The hardness of his arousal pressed between her legs through his trews and her dress. Leila cried out and moved her hips the way he'd shown her.

The Lion worked at the top of her gown with blind fingers while he kissed her hungrily. Finally, he managed to tug it down enough to reveal her breasts above the lowered neckline. He lowered his head and caught one nipple in his hot mouth.

More tingles, more heat, more pleasure. So much, she could only gasp at the overwhelming and wonderful sensations whirling through her. She had worked free his doublet and pushed it from his body, so he wore only the linen shirt beneath. She was just beginning to lift it from his torso, revealing the banded muscle of his stomach beneath, when his hand slipped under her dress to her naked calf.

"Do ye trust me, Leila?" he asked.

Leila.

Her lips curled into a languid smile. She liked her name on his lips like that, without "lady" before it. It was intimate, sensual. Like him.

She nodded in reply, for though she should not, she did trust him. After all, mayhap the vision of her death might be one that changed. She knew better, of course. She'd had the dream too many times. But mayhap...

His fingers caressed up her legs in long, climbing strokes, over her knee, along the inside of her thigh, nearly to the apex of her legs. Her mind went blank of all thought.

His breath was coming faster, along with hers, as he crept his fingers higher still. So close. So close.

His fingertips grazed the cleft between her thighs. She sucked in a hard inhale.

"Ye're so damn wet." His face flinched in a look almost pained.

"Should I be?" she asked breathlessly.

He swallowed and studied her for a moment. He touched

her sex once more, lingering, gliding in the slickness of her desire. When she cried out, the natural huskiness of her voice was almost hoarse.

"Aye," he answered. "It's what prepares a woman for a man."

She nodded, knowing how such things worked. One could not heal without understanding the baser functions of the body. But he did not need to know how much she knew. "How?" she asked wickedly. "Tell me as you touch me."

His finger circled the bud of her sex and pleasure sparkled and radiated everywhere.

"It makes yer passage soft and warm," he said brokenly. "Ready for a man to glide himself into." A digit nudged at her entrance, easing in just a scant fraction of an inch.

Leila's head fell back with a moan. She wanted to sink down on his finger, to force it up inside of her, to douse the blazing desire before she burned to a cinder. But he shifted his hand upward once more to stroke the nub that sent stars flashing behind her lids.

"Do you want to glide yourself into me?" she asked.

He groaned and his jaw clenched. "This is about ye. No' about me." The circular caress became faster, almost a flicker, back and forth, back and forth until her blood was molten in her veins.

"Aye, Leila." His voice was low and gravelly. "Come for me, lass."

Her crises washed over her like a shower of sparks: brilliant, hot and glowing. He caught her mouth with his, drinking in the cries of her delight. Her heart was racing, and her breath came too fast, but she scarcely noticed. Her entire being felt as though it was flying, floating high up above the puffy white clouds and toward the intensity of a beautiful hot sun.

She opened her eyes and found the Lion studying her face.

Her mouth opened, but she had no words to say. At least not before he spoke ahead of her.

"I shouldna be here." His gentle tone did not dull the sting of his words. "I shouldna have done what I did." He eased her off of his lap.

"Stay with me." She allowed him to set her away from him and help her to standing.

"I canna. Leila, ye're..." He shook his head, not finishing his sentence.

The glow of her release cooled with his implication. "I know. You're Deputy to the Keeper of Liddesdale and I'm your prisoner."

His mouth curled into a sardonic smile. "It isna that. Ye're too damn beautiful. I think of ye often. Day and eve. 'Tis foolish, I know, but I canna seem to stop. To stay here with ye would be too tempting when I have matters that must be tended to."

She wanted to goad him, to press him as to what would be too tempting, but she already knew. It was evident in the arousal that still strained in his trews after she'd had her own relief. He had given her pleasure even as he had remained frustrated.

Without another word, he gathered up the tray, inclined his head and slipped from the room, leaving her alone with the branding of memories from what they'd done. Emotions tangled against one another until she could scarce sort love from fear.

For no matter how much she tried to resist, she could not stop herself from the incredible lure of The Lion. Once, not so long ago, she wondered how she could love a man she knew would kill her, but now she understood just how easy it could be.

CHAPTER 12

Sleep did not come easily for Leila. Despite the luxurious relaxation of her body following her release, her mind was like a hive of bees, all darting this way and that in chaotic abandon.

Her gaze wandered back to the solid wooden door. Not with fear as before, but with anticipation. No longer did she dread Alban would swing it open and make good on his threats. Nay, now she wished it would part to reveal the Lion in the doorway, still hot and hard. Ready to show her how a woman's wetness helped to accommodate within her that most intimate part of him.

With Niall guarding her door, she'd put aside the shaft of wood she'd peeled from the bed. The ache of her fingers from prying it free had eased with her balm he'd brought her. Her eyes flicked back to the door.

Was he still there?

She shifted in the straw mattress. Bits of hay jabbed at her through the thin, rough sheet. Her right side was no more comfortable than her left.

Was he still there?

She drew back the thin blanket and slipped from the bed to the floor, her gaze fixed on the door.

A cool current of air swept in from the crack beneath it as she approached. "Are you there, Lion?" she asked.

"I am."

She put her hand to the solid wooden surface as though doing so might allow her to feel him through it.

"Do ye need something, lass?" he asked.

She almost laughed at the question, as if she were a guest rather than a prisoner. Aye, she needed much. Her freedom, her family, him.

"Nay," she replied instead. "Only to bid you good night."

"Rest easy, Lady Leila," he replied. "I'll ensure ye're safe."

She pressed her lips together. His reassurances of her safety had been humorous at first, at least in a macabre sense, when she was determined to resist him. Somehow, however, he had slipped past every defense she'd erected and was working his way into her heart. Now his reassurances of her safety, and the reminder of how integral he was to her demise, had lost all humor.

Saying nothing further, she walked backward toward her pallet as she left her attention on the door. Where he remained on the other side. The Lion. Her destiny.

She settled into her bed and drew the covers over her. This time she did not fight the memories of what they'd shared, nor did she try to fight the pull of her thoughts toward him. She ran to them, let them embrace her with comfort and warmth. It was then that sleep finally claimed her, wholly and completely.

Her dreams were senseless shifts of images of her loved ones. She tried to cling to their faces, but the harder she tried to focus on them, the more they pulled away. A tingling sensation washed over her, one so familiar, she could register its presence even in her sleep. It was the same with every vision she received, whether she was asleep or awake.

The village around her was one she instantly recognized, the one located just outside of Werrick Castle beside the pestilence hut. Her nose stung from the smoke hanging thick and acrid in the air and her eyes watered against it. Within the hut came the cries of the dying as they begged for water and pleaded for relief.

Werrick Castle loomed on the horizon as it always did, like a sentry guarding the village and all its people. Her heart leapt at the familiar site. Father was inside, as well as Isla and Nan and Bernard and Peter, and all the servants she'd come to love as family.

She raced toward the castle, alight with joy to see them all once more. A violent gust blew at her, sending her staggering backward as a shadow appeared behind Werrick Castle. It was like a cloud, but thicker, darker, glistening as if a sheen of oil had been slicked over its surface.

It rolled through the sky like something living, bringing with it the sickly-sweet odor of illness. Terror gripped Leila. She stopped struggling against the wind and was blown onto her back. She watched, helpless, as the mass stopped over Werrick Castle, casting a shadow of death on all those she loved.

Her right shoulder burned where Death had left his mark. "Nay," she cried. But the cloud did not leave despite her pleas. Everything in her sagged in defeat, for there was nothing she could do to stop it. The pestilence would descend upon Werrick Castle.

The wind ceased abruptly, and water rushed over her feet. She jolted upright as the scene changed into the rushing river where the sky was gray, and the banks laid white with a dusting of snow. She gasped harshly. Not this. Not him.

He was there, bathed in the chilly winter light as he stalked toward her, his face set with determination. Except now she knew that face in passion, when his lips were not thinned, and his eyes were tender.

"Leila." He was next to her now. A hand at her back pushed her onward.

The water was up to her calves, so cold it burned like Death's mark on her shoulder. She shook her head.

"Leila," he said her name again in a gravelly voice. His hands came up to her shoulders.

The river was at her thighs now, stealing her breath and filling her with fear while he pushed her down. The frigid water stung like a thousand arrows and left her momentarily stunned as it filled her nose, her mouth. That was when she struggled for her life, and when he pushed down all the harder, intent on her death.

∾

NIALL ADJUSTED his back against the hard-stone wall. He'd slept in worse places. Admittedly, his cock hadn't been raging with lust in such conditions, but he'd definitely managed rest in locations more rugged than the interior of a keep.

He wasn't worried Alban would approach without his notice. Niall had never slept deeply. No warrior ever truly did.

Nay, his inability to sleep had more to do with her husky voice bidding him good night from the opposite side of the door. It was the flushed pleasure on her lovely face when he brought her to release with his hand, the sweet scent of her desire flavoring the air and driving him nearly mad. It was how she had asked him to stay and how damn hard it had been to decline.

He gave an irritated grunt and shifted against the wall once more. The stone stair beneath his bottom was hard and cold and only served to heighten his discomfort. A whimpering sound pierced the air.

Niall jerked upright.

A cry came this time, a protest from the other side of the door where Leila slept. Niall regarded the door warily and settled back once more. Alban wouldn't have been able to get inside unless he'd gone through the window, which wasn't likely.

Niall had just decided to ignore what was most likely a night terror when the thrashing of a struggle sounded, along with cries of fear. He scrambled to his feet, his fingers fumbling with the ring of keys.

By some miracle, he managed to choose the right one on the first try and flung the door open. He'd expected to find Alban in the room, based on her wild screams, but she was alone in the bed, flailing as though fighting for her very life.

"Leila," he said softly.

She did not wake. He approached the bed. "Leila."

A sob burst from her. "Nay." She began to struggle again.

Niall reached for her shoulders to gently wake her. She shrieked and fought against him with balled up fists.

He pinned down her arms with his elbows and held her shoulders in place. "Leila, ye're having a dream. Wake now."

Her eyes flew open. "The Lion," she whispered. "You've come for me already." Her breath came faster, and she yanked free of him. "Please don't do it." Her voice was small. "I cannot bear for it to be you."

Chills raked down his spine at the frightened hurt in her tone. What was she talking about?

He put his hands up and stepped back from the bed, so she did not perceive him as a threat. "Leila, I think ye're still dreaming. Ye need to wake, lass."

She blinked and looked around her, as though coming to the realization as to where she was. "My family," she said. "Have you had news of Werrick Castle?"

Niall stared at her. Was this still part of her dream?

"I've no' heard anything of Werrick Castle," he replied slowly. "Is there news I ought to have been informed of?"

She sat up and hugged her knees to her chest. Her hair was tousled around her shoulders and her eyes wide as she turned her gaze up to study him. She shook her head, her brows furrowed with concern. "Nay. 'Tis nothing."

He ought to have accepted what she said and walked away. He never should have even entered the chamber in the first place. But he was there now, and her stricken face revealed more than she would allow herself to say.

"If ye tell me, I can help." He offered.

Her eyes filled with tears, but she wiped them away and shook her head. "'Tis only a night terror. Like you said."

"Do ye want me to stay with ye?" He stepped closer slowly to show he wasn't a threat to her, that he meant well.

She drew in a shaking breath. "Aye. Please."

He nodded and went to the door to close and lock it. That done, he lay down in front of it.

"Do you mean to sleep on the floor?" Leila asked.

He tucked his hands behind his back. "I was sleeping on stone on the stairs. I must say, the wooden floorboards are an improvement."

"Would you—" Her gaze slid away uncomfortably. "That is, I would not..." She shrugged shyly. "Growing up, my sisters and I slept together in one large bed. I found it comforting. I still had night terrors but having them near me did much to allay my dreams."

"Ye want me to sleep in yer bed with ye." Niall lifted his head from the cradle of his hands to stare pointedly at her.

Leila nodded.

"I dinna think yer da will take kindly to that." He lowered his head once more.

"You also abducted and imprisoned me. I do not think you will ever be redeemed in his eyes."

Niall sat up. Her point was an excellent one, though he found it odd that the truth of it should gnaw at his mind so much to hear it. He had never cared for Lord Werrick's approval prior to having met Leila.

Niall got to his feet and made his way to the bed. His pulse doubled its beat as he neared her. Aye, Leila still wore the red wool dress, and he was fully clothed, but lying beside her as they both slept, sharing heat and air, would be almost impossibly intimate.

Her demeanor was reticent as she shifted over on the mattress to make space for him. He took a long, deep breath in an attempt to settle his racing heart and slipped under the blanket beside her. The sheets there were warm from the heat of her body and everything smelled like clean, dried herbs. Like her.

He extended his arm toward her, offering his chest to lay upon. She readily accepted and snuggled close to him with her head nestled against his shoulder. The delicate scent of rosemary wafted from her hair.

He liked having her laying against him, not just for the slight weight of her lithe body nestled to him, but also the feeling that he could protect her from anything.

He preferred her being with him like this rather than regarding him with raw fear as she had when he first entered the room. The chill he'd felt then resurfaced in the form of goosebumps over his flesh.

You've come for me already.

What had she meant by that? He remembered the first time he'd seen her. She had spoken to him cryptically then as well. It was as though she thought he intended her harm.

"I would never hurt ye," he said softly into the darkness.

She offered no reply, save for the smooth, even breathing of her apparent slumber. Sleep claimed him not long after. But before it did, he could have sworn somewhere between wakefulness and slumber, he heard the quiet sound of a sob.

CHAPTER 13

Leila woke to a stream of sunlight spilling into her chamber and a lonely bed. She did not know how long the Lion had lain at her side before he'd left, but the sheets no longer held his warmth or scent.

The dream came rushing back at her once more, along with the sharp ache at her shoulder. She pushed down the sleeve of her kirtle where the five bone white spots stood out on her skin.

The Lion had promised never to hurt her, but she knew better. A new heaviness settled on her heart, more than just that of her own impending death. It was that cloud over Werrick Castle. She pushed the heels of her hands against her eyes, as if she could blot the image out and obliterate its meaning.

Who was the one who would fall ill?

Would it be Isla who worked with the villagers and exposed herself to the illness every day? Mayhap Bernard from his time praying over those dying from the great mortality? Mayhap Father?

Her chest squeezed painfully. Illness was coming to Werrick Castle.

She craved the gentle comfort the Lion had offered so willingly the night before, enough that it dragged her from the warmth of her bed and to the door. "Are you there, Lion?"

No reply came, which was answer enough.

He was gone.

He remained away for a majority of the day and did not return until later that afternoon. Her meals were carried in by the maid who offered little more than a wary glance with each visit. Other than that, Leila was left with the hauntings in her mind of all the terrible things to come.

A knock sounded. "Lady Leila, 'tis Niall." The door opened and the Lion entered.

"Niall?" Leila stared at him. "Are you not called the Lion?"

He lifted his lips in a boyish half smile that lightened his face. "More so by people who are not well-acquainted with me." The morning light caressed his hair and hazel eyes and cast him in gold. "I'd like it if ye called me Niall."

There was a quiet note of intimacy to his voice that left a delicious awareness dancing over her skin. She offered a shy nod.

"Alban has left. I saw to his departure myself this morning." Niall offered a courtly bow. "My lady, you are safe."

"Thank you." She twisted her fingers together even as her stomach knotted with worry. "Is there any word from Werrick Castle?"

The skin around his eyes tensed. A look of suspicion? Apprehension iced over Leila's veins. She would need to be careful with what she let Niall know. He appeared convinced of her innocence. But if he knew she could see into the future, that she sometimes glimpsed the past, would he be so understanding? Would he continue to be so kind?

Or would he truly be the one to kill her?

She knew the answer already, of course. A shiver rattled through her.

"There isna word from Werrick." He glanced down at where her arms were folded over her chest, where her raised flesh from the cold showed on her forearms. "I'll have yer cloak brought to ye. I shouldna have forgotten it."

She nodded her thanks.

"Are ye sure ye're well?" he asked. "Ye seem melancholy."

She swallowed down the sorrow rising within her for her family. "I'm well, thank you."

It was the same answer she continued to give for the next four days, any time Niall asked how she fared. Each of those nights, he had brought food for them to share as they spoke about their lives and their families.

It had been kind of him to share food with her when she would otherwise simply have had stale bread and cheese. It had been even more generous of him to crack his heart open and let her glimpse inside at the boy he had been. He had been absent a mother's love and his father was seldom home. Niall's poor behavior as a youth had awarded him attention and ultimately led to his rebelliousness.

He did not guard her through the night again. There was no need with Alban on a scouting mission. Nor had Niall kissed her again. She was most chagrined about that, even as she appreciated his company.

It was late morning on the fifth day after Alban's departure that a key rattled in the lock. She had scarcely heard it as she'd been so lost in her thoughts. Each night brought dreams of the cloud over Werrick Castle, and of her own death.

She'd refrained from asking after Werrick Castle, but it was never far from her mind. The door opened, drawing her from her thoughts. Her foolish heart lifted in anticipation of seeing Niall and the reprieve he offered from her constant worrying.

Except it was not Niall who entered the chamber, but Alban.

Leila jerked back reflexively. The stake she'd pried free from the bed lay beneath the mattress on the other side of the chamber, too far away to be of use.

"Ye're still alive, it appears." Alban scoffed. "The old priest who will send ye back to hell is taking his time traveling from Edinburgh." His gaze slicked down her body. "Meaning ye're still here and I've returned."

The door was left open at his side. If she could dart past him, she might be able to slip out before he could stop her, mayhap make her way down the stairs. Then what? Be caught by the guards and returned to her chamber?

She ground her teeth in frustration. He was too quick to attempt an escape.

He smirked. "We were near the English border yesterday. Did ye know that?"

Leila regarded him warily, dreading whatever it was he wished to share.

"The village outside of yer castle isna doing well." Alban inspected his hands casually as he spoke. So casually, in fact, it made her realize the door had been left open intentionally. He wanted her to try to escape, to use it as an excuse to kill her himself.

"Most of the villagers are dead." He shrugged. "Even more than here. Guess yer protection isna aiding them with ye gone."

"I'm no witch. I can't cast protection spells or create curses," Leila protested.

Alban smiled, a cold, cruel curling of his lips. "Ye're no' there to protect Werrick Castle anymore, either."

Leila's knees went soft. She knew what he meant, but she did not press him to continue. Not when she didn't want him to say more, as though not hearing might make whatever bad tidings he brought not be so.

"Lord Werrick is said to be brought down with the pestilence." Alban's eyes narrowed as he wielded his words as a cruel weapon. "His neck swells with the putrefaction of his body and he grows weaker by the day. Once he is dead, Werrick Castle will fall, and no one will give a damn if what is between yer legs stays intact or no'."

Father.

Leila practically fell backward onto the stone wall, bracing herself upright against its strength. To imagine her father, his slender frame withered with the effects of the pestilence, his body searing with the same pain as hers had. Her eyes filled with tears and the room blurred.

She knew well the dangers of the pestilence for people who were her father's age, who were of the same sparse frame. He had done everything for her, giving her a life she never deserved, always showing her love and acceptance, and she could not even be there to tend to him through his illness.

When she had thought seeing him in the prison would be her last opportunity to say goodbye, she had assumed it had been her life that would end. Not his.

Alban walked toward her, his steps slow and menacing. "As soon as yer da dies, I'm coming for ye, ye little—"

"What is the meaning of this?" Niall's voice boomed in the room.

Alban spun around. "I wasna touching her." He slid a glance to Leila. "No' yet," he muttered.

"Lord Armstrong asked for ye," Niall said, the authority of his tone undeniable. "Ye're no' to see the prisoner. Get ye gone. Now."

Alban skulked out of the room with a hateful glare.

Niall closed the door and locked it before rushing to her side. "Leila, what is it?"

She had been staring at the distant wall, not seeing it, but instead imagining her father as Alban had described him. "My father." She could no longer feel her legs.

"What's happened?" Niall caught her before she slid to the ground.

She sucked in a ragged breath through the pain lancing her heart. "He's ill with the great pestilence."

What she did not say was that his chance of survival was lower than most, that while she was locked in a tower at Liddesdale Castle, he might die.

∼

NIALL HELD Leila in his arms as she sobbed for the fate of her father. Yet, even in the length of time that he quietly comforted her, he could not stop the thought that kept nipping at the back of his mind.

She knew.

How many times had she asked him for news of Werrick Castle? Her questioning had started after the night of her dream when he'd gone in to ensure she was safe. It was only after the dream that she had fallen into a morose state. She'd tried to hide it from him, but he could make out the flatness of her gaze from behind her smiles and forced laughs.

'Tis you.

She'd known Niall before she met him, of that he was certain. But how? And in what sense?

Of one thing he was certain: there was more to Leila than he allowed himself to see and he needed to stop being blind. A knock came from the door.

"Lord Armstrong requests to see ye, Niall," Brodie said from the other side.

Niall released his hold on Leila. "Forgive me."

She said nothing, and instead turned to the bed, which she lay upon with her back set to the door. Niall exited the room quietly, giving her the solitude that she needed as she nursed her hurt.

He strode into the great hall where Lord Armstrong waited for him. Niall's steps were nearly silent on the thick layer of rushes beneath his feet.

Lord Armstrong seldom looked pleased as of late. This time, however, the frown on his face was not one of anger, but of sorrow. "My daughter is ill," he said by way of greeting.

Lady Davina was a young woman of eighteen, a frail thing whose countenance had never been strong. It did not surprise Niall that she would fall ill. If anything, he was surprised it had taken so long to strike the poor girl.

She was a kind and gentle soul; everything her father and brother were not, as if all the evil had been spent on them and there was nothing but goodness to give Davina.

"I'm verra sorry to hear such news," he replied with heartfelt sincerity.

"There are no' any physicians or healers here to see to her," Lord Armstrong said. "All have died or fled. There isna anyone to tend to her, save the few servants who will go near her and they dinna have the learning needed to heal her."

"Mayhap it isna the great mortality, my lord. One of my men—"

"She bears the mark of the pestilence." Lord Armstrong looked down into his lap briefly and did not speak so long, Niall was left to wonder if he was gathering his strength to continue on.

Lady Davina had a way of warming even the hardest of hearts, including that of her own father. It was no secret Lord Armstrong cared for his daughter greatly. It was rumored he continued to put off her marriage to her betrothed for fear of never seeing her again.

It was a valid concern since Lady Davina was displeased with her life in Liddesdale.

"The prisoner is a healer, aye?" Lord Armstrong asked. "The witch."

Niall raised his brows. "Ye would have her tend to Lady Davina, even as ye suspect her of having caused her to fall ill?"

The Keeper of Liddesdale put his fingers to his lips as though in consideration of Niall's logic. "Lady Davina is a pure soul. I hope the witch can see that and help her live." He heaved a soul-deep sigh. "There isna anyone else to aid her and I canna lose my daughter."

"And ye wish me to speak to Lady Leila on yer behalf," Niall surmised.

"She's yer responsibility. And that includes convincing her to aid Davina."

Niall would have to ask Leila to help Alban's sister, even as Leila's own father lay in England with the same ailment and she was unable to care for him. The twisted fate was cruel.

Still, Niall nodded. "I'll speak with her."

Lord Armstrong waved him away with a limp hand and lowered his face into his palm as Niall departed.

Leila was still on her bed when Niall entered her room. "Thank you for coming back," she said without turning to look at him.

"How did ye know it was me?" he asked.

"You are always quiet when you open the door, as if you don't wish to disturb me." She sat up and regarded him with red-rimmed eyes.

"I..." He rubbed at the tension along the back of his neck. How in God's teeth was he going to ask this of her?

She got to her feet. "What is it?"

"Lord Armstrong's daughter is ill." Niall slid his gaze away and noted the tray with her food set atop of the trunk, the food untouched. "There's no' anyone left to properly treat the lass."

"I will," Leila offered. "If he'll allow it."

Niall returned his attention to Leila. "Ye canna even attend yer own da, yet ye would willingly see to Lady Davina without knowing anything about her, or her condition?"

Leila swallowed and lifted her chin with that iron spirit he so admired. "My father's illness has naught to do with her. She is someone in need of help and I am in a position to give it."

"If she dies, ye will be held accountable."

"And if she lives, I have saved a life."

Frustration ground into Niall at her stalwart determination to help this person of whom she knew nothing. "You will die if she does. She is ill with the pestilence."

Leila gave a mirthless smile. "My life is already in forfeit."

He opened his mouth to protest her claim, but she put up a hand, silencing him. "I understand you believe a priest is being brought in to declare whether I am guilty or not. I tell you they have already made up their minds and are only doing this to appease the masses. I was not brought to Liddesdale to be tried; I was brought here to be killed."

"That isna—"

"I will do it." Leila folded her arms over her chest, unwilling to listen to his arguments.

And he did have arguments to rival her claim. No man of God would judge her as a witch if she was not.

"Have ye any demands if ye do this?" Niall asked in an encouraging tone.

She glanced down at herself. "A bath and a clean kirtle. It will only benefit her health if I can be clean when I attend to her." Her cheeks colored to a lovely shade that was made all the prettier by the crimson gown. "I'm sure I must look dreadful."

"Ye're the bonniest woman I've ever laid eyes on." Niall's feet carried him to her. He had told himself before that he would not kiss her again, touch her again.

He had not promised he wouldn't crave her again, for such a thing was impossible.

His longing for her had redoubled in the span of days since they had kissed, since he'd stroked her to pleasure. Her cries echoed in his ears and the image of her heavy-lidded eyes bright with desire filled his thoughts and dreams.

It was because of all those things and more he had kept his distance from Lady Leila. And it was for all those things and more, he could not stay away. Despite her incredible outward beauty, she was far lovelier within. Her strength, her spirit, her kindness.

His hand rose of its own accord and delicately stroked her soft cheek. She pulled in a quiet breath. "I'd meant to stay away from ye," Niall confessed. "But I canna."

She searched his eyes. "I do not want you to."

Niall groaned and captured her lips with his own. It was a tender kiss, a hope for what was to come later. For now, he had her reply to deliver to Lord Armstrong and she had a life to save.

CHAPTER 14

Leila's skin practically glowed with the refreshment of her bath. Granted, the water had been cold, and the soap was lacking the scents and benefits of the herbal mix Isla added for her at Werrick Castle, but at least she was clean. The kirtle she had been given was as fine as the other two, this one of a soft blue wool.

Once she was clean and ready to go to Lady Davina, Leila was led through the castle by a servant who had been waiting for her at the bottom of the stairs. The woman's dark hair was tinged with gray beneath her mobcap and she held Leila's basket at the crook of her arm.

She bobbed a quick curtsey. "I'm Ana. I've been tending to Lady Davina since she fell ill three days past."

She led Leila, with Brodie in tow, to Lady Davina's chamber. The servant's manner was perfunctory, but her demeanor was kind. She had been a member of the kitchen staff before her assistance was needed with Lady Davina. And while Ana had no knowledge of healing, she had willingly risked herself for the earl's daughter and sought to aid Lady Davina in any way possible.

"'Tis kind of ye to assist us, Lady Leila." Ana's heavy brows knitted together. "I heard ye dinna have a welcome reception to Liddesdale and that ye're being held on suspicion of witchcraft. I dinna know anything about any of it, but I know we all care greatly for Lady Davina and our hearts are all grateful to ye for yer aid."

"I have aided many villagers near my home in Brampton." Leila chose her words carefully. "You must understand I cannot cure the pestilence. I can only help ease her discomfort. The strength to survive will need to come from her. Knowing that you have seen to her needs, ensuring she had enough food and water, is the best thing you could have done for her, Ana. If she is able to survive this, it will have been from your efforts."

Ana's face colored in a blush. "Aye, well, she's in here." She pushed open the chamber door and bustled inside.

Leila followed and was met with the sickly-sweet odor of illness. The room was shuttered in darkness and a fire roared in the hearth. After having been in so cold a room for so long, the excessively hot chamber made Leila feel as though she were being roasted on a spit.

"Ana?" The feminine voice was softly spoken and wispy.

Leila looked to the bed and found a slender woman with flushed skin and lank strands of red hair lying beneath a mountain of blankets and furs. A sheen of sweat glistened at her brow.

"Aye, my lady." Ana bent over the hearth to settle another log into the flames. "I've brought—"

"Nay." Leila put a hand on the new log Ana reached for to keep her from adding it to the flames. "Please do not add more. We will need to air the room out. It is far too hot as it is."

"Whoever is here, you must leave." Lady Davina's voice was frantic. "Please, I do not want you to become ill."

Leila went to her side. It did not escape Leila's notice that as soon as she redirected her attention, Ana shoved the log into the greedy flames. No matter. Leila would have it all sorted out in good time.

"Lady Davina." Leila approached the ill woman.

An angry black lump swelled at the side of her slender neck, making her head lean to the right, where Leila stood. Her eyes slitted open, so bloodshot, Leila could not make out their color.

"Please go," Lady Davina panted.

Leila sat on the chair beside the bed and took Lady Davina's hand in hers. The young woman's small hand nearly burned Leila's fingers. "My name is Lady Leila. I have been ill before with the pestilence and from what we have seen, once one is ill with it, they cannot get it again. I have worked with my own healer at Werrick Castle and am here to help you."

Davina's hand closed on Leila's fingers in a weak grip. "Bless ye for yer care. Thank ye for coming to my aid. Ana hasna been ill. She must—"

"They'll have to drag my corpse from this room before I leave ye." Ana set about organizing the small bottles beside Davina's bed.

"Ana, please boil some water for a tea." If the servant was going to stay, Leila would at least put her to work. "While we wait on the water, I want you to open the shutters and move off most of these blankets. 'Tis far too warm in here."

The servant's eyes went wide. "But letting in the air will bring contagion."

"She is already ill, and the fresh air will do her good." Leila reached for the ginger balm in her basket, the one infused with willow bark and meadowsweet root, to aid with pain relief. "Water is much the same as air." She spoke as she worked, saying the same thing to Ana now that she had been telling the villagers for years, each time she was called to a sick bed. "Free flowing is best while stagnation allows filth to gather. You should not drink from a murky puddle any more than you should breathe fetid air."

Ana nodded, understanding immediately as many often did after Leila's explanation. She and Isla had compared their experiences through the years, and they both had noticed the introduction of fresh air improved the patients in nearly all cases.

She turned her attention to Lady Davina while Ana set to work to comply with Leila's instructions. "Lady Davina, I need to put a balm on your neck, and it will hurt. But the effects are worth the discomfort."

Lady Davina squeezed Leila's hand with her hot palm. "Thank ye."

Leila cast a quick glance to the cauldron of water set to boil over the flames. It could not boil fast enough to suit her. Not when the fever had clearly been burning in the young woman for a while. The sooner Leila could get the tea down her throat, the higher the likelihood of Lady Davina's survival.

Leila withdrew her hand from Lady Davina's grasp and popped the cap from a pot of balm before taking her hand once more. "Forgive me," Leila whispered. She scooped the balm onto her fingertips and carefully, oh-so-gently, spread the greasy salve over the swollen lump at Lady Davina's neck.

The young woman pressed her lips together, her fingers gripping Leila's as a tear ran down from the corner of her eye. Leila's own eyes welled with tears to know the amount of agony she caused with her ministration. "It will be better soon, I promise," Leila whispered.

"Thank ye," Lady Davina gritted out from between clenched teeth.

Leila's heart flinched. How could this considerate, gentlehearted woman be Lord Armstrong's daughter?

"The water, my lady." Ana extended a mug of hot water to Leila.

The tea was steeped quickly, comprised mostly of meadowsweet root, and carefully fed to Lady Davina, ensuring all of it went down her throat. It had been a difficult feat when her head could not straighten due to the lump at her throat, and swallowing appeared to be not only difficult but painful.

Still, never once did the young woman complain or fight against the remedy. As Leila administered to Davina, Ana complied with the rest of her requests. All blankets but one were removed from Lady Davina's bed and sent down to be boiled clean. The shutters were opened to allow in light and one casing left ajar to allow in some fresh air.

Ana paused in her work and stared down at the sleeping Lady Davina. A smile curved her lips. "I havena seen her sleep so well since she'd been ill." She wiped at her eye with the corner of her apron. "If nothing else, ye've given the wee lass a reprieve from her constant agony."

"We shall pray to God for him to do the remainder of what is out of our hands." Leila stroked a strand of hair from Lady Davina's face. "She is far stronger than I think many realize."

"I hope ye're right." Ana bobbed a curtsey and set about changing the water they'd used to wipe Lady Davina's face clean.

Leila hoped she was right too, for though her own life did not hinge upon it, Lady Davina's did. Because it was true what Leila had told Niall, her fate was marked long before her capture.

No matter the outcome of Lady Davina's condition or the witch trial, Leila would die. And no matter how kind and tender Niall had been with her, no matter that she had tried to harden her heart to him, Leila's resolve had begun to melt.

As much as she tried to deny it to herself, she knew the terrible truth: she was in love with Niall Douglas. There was only one more step in her fated destiny: her death.

∼

NIALL'S HEART pounded with anticipation at seeing Leila once more. He had seen little of her after she was tasked with tending to Lady Davina. She was even ordered to sleep in the young lady's room on a pallet at the foot of her bed, like a servant. Leila had not complained at the insult. Instead, she had lost herself in her efforts to save Lady Davina.

Nearly a sennight had gone by when the announcement was made through the castle that Lady Davina was declared well, and Niall was summoned to return Leila to her chamber. He rapped on Lady Davina's chamber door where Brodie stood guard and waited with an impatience unlike any other he had felt before.

Leila stepped into the hall, more beautiful than he had ever seen her. A rosiness of health and happiness touched her cheeks and lightness sparkled in her blue eyes. Even her hair appeared as glossy as silk and left him with a yearning to reach out and skim his fingers over the cool smoothness. It went against everything in Niall to present himself as a soldier before this woman he had not stopped thinking about for the entire time she'd been busy aiding Lady Davina.

"I am to escort ye to yer chamber," he said with as much authority as he could summon. Even still, his command came out soft enough to bring a knowing smile to her lips.

Their eyes met and held with the same burning need. "This way," he said gruffly.

She followed him like a biddable captive. He kept his steps paced slow, though his need to be alone with her felt as necessary as his need for air.

The walk to her chamber was interminable, as was the climb up the stairs. He hated having to lead her back to her chamber, to lock her up like a prisoner when she deserved to be set free.

Father Gerard would surely arrive soon. Mayhap when he learned what she had done, he would see Leila was no witch and proclaim her innocent. Niall grasped Leila's hand as he led her up the last few stairs. Her fingers were warm for once, not icy with the cold.

The connection between them was instant, like tinder set to kindling. He opened the door to her chamber and immediately spun around to face her. They fell into one another's arms, mouths slanting over one another's, tongues tangling in lust. Niall edged her back against the wall and pressed his body to hers. She moaned into his mouth and arched into him, encouraging his arousal.

"I havena been able to stop thinking of ye," he said between kisses. "Ye're in my mind, my dreams. I've been waiting for this moment the entire week." He ran his mouth down her neck, breathing in her clean, herbal scent.

"I've missed you, Niall." Her words made the column of her throat vibrate beneath his lips. "I cannot stop myself from wanting you, though I know I should not allow myself."

He cupped her breast in his palm and brushed the pad of his thumb over the hardened nipple there. "We shouldna be doing this," he groaned. "But I canna help myself. Leila, I..." He straightened and stared into the most beautiful blue eyes he'd ever beheld in all his life. "I love ye."

Her mouth opened, but she didn't speak. Instead, she ducked away from him and lowered her head. He looked at her in question as the door flew open.

Alban stood there with his lip curled as he regarded Niall. "Father wishes to see ye." His gaze slid to Leila in a way that made Niall wish he had his sword in his hand. "Davina has survived because of ye." He nodded in a gesture of gratitude that was more than Niall had ever seen him display.

With that, Alban led Niall from the room, rather than

staying there with Leila and tormenting her, which was a greater show of appreciation than any words he could muster from his withered heart.

When Niall approached, he found Lady Davina at her father's side. She wore a pale pink gown that made the vibrance of her red hair stand out like fire. Healthy color touched her cheeks and the smile set on her lips bespoke of a full recovery, as had been rumored.

Lord Armstrong spoke softly to his daughter and tenderly touched the top of her head. She nodded once and the smile melted into an expression of obedience. Without another word, she left the room. An affectionate sheen gleamed in Lord Armstrong's eye until he set his gaze on Niall and the look frosted into ice.

"Father Gerard is dead," he said abruptly. "The pestilence took down the party of men he traveled with, as well as him. This happened some days ago, but I had wanted to ensure my daughter could be healed before letting it be known."

Niall's heart slammed into his ribs, but he kept his face impassive. "Will Lady Leila no' be tried then, my lord?"

"Oh, aye, she will." Lord Armstrong fixed Niall with a pointed look. "By the most trusted man in all of Liddesdale."

Niall's stomach slithered low in his gut.

Lord Armstrong steepled his fingers. "Ye'll question her and will bring your final findings to me."

"Aye, my lord." Niall lifted his chin. His word, his honor, would be what held Leila between life and death. The woman he had told only moments ago that he loved. The woman he *did* love.

"This was sent to me from the monastery where Father Gerard passed." He handed a parchment to Niall. "It will aid ye in the questioning."

He accepted the parchment with a nod. She would be innocent, surely. Though even as he thought such a thing, his insides twisted into knots.

"I'll expect yer findings as soon as ye've finished the questioning." Lord Armstrong waved his hand dismissively to Niall.

"Aye, my lord." Niall folded the parchment in his hand and strode from the room. Once he was near the tower, where the hallway was empty, he unfolded the parchment and reviewed the carefully scripted lines. The tension at his shoulders began to relax as he read. For he was certain she did not fly in the air, nor that she consorted with the devil through intercourse, nor that she controlled the weather.

He read further on and the fear tightened through him once more. *Can they see the future?*

Niall would ask the questions as he was directed. All of them. But his heart was already heavy with what he suspected her answer would be. If she truly was a witch, like the one who had killed his father, could he lie to save her?

CHAPTER 15

Leila hugged herself in the cold quiet of her room. It had been so easy to adjust to the bustle of activity when she'd been healing Lady Davina. Her mind had been focused on caring for someone ill rather than overwhelmed with worry for her father.

Lady Davina's room had been as sumptuous as Leila's had been back at Werrick Castle, with tapestries and plush bedding, as well as various other luxuries that extended beyond a simple bed and an abandoned trunk.

Even more delightful than her surroundings had been the companionship. Ana's matter-of-fact personality and the gentle kindness of Lady Davina. In the last few days, Lady Davina had been awake and speaking, her concern always on others.

Leila squeezed her arms tighter around herself. She was a prisoner again, confined in the cold tower chamber, alone, empty. A familiar burning ache clenched at the back of her throat.

Footsteps sounded against the stone stairs leading up to her chamber, crisp with authority, but still gentle. *Niall.* The loneliness began to ebb at the very thought of seeing him. He had said he loved her in those precious seconds that they were alone. Before she had been able to wrap her heart around his declaration, before she could even compose a reply, he was gone.

He let himself into her chamber and locked the door behind him. Leila rushed forward, anticipating the softness of his lips on hers once more, the strength of his body like a wall against her. But the fullness of his mouth was drawn into a grim line and he did not come at her with mutual eagerness. Nay, he stood for a long moment, as though unsure of what to say.

"What is it?" Fear turned her heart to a block of ice. "My father."

"Nay, 'tis no' yer da." He glanced down at the parchment in his hand. "Father Gerard is dead."

She frowned in confusion. "He was the priest who was to determine if I am a witch or not, correct?"

Niall nodded and extended the missive in his hand for her to see. "I'm to take his place."

"You're to judge me?" she asked slowly.

A muscle in his jaw. "I have questions to ask ye."

"I'm no witch," she said with vehemence. If he loved her as he had so recently claimed, surely, he would not even question her innocence of such a preposterous charge. "Ask me your questions."

Regret shadowed his features as he unfolded the missive. "Do ye consort with the devil?"

Leila scoffed at the ridiculousness of it. "Nay."

"Do ye..." He shifted uncomfortably. "Do ye fornicate with demons?"

She couldn't stay her mirth at that question. "Nay, of course not."

"Do ye propel yerself through the air?"

"Are you asking if I can fly?" Leila shook her head. "What is this foolishness they've given you?

"Please answer the question," Niall said softly.

Leila sighed. "I do not fly through the air."

"Do ye see the future before it happens?" He kept his gaze fixed on the parchment when he asked that question. As though he did not wish to see her reaction.

The questions no longer seemed as humorous or silly. Her pulse ticked with wild abandon. She could say she did not and lie.

Yet, she could not agree to it and damn herself. Rather than speak, she let silence fill the space between them.

"Leila." He said her name with a flinch to his brows. "Ye have to answer the question."

"I..." She pressed her lips together.

"Mayhap the next question, then." He ran his finger down the page. "While ye consider yer answer to the last one."

She nodded, but her mouth went dry.

He cleared his throat before speaking. "Have ye seen events that happened in the past in visions?"

Tears burned hot in her eyes at her frustration.

He dragged his stare from the parchment up to her. "Leila."

"Aye," she whispered.

"Aye?" His brows raised; his face furrowed, as one does when they await a blow.

"I have seen the past in visions." She closed her eyes as she made the admission, unable to bring herself to look at him. "And I see the future before it comes to be."

"Ye knew about yer da before he fell ill." There was no accusation in Niall's tone.

Leila opened her eyes. "I knew the pestilence would befall Werrick Castle. I did not know it would be my father who would fall ill."

"Ye knew who I was when we met that day in the village outside Werrick Castle, dinna ye?"

Leila turned her attention to the scarred wood floor where lines crisscrossed themselves. "I did."

"How?"

"I have seen you often in my visions. I've known for the whole of my life that I would meet you."

"What did ye see of me?" His expression was unreadable, and it plucked at a chord of unease within her.

"That we would be lovers," she said quietly.

The skin around his eyes tightened. "Is that why I canna stop thinking of ye? Why I dream of ye now? Because ye make yer visions say we are intended to be together?"

Leila shook her head, helpless. "I've never been able to control what I see, or what the outcomes are, or even when I will have a vision. I've been plagued by them my whole life. It is not the gift some believe it to be, but a curse, and I loathe it." Tears were blurring her vision and her voice was harsh, but she could not stop now that she had started.

"I have always been different than my sisters. You know the origin of my conception. You heard it when I spoke to my father." Her cheeks blazed with humiliation. "These visions have been with me for as long as I can remember, dark images of what was to come and no way to properly gauge when it would, or how to stop it."

She drew in a pained breath. "I stopped sharing most of what I saw, because doing so raised more questions than I could answer. These visions are fickle things, sometimes easily misread. Sometimes, I never had visions of dangerous events that came to pass. But even though I ceased sharing what I saw, they were always there. Not just the future, but the past and the terrible things that happened." She hugged herself again, though this time against the hurt within her rather than the chill of the room. "My mother. I dream of her often, of what happened to her."

"Leila." He said her name gently. When she looked up, she found his forehead creased with concern.

"I've tried to keep from loving you, Niall." A tear slid down her cheek. "I've fought it since you loosened the bindings on my wrist, and tried to keep my heart dammed from every kindness and good thing you've done. Loving you is…"

He reached for her and took her into his arms. His body was solid with strength and the wonderfully familiar scent of him, of leather and cedar, caressed her soul. He tenderly touched the underside of her chin and lifted her face.

"Loving me is what?" he asked.

She licked her lips. "Dangerous."

He released her abruptly, as though she had burned him. "How so?" His demand was harsh, though she knew he did not speak thus out of anger. Not when his eyes were wide with fear.

She considered the situation from his perspective then; considered how she would feel if he told her she would kill him. Something deep within her splintered. She should not have said anything at all. She ought to only have shared that they were meant to be lovers and nothing more.

"Leila, tell me." Niall swallowed. "Please."

She closed her eyes and the heat of another tear slid down her face. "I will not survive my time at Liddesdale, and you will be the one to kill me."

∽

"Nay!" The protest erupted from Niall's mouth before he could stop it. He closed the distance between himself and Leila and drew her into his arms one more time, reveling in the sureness of her sweet body against him, where he could keep her safe and protected. "I willna ever hurt ye," he vowed against the cool sleekness of her dark hair. "I love ye."

"And I love you, Niall." She drew in a shaky breath and pulled away to regard him. "But, aye, you will kill me."

He shook his head. "How can ye be so certain?"

"The more often I have a vision, the more likely it is to come to pass." She looked down at her hands. Her fingernails had healed in the time she'd assisted Lady Davina. "Like a siege we had at the castle once, like the pestilence sweeping over the land...and like you."

He wanted to take her hands in his, to caress the smoothness of her skin as they talked, to reassure her. Her claim, however, stayed his affections. How could any woman trust a man she anticipated would cause her harm?

"How often have ye had visions of me?" he asked.

"Since I was a child." She played with a loose thread on the edge of her sleeve, focusing on that instead of turning her gaze to him. "I have always had visions and dreams of you killing me. It was not until I was older that I realized I would also be your lover."

Lover.

That word conjured carnal images of their bodies splayed on his bed, glistening with sweat and panting with exhaustion. He ground his teeth. "How do ye know 'tis a vision when ye have it?" His demand came out with a steadfast denial even he was able to detect.

"I feel it." She closed her eyes and her face went serene with apparent concentration. "It tingles warmth through the back of my neck and spreads everywhere with a sense of calm. I see it all around me as though I were existing in another place and time, rather than where I presently stand. I can feel the ground beneath me, the wind blow and I can smell whatever scent the air carries. I am *there,* even though I am not."

"How?" he asked.

She opened her eyes. "I know not. It has always been a part

of me, and I've always loathed it. I am helpless to control what I see, what I experience." She shuddered.

This time, he did lift her hand. The connection between them was instant, alive with a pleasant tingle.

"How?" he said again. "How do ye anticipate I will kill ye?"

She stared into his face with more tenderness than he would ever use to gaze upon his own killer. "Are you certain you wish to know?"

"Aye." If he knew, he could prevent himself from doing it. No matter the cost. He would die rather than take her life.

"Drowning."

Drowning? The death of a witch.

Niall shook his head vehemently. "Nay. Ye canna be correct." He pulled on her hand to bring her closer to him again and folded his arms around her, as though he could protect her from everything. Including himself.

He reveled in her petite body that he knew possessed the strength of a warrior, in the cool smoothness of her hair that somehow always smelled clean and wonderful, in the determination of her spirit that he found even more beautiful than her external loveliness. "I love ye," he whispered vehemently. "I would give my life rather than take yers."

She lifted her face up and placed her hand on his jaw. Her gaze slid to his mouth and the familiar stirring of lust rose within him. She eased upward on her toes even as he lowered his head. They met somewhere in the middle, their lips connecting in a gentle kiss.

"I love you, Niall," she said against his mouth.

"I'll never hurt ye," he vowed again.

She swept the tip of her tongue against his and any idea of speaking burned away with the flame of desire. Their declarations of love came in the slant of their mouths against one another's, in the panting of their shared breath, in the arch of their bodies as they moved together with desperation.

Leila's hands molded over his body, over his arms, his chest, down the rigid lines of his stomach. He groaned at her exploration, proud of the body she found so appealing.

He cupped her bottom with one hand, drawing her pelvis to his. She moaned into his mouth and rubbed herself against him in the most maddening, wonderful, enticing way. He kissed the sensitive skin behind her ear and along the length of her graceful neck as his fingers worked at the neckline of the kirtle. The gown was too big and gave easily under his touch, springing free her pink-tipped breasts.

Leila gasped and pushed her chest toward him, as though in offering. One he would gladly accept. He cradled the silky warmth of one in his palm and teased at the bud with his thumb. With the other, he closed his mouth over the pert nipple and flicked his tongue against the nub until it went hard.

Her hands clutched his head to her. He loved her pleasure, her breathless whimpers, the way her eyes grew heavy-lidded and sensual, the brilliance of her own passion for him. His fingers shifted from her bottom to the hem of her kirtle and then up to the shapely calf beneath it. The cries of her climax had echoed in his mind since the first time he pleasured her. He wanted to hear them again, to think of them later as he stroked himself.

Higher and higher, his hand crept up her long, lean legs. Quicker and quicker her breath came, in obvious anticipation. He ran his thumb against the side of her inner thigh, a breath away from her sex. Her leg quivered beneath his touch. He did the same on her other leg, teasing.

She gave a whimper of frustration and parted her legs wider for him. This time, he ran his fingers along her damp slit. She sucked in a sharp breath and her hips bucked.

"Is this what ye want?" He slid his touch over her, pausing at the top to gently swirl a circle over the little bud.

She gave a long, eager moan even as she shook her head.

Niall removed his hand from beneath her kirtle and cast her a questioning look. "Did I hurt y—"

Her finger came to his lips, silencing him. Wordless still, she reached toward him and slipped free the first button of his doublet. His heart slammed hard in his chest and thundered in his ears.

"Leila, I—"

She paused from her task of slowly, painstakingly working down the line of buttons of his doublet. "I don't simply want release this time, Niall." She undid the last button and pushed his doublet from his shoulders. Her smile curved up, edged with a wickedness that went straight to his cock. "I want *you*."

CHAPTER 16

Leila's heart raced at her own brazenness as she nudged Niall's doublet to the floor. The white leine he wore beneath was of average quality linen, thick and opaque. The open neckline revealed the muscles of his neck and the hidden strength along his chest.

Her hands trembled as they skimmed down his firm torso to the hemline of the leine.

"Leila." Her name came out in a deep baritone.

She stilled and lifted her gaze to his burning stare.

"Ye're a lady." He tensed. "I canna—"

She shook her head. "Don't say anything more."

"Yer maidenhead—"

She put up a hand to stop him. "I know my future," she said carefully. "I will not throw away this one chance at happiness because it isn't proper."

His brows furrowed with a pained expression. "I willna hurt ye, Leila. I'd never hurt ye."

She traced her fingertip over the sharp line of his jaw. The whiskers prickled over her skin and caught at her short nail. "Love me, Niall."

He gave a wounded groan and lowered his mouth to hers, capturing her lips in a searing kiss, one filled with passion and promise. Her hands found their way to the hem of his leine once more and drew it upward. He grasped it with her, tugging it over his head and tossing it aside, before reaching for her once more.

His body was beautiful in movement, muscles bunching, shadowed valleys shifting. A golden line of hair trickled down his rippled abdomen from the base of his navel where it dipped into the waistline of his trews. He pulled her to his hard body, pressing her to his hot skin as he kissed her.

Her hands moved over his exquisite back, seeing with her hands every carved line of his strength.

"If ye keep touching me like that, I willna last long," he said in a low voice.

She ran her fingers along his sides and down the bands of his stomach to the sprinkling of hair that descended into his trews. "Like this?" she asked innocently.

He growled and caught her hands. "No' yet. No' when ye're still fully clothed."

Leila lifted an eyebrow and slowly turned around to put her back to him where her kirtle was tied closed. Niall swept her hair aside and grazed his lips against the sensitive dip where her neck and shoulders met. She gasped in happy surprise as prickles of pleasure played over her skin.

He curled his strong arms around her and held her body snug to his own, so her bottom pushed against the length of his arousal. "I want ye so verra much," he whispered beside her ear, his breath warm and tantalizing where it swept over her. He stroked her skin from her neck to her shoulder and back again before tracing the same path with his mouth, his tongue.

Leila pushed back into him, arching against his erection with a moan. Desire pulsed at her core.

"I want ye," he repeated in a low groan. "But I want to take my time with ye. To savor ye." There was a gentle tug at the back of her kirtle as he pulled free the bow tied there. "To savor us."

With one hand, he ran his fingers up the column of her throat, leaning her head back against his powerful shoulder. He nuzzled his nose to her neck, followed by the heat of his lips and then the rasp of his whiskered chin. As he made her nearly melt with kisses, the fingers of his free hand worked at the back of her kirtle.

He pressed his lips just below her ear.

He slipped a lacing free.

He nipped her earlobe gently.

Another lacing slipped free.

"*Mo chridhe*," he murmured into her ear, "I canna wait to unveil ye."

Another lacing slipped free.

Mo chridhe. My heart.

Leila closed her eyes at the caress of his endearment, at what it meant. The kirtle now gaped at her back and let in tendrils of icy air in contrast to the burn of her longing. Niall held her shoulders with both hands now and swept his fingers down over her chest, brushing the tops of her breasts.

She leaned back on his strength, wanting to feel every part of him touching every part of her. Slowly, he pulled her around to face him once more, his eyes alight with desire, his naked chest rising and falling with his ragged breathing. Leila pulled at her kirtle, peeling it from her body so she stood before him in only her chemise. Unlike the linen he'd worn, hers was fine. Thin. Her body was no doubt visible beneath it.

Leila grasped the hem and drew it upward. Niall gave a long, low exhale as she pulled it over her head and let it fall away. She hesitated, wondering what he might think of the puckered scars left from the arrows that had struck her as a girl: one on the upper portion of her left arm, one beneath her right breast.

Those, as well as the white marks upon her skin that Death had left behind that always remained cold to the touch.

"Leila." He uttered a curse under his breath. "Ye're even more perfect than I imagined ye."

Heat effused her at his compliment. His gaze did not linger on her scars, but on the whole of her, raking over her with searing desire.

"You imagined me naked?" She smiled coyly to cover her shyness.

He skimmed his hand over her waist. "That isna all I imagined." His gaze seared into hers.

Leila's throat went dry. "Pray tell what other things you imagined."

His lips lifted at one corner in a boyish grin. "I think I'd rather show ye." With that, he swept her legs from beneath her, so she fell back into his strong arms.

She laughed at the surprise of it and he carried her to the bed where he lay her on the mattress. Sitting beside her, he cradled her jaw and leaned toward her to kiss her slowly, thoroughly with the stroke of his tongue and the nip of his teeth.

He eased over the top of her on all fours. Leila's breath caught at the image of his beautiful body poised over her. While she was a maiden, she knew enough about intercourse. One did not deliver babes without knowing of their origin, and everything in her hummed with anticipation.

Except that he still wore his trews.

He cupped her breast and leaned over her. His tongue flicked against her nipple and set her alight with a new wave of desperate desire. If he noticed her scars, he did not mention them, and for that, Leila was grateful. Instead, he loved her breasts with his hands and mouth and little scrapes of his teeth, alternating between the two until Leila was squirming beneath him.

She rubbed her thighs against one another for the scant pressure it provided to the lustful pounding at her core.

He glanced down at where she writhed in carnal frustration. His finger tickled down the side of her stomach. She twitched beneath him; her skin overly sensitive.

"Do ye need relief, *mo chridhe*?" he said with silky seduction.

She whimpered, a small, pathetic sound that gave voice to what words could not. His touch swept lower, lower—dear merciful heaven—lower... His fingertip brushed the apex of her legs and Leila cried out.

Niall kept his gaze on her as he crawled backward. With purpose, he nudged her legs apart, spreading her thighs. Leila flushed at the idea of her sex being blatantly splayed before him.

He met her gaze, then leaned over her and let his tongue drag against her center.

Leila's hands fisted the bed sheets as he repeated the motion, more firmly this time. He lowered himself to the bed with his face firmly settled between her thighs as he licked at her center with the most delightfully wicked tongue.

His finger gently probed her as he tasted her, carefully stretching her as he eased the digit inward. There was a little discomfort with the action, but nothing that could draw her from the haze of pleasure building around her. He continued to nudge his finger into her until the slight pain melted into something euphoric and her hips bucked up to meet the glide of his hand.

Her core drew tight with anticipation. Niall's finger and tongue were hot and wet against her, encouraging her over the edge. She soared into her crises on the wings of love and bliss. When she gently floated back, she found him climbing off the bed with his hands settling on the ties of his trews.

She rubbed her thighs together as currents of pleasure tingled throughout her body.

"Ye're certain?" Niall lowered his gaze at her. His stomach flexed hard with each breath, as though he labored to maintain control of himself. "It canna be undone once we've…"

"Aye," Leila replied with more certainty than she'd ever felt before. "I want you." For if she did not survive her capture at Liddesdale, she would at least feel the full force of his love before she succumbed to death.

~

Niall watched Leila as he pulled free the first tie of his trews. She was lovely where she lay, her lithe, lean body bathed in a wash of sunlight, gleaming across lines of delicate muscle. She returned his regard with curiosity in her bright eyes and a flush to her cheeks, brought on by her crises.

He still had the intoxicating taste of her on his tongue, even as his ears echoed with her hoarse cry as she fell under her release. His cock raged with these sensations and the driving need to possess this extraordinary woman.

He drew free another tie and her teeth sank into her lower lip. He wanted to pull that lip free and glide his thumb into her mouth or kiss her until she was writhing again. Her gaze dipped over his torso, down his legs and back up again, flitting occasionally to where his arousal strained at his trews.

He tugged at a third and fourth tie and shoved the garment to the floor, so he stood before her completely naked. Leila's blazing stare roamed over him, taking in every inch of him.

He leaned over her on the bed and ran his hands along the sides of her thighs and hips. She arched up toward him as he lay his body over hers. Though her limbs were lean, there was still a womanly softness in the roundness of her breasts and hips. He kissed her with the force of his love, and she met his passion with eagerness.

Her tongue swept against his, and she parted her thighs, cradling him. He found her with his hand first, stroking her and gently stretching her to better accommodate him. She gave a frustrated whimper and pressed against his hand.

He shifted so their pelvises were directly against one another, and his weight was braced over her with his left arm. His heartbeat thrummed erratically in his chest. He removed his hand from between them and used it to guide his cock to the warm heat of her entrance. Excitement and anticipation quivered low in his belly. He wanted this, needed this. Needed *her*.

Leila's full lips parted, and she gave another frustrated whimper.

He guided himself carefully into her, just a bit at first. The grip around him was a tease, encouraging him to plunge himself fully into her sheath, to let it wrap and squeeze around him. His muscles shook with the force of his control. He paused at the delicate barrier within her.

He'd never been with a virgin. He'd never wanted one. But he knew what he had to do, and he knew it would cause a pain within Leila. His heart caught, but she nodded, her chin set with defiance.

His brave, beautiful Leila.

He released his hold on his cock and slid his hand over hers, letting their fingers interlock against one another as he nudged past her maidenhead. She blinked in surprise and the muscles of her neck tensed.

"Forgive me, *mo chridhe*." He nuzzled her lips with his own and flexed his pelvis forward, going slightly deeper.

Her brow flinched and she lifted her hips to meet him. He opened his mouth to tell her what she did was not necessary, but she kissed him hungrily and drew him toward her with her arms.

He eased out of her slightly before easing back in, his movements slow and careful. His back ached with his restraint even as he entered her again until their pelvises were pressed against one another. He ground his teeth and held himself there for a moment, letting her get used to the sensation of him fully filling her. She was so damn tight, it nearly hurt. The breath panted from his lungs as he began to move within her, slowly at first, then faster.

Leila's eyes closed with pleasure and a quiet moan sounded in the back of her throat. A groan tore from somewhere deep in Niall's chest at her enjoyment. This was what he'd wanted, their mutual pleasure. Suddenly, the squeezing grip around him was no longer painful, but euphoric; his muscles no longer tense, but gliding with ease along with hers as they arched and moved against one another.

Heat tingled through him and his bollocks tightened with the temptation to release. He angled his hips over hers to ensure he rubbed at the bud between her legs with each push and increased his tempo. The change in pitch of her moans told him he succeeded in hitting just the right spot.

She clung to his shoulders as he thrust. Her center squeezed at him and began to tense. He gripped her hips and drove into her as she cried out. Pleasure melted over Niall as his own release took him with greedy, hot spasms of bliss.

Muscles shaking, breath panting, he lowered himself to the side of her so as not to crush her and held her as their frantic heartbeats slowly calmed. She nuzzled against his chest and distributed featherlight kisses across his skin.

"I dinna hurt ye?" he asked.

She grinned up at him. "It was even better than what I had expected from my vis—" She stopped short of saying the full word.

Her visions. And he knew why. Their love was not the only vision she'd had of him.

"I willna ever hurt ye." He stroked a lock of hair from her sweaty brow. "I'll no' ever kill ye, to be sure. They'd have to cut out my own heart to make it so." He said it with all the power and conviction in his soul.

Nothing could make him hurt Leila.

She tucked her body closer against him. Five white dots were evident on her shoulder. He ran his fingers over them and quickly withdrew his hand. The spots were cold as ice. "What is this?"

"When I was ill with the pestilence, Death came for me," she replied against his chest. "But he knew he could not have me yet and so he left me with this reminder." A shiver wracked her slender body and left her skin prickled with chills.

He leaned back to regard her. "Death?"

"My visions are seldom pleasant." Her gaze slid away. "'Tis the only time one left a mark between the world of seeing and the world I live in."

"And these?" he let his fingertips skim over the large white scars on her arm and just below her breast.

"Aren't women supposed to ask men about their scars and not the opposite?" She lifted her brows at him.

He chuckled lightly. "Ye can go over my whole body later, if it pleases ye to do so."

"I believe I may be tempted to make good on such an offer." She let her gaze wander down him in a way that made his cock stir from its languid state.

"Arrows." She brushed her fingers over the scar at her arm. "We were being attacked at Mabrick Castle when I was a girl. I had a vision that my sister, Anice, would be struck."

"Ye put yerself in front of her?" Niall settled his fingertip in the dent of the puckered wound. Arrows were nasty things. There was no simply pulling them free. The tips were attached to the shaft with a bit of wax, so the head broke off when the shaft was tugged. The only way to get the remaining tip out was with a scooping instrument. The process was messy, painful and left behind deep scars.

And Leila had been only a girl.

"It was the only time I was able to change what I saw," she said.

His head snapped up. "Ye can change it?"

She gave a discouraged shake of her head. "It hasn't happened since."

"But it doesna mean it's impossible." Hope lit through Niall.

His will was stronger than any damn vision. He would do anything to keep Leila safe, including defying the future. And it would all start with approaching Lord Armstrong and declaring Leila innocent.

CHAPTER 17

Niall remained at Leila's side for as long as he dared and spent the time holding her in his arms as they spoke of their lives. Each was careful to avoid any talk of the future.

Lord Armstrong awaited Niall's answer and that knowledge lingered in the back of Niall's mind. He ran his fingertip over Leila's slender waist. "I must return to Lord Armstrong and tell him ye're no' a witch."

Leila frowned slightly. "He won't believe you."

Niall studied her carefully, putting weight to her words. "Did ye have a vision of it?"

"Don't you do that now too." Leila sat up in the bed and drew the sheets over her beautiful breasts. "Everyone thinks everything I say has to do with a vision. Some things do not require the sight to know. Like Lord Armstrong's dislike for me, his underlying hatred of my father, and his need to cast blame at someone's feet for the death of his people."

"I am his deputy because he wants a man who is honorable working with him." Niall caressed her face and tilted her chin up to better see her lovely face. "He will listen to me."

Leila turned her gaze from his and he knew she did not

agree with what he said. She would see Lord Armstrong's fairness. While Niall had not agreed with Leila's captivity, he knew the Scottish earl would weigh on the side of fairness and justice.

Niall brushed his lips against Leila's in a tender, sweet kiss. One chaste enough not to lure him back into her arms. He dragged himself from her bed and pulled his discarded clothing from the floor to dress.

She followed suit, donning her chemise and the kirtle over it. He helped lace up her back, kissed her once more and made his regretful departure. Despite his words of comfort to Leila, however, he found his pulse quickening with trepidation the closer he came to the great hall.

The earl stood by the hearth with his hands extended toward the fire and two hulking, wiry-haired dogs at his side. "'Tis cold as sin in this castle," he groused.

It was colder in the tower where Leila was being held, but Niall did not dare say such a thing. "I've spoken with Lady Leila regarding the charges of witchcraft." His heart slammed so hard as he spoke, the earl could probably hear his ribs rattling.

Lord Armstrong didn't bother to turn his head to look at him. "And?"

"She's no' a witch."

At this, Lord Armstrong did turn toward Niall. "Nay? Ye were once so certain of her engagement in witchcraft and now you deem her innocent. Ye asked her the questions ye were given?"

Regret knotted in Niall's stomach. He wished he could take back those early words of certainty that Leila was a witch. Despite her ability to see into the future and the past, he couldn't find it in him to call her a witch now. Not when she was just a woman helpless against an unwanted power she could not control.

"Aye, I asked all the questions," Niall confirmed.

Lord Armstrong narrowed his eyes. "And she answered nay to every one?"

"Aye," Niall lied. He hated the dishonesty and the pressing need of the situation's severity.

"Lies," Armstrong hissed.

Niall held his ground despite the chill running through his veins. If Lord Armstrong caught Niall speaking anything but the truth, it would cost him his position and Leila her life.

"She lies," the earl snarled.

The tension in Niall's shoulders did not relax at the realization that Lord Armstrong was not accusing Niall of lying, but Leila. Not when her life was still at stake.

"I asked the questions I was given," Niall replied. "The lass isna a witch."

"She's made a fool of ye, Lion." Lord Armstrong scoffed. "She's lying to ye."

"I dinna feel right in charging her with these crimes, my lord." Niall kept his voice even for fear doing so too vehemently might arouse suspicion. "Why would she have helped Lady Davina if she was a witch? Would she no' have let the daughter of the man who arrested her die?"

"Of course she cured her." Lord Armstrong's voice rang out against the stone walls of the great hall. "It was a clever attempt to prove her innocence, but I'm no' as naive as ye, lad. I knew what she'd be about and that's why I tasked her with aiding my Davina."

"My Lord, I—"

"The people need a reason to explain this sickness that has killed so many," Lord Armstrong said in a loud tone. "I've found them a witch whose death will ease the losses they have suffered."

Niall bit back his objection. The earl's statement told Niall everything he had not understood before. Lord Armstrong did not believe or disbelieve Leila was a witch. Doubtless, he did not care. He only wished to appease his people's need for vengeance.

Niall also was aware that no amount of protest or reasoning would alter the earl's decision. "What are we to do with her, my lord?" A knot formed in Niall's gut even as he asked the question.

"What one is supposed to do with witches, what the people expect us to do." Lord Armstrong gave a maniacal grin. "We drown her."

Niall's stomach sank. It was exactly as Leila had said.

"This may cause a war with Lord Werrick," Niall cautioned.

But Lord Armstrong's dark joy did not melt away at the threat. If anything, his smile grew wider. "So be it." He reached down and stroked the head of one of his dogs. "That's if the earl lives. The witch isna there to get him through his illness."

"When is her sentence to be carried out?" Niall had to work to keep his features impassive as he spoke, lest his emotions break free. His rage and disgust for the man he had once regarded with such esteem.

"The sooner the better." Lord Armstrong nodded to himself. "On the morrow, if it can be done in time. If no' the day following."

Niall nodded even as he considered how he might be able to put off her execution for as long as he could. "I'll handle the arrangements."

Lord Armstrong sighed heavily. "Nay, Alban will see to it. I've no' been giving the lad enough responsibility and ye've done much with the prisoner of late. Mayhap too much." He put a hand to Niall's shoulder and squeezed it, the way Niall's father used to do. "Ye're a good man, Lion. I'm grateful to have ye among my men."

Niall nodded his gratitude at the compliment even as disgust roiled in his gut. For he was not a loyal man of Lord Armstrong's. Not anymore. Not when the earl would so readily sacrifice a young woman's life for the sake of slaking his people's bloodlust.

Lord Armstrong released Niall's shoulder. "Go on with ye."

Niall turned at once and strode from the great hall directly toward Leila's chamber as his mind worked through a forming plan. Brodie grinned at Niall as he approached. "Back so soon? I think ye've taken a liking to the lass."

Niall edged closer to Brodie. "Dinna be here as guard tonight, aye?"

"Ye're breaking her out," the younger man spoke with certainty.

Of all people Niall could trust with his life, it was Brodie. But it was not Niall's life at stake, and so he did not reply.

"She saved my sister, if ye recall," Brodie said.

"Aye, I do."

"I'll be on guard tonight." Brodie straightened against the wall with his head held high. "I owe the lass a life for saving my sister."

"Pray God ye willna have to give it." Niall clapped the other man on the back in silent appreciation.

"Dinna get caught," Brodie warned. The skin around Brodie's eyes tightened with sincerity. "Get her to safety."

And that was exactly what Niall planned to do. He made his way up the stairs to Leila's room to share the plan with her, for this night, Niall would be breaking her free.

∽

Leila was glad to be back in her trews again. She was even more grateful for the belt of daggers once more secured at her waist.

The light around the shutters of the chamber indicated dusk

had descended some time ago and the world was tipping toward nightfall.

With the coldest time of the year upon them, the final meal of the day was eaten just before the sun began to sink in the horizon. By dusk, everyone was in bed, buried beneath furs to ward off the pressing chill. Though the evening had only begun to stain its inky darkness through the castle, most would already be heavily asleep, lured there by drink and hearty fare. That was when Niall would come for her, so that they might leave under the cover of darkness and put enough distance between them and the castle before anyone roused to note their absence.

She strained to listen for a noise at her door, the careful pat of Niall's footsteps as he climbed the stairs, the light jangle of keys as he unlocked her door.

Nothing.

She ran her fingertips across the worn leather belt and let them glide over the hilts of several daggers. Niall had returned it to her earlier that day in anticipation for their flight from Liddesdale Castle.

She bounced on her heels several times and moved through the steps of battle. They were motions she'd repeated time and again in her life. She had grown up learning to fight along with her sisters. The attack on Werrick Castle that had led to the rape of their mother had forced their father to make the decision to send them away or train them as warriors. Leila was glad he'd chosen the latter.

She spun about and dipped low as she slid a dagger free before leaping up as she sliced with her blade. Her invisible opponent received a mortal wound. She did not pant with her exertions. If anything, her blood sang in her veins with the familiarity of practice.

When she'd first been locked in the chamber, she'd been too

resigned to her fate to continue her routine. But now, they would fight.

She would be freed by Niall and together they would run to Werrick Castle. To safety. To her father's side to ensure he was still safe. If he was still alive.

If she would even live. The memories of being pushed beneath the icy water threatened to consume her. Her heart crumpled at such thoughts and she tried to push them away, lest they debilitate her energy. She couldn't think of failure, nor death. They would be successful in their attempt to escape and her return would find her father alive and well.

She stretched out her muscles and stared at the door, eager for freedom. Steps sounded on the stairs and she fell still. She pulled a dagger free and curled her palm around the hilt. With her weapons and old clothes, she was no longer a prisoner. She was powerful, capable. She was a warrior who would not be kept down.

The keys jangled in the door; the sound lovingly familiar. Regardless, she crouched low and prepared to strike.

Niall opened the door. His gaze went to her dagger, then up to her. He grinned, understanding the way any warrior would how it felt to be armed once more. He closed the door and strode to her.

She straightened at his approach. "Is it time?"

He nodded and drew her into his arms. Their mouths found one another in a quick but passionate kiss. "It is good to see ye as a warrior once again, *mo chridhe*."

"It is good to be strong again."

He stroked her lower lip with his thumb and gave her a searing look that told her he couldn't wait to resume their kisses when they could let it lead to more. "Ye've always been strong. Now ye're just armed."

He grasped her hand and pulled her toward the door. Together, they crept down the winding stairs to the bottom.

Brodie nodded at them and closed his eyes, body tensing. This was the part of the plan Leila had dreaded the most. A muscle worked in Niall's jaw as he drew back his fist and struck Brodie hard with his fist. The younger man staggered back against the wall and slid down.

Niall lunged toward him, caught the guard and slowly lowered him to the ground. Carefully, he dragged Brodie up the stairs and out of sight where he would remain until morning.

Loathsome though the task was, hitting Brodie to make him lose awareness was preferable to having to kill someone else. At least Brodie could make his injury last as long as need be. Another reiver who was not in on the escape would go to Lord Armstrong as soon as they roused.

Niall led Leila down the hall, their steps hurried yet silent on the floor. They passed no one as they made their way through the castle, nor even as they wound their way down a second flight of stairs. He stopped before an exceptionally large tapestry and reached behind it, drawing free a gambeson and helm. He'd told her he would try to get them without being seen and it appeared he had succeeded.

She slipped the gambeson on as footsteps sounded in the hallway, coming directly toward them. Niall plunked the helm on her head as her fingers frantically worked at the ties of her gambeson. The footsteps came closer.

Niall swept a hand over Leila's shoulder and the weight of her hair fell behind her. She finished the final tie as a servant rounded the corner and passed them by without even a glance. The tension in her shoulder eased somewhat but did not fully abate. It would not, not until they were away from Liddesdale and riding back toward home. Until she was completely free.

Niall led her through an iron-bound door to the chilly, open night. The frigid wind stung her cheeks and tingled over her skin. Still, she paused for a brief moment and reveled in the crisp air in her lungs. Though it was bitterly cold, and the night black as ink, it was her first breath of such freshness in over a fortnight.

Niall strode on ahead of her and left her scrambling to catch up. She kept her pace even in the hopes she did not appear to be rushing. Already, it had been foolish to pause. She couldn't do anything to arouse suspicion.

Niall led her through the bailey toward the portcullis.

"Halt." A guard approached and stared at them in the darkness.

"We must leave." Niall said. "We heard news of English reivers nearby and must see to them."

"Are ye the Lion?" the guard asked.

"Of course I am," Niall replied. "Open the gate."

The man hesitated and rubbed the back of his neck. "Aye, of course." He waved to the battlements and the portcullis gave a long, low groan as it started to slowly lift open.

Tension hovered in the air and there was a subtle stiffening to Niall's shoulders. This was not going as smoothly as he would have liked.

Leila held her breath, hoping the reiver wouldn't ask after her.

He did not and within the passing of several agonizing minutes, they were free to exit through the castle entrance.

"Walk normal," Niall said quietly. "But as soon as I say to do so, run."

Leila's pulse leapt and she had to force her feet to maintain the slow pace. The village was quiet; the streets empty save for the few dead who were laid out for collection. Within the cottages, neighbors kept to themselves and did not emerge.

Niall led her around the corner of a cottage and grasped her hand. "Run."

Together, they raced, Niall threading through a maze of streets Leila did not know. Shouts rose up from behind them, coming from the castle, and Niall's grip on her hand tightened.

He turned abruptly, pushed open a door to a cottage and shoved her inside.

Leila stumbled into the dark, empty single-room home. The air was musty with disuse and cold in a way suggesting a fire had not been lit within for many years.

A low tingling started at the back of her neck, the first signs of a vision coming as the room lit with a golden glow.

CHAPTER 18

Leila had long since learned not to fight her visions. For whether she wanted them or not, by will or by force, they came.

"Leila," Niall's voice came from the distance of another world, but she did not respond. She could not.

The tallow candle flickering on the table was little more than a nub of fat set within a greasy puddle. Oily black smoke coiled up from the flame and clogged the air with its foul odor. A man sat in a single chair by the hearth where a meager fire struggled to come to life.

The door creaked open behind Leila and the man got to his feet. He was short, his hair dark and shaggy where it fell over his eyes. He bowed with reverence. "My lord."

Lord Armstrong swept into the cottage and cast a disdainful look about. The silver streaks were gone from his red hair and the lines of time on his face had smoothed. He was a young man once more, his shoulders square with arrogant youth and limitless vitality. "Ye know why I'm here, Fingal."

The other man, Fingal, nodded. "Renault the Honorable has gone too far with his righteousness, aye?"

Lord Armstrong gave a grunt of assent. "Lady Elliot may provide us with a way to free ourselves of his burden, the withered old slut."

"The one who threatened Renault when his lad held her husband for ransom?"

"No' threatened." Lord Armstrong's mouth curled into a smile. "Cursed."

Fingal's dull eyes did not brighten with understanding even as Leila pieced together what would come next.

"Poison the bastard and lay the blame at Lady Elliot's feet." Lord Armstrong lifted a white handkerchief to the underside of his nose and narrowed his eyes at the offensive tallow candle. "Then we will be free of him, and the old woman can be drowned as a witch. We'll be done with both of them."

Fingal's mouth opened as he bobbed his head. "A bonny idea, my lord. A bonny idea." He pursed his lips. "The people like Renault, though."

"They willna know we ordered his death," Lord Armstrong said with barely tethered patience. "And his son is of age to take his father's place. The lad's no' as good as his da, but there's goodness in him yet, or so the people say." He lifted his shoulders in a shrug that indicated he didn't care one way or the other. "He'll be malleable and no' as obnoxiously righteous as his da."

"I'll see to the poison, my lord." Fingal bowed.

Lord Armstrong lowered the handkerchief, grinning. "And I'll see to Niall."

Leila sucked in a sharp gasp. A hand went around her face, smothering her in the darkness. A man's body was at her back, locking her against him. She shook her head aggressively and drew an arm back. The hand loosened.

"Be silent," Niall whispered.

The strong torso at her back was familiar now, as was the scent of cedar and leather. Footsteps sounded outside, along with the call of orders, as Lord Armstrong's guards searched for them.

Leila took off her helm and twisted to better look at Niall. He tensed his hold on her in warning.

"Niall," she breathed. "I have to—"

The door rattled. Her heart jolted.

She clenched her teeth to keep from speaking. She had to tell Niall about what she'd seen of his father, of Lord Armstrong. But to speak now would give away their position.

Her mind reeled with what she had learned, or she would have protested as he eased her around behind him, putting himself in front of her. A splintering crack shattered the silence around them as the door flew inward and a cluster of guards ran in.

"Niall," Leila said. "Your father—"

"There they are," a man shouted over her. "Get the witch."

Niall loomed up over the man and raised his sword.

Alban ran in front of his guard and blocked the blow. "I wouldna do that if I were ye, Lion." He smirked. "Or mayhap I should let ye. If any men are killed, she will die this night."

"Ye mean to kill her anyway." Niall lunged at Alban and swung his blade.

Alban blocked the blow and called out to his men.

"Nay," Leila cried. "Niall, please! Don't do this. I saw your father."

"His father is dead," Alban growled and thrust his blade at Niall. Leila took that exact moment to flick a dagger free from her belt and send it hurtling through the air toward Alban. One of his guards threw up a targe, blocking her attack.

"It was from the past," Leila said desperately. "A vision—"

Hands grasped her, so many hands. Too many to count. They pulled at her, tugging her away from Niall, dragging her from him. Fingers clasped firmly over her mouth, sealing her words within so she couldn't speak.

She tossed her head, but the grip did not abate. She gnashed her teeth, but the man kept his hand cupped in such a way that she could not catch his skin. She writhed and thrashed and screamed as well as she was able, but the restraining hands did not release her.

"Leila," Niall cried.

"Take her to the dungeon," a low, familiar voice said.

Shivers rippled over her skin. Lord Armstrong had arrived.

Niall didn't know what Lord Armstrong had done to his father. What he might end up doing to Niall. She screamed as loud as she could, but every word of her warning was muffled by the hand in front of her mouth.

Lord Armstrong did not so much as look in Leila's direction. Instead, he kept his focus on Niall. "I would like to speak with ye in my solar."

"No more out of ye," a guard growled into Leila's ear.

Something hard thwacked into her head. Pain sent stars winking around her, followed by a terrible dizziness. She closed her eyes against it. Darkness filled her vision. Darkness with a glowing white skeleton in the distance, grinning at her, as Death laughed and laughed and laughed.

The white dots on her shoulder burned with an intensity that brought her to awareness once more.

Niall.

Her heart stung at the thought of him. Would Lord Armstrong kill him?

Her brave Lion, who would have fought them all to the death if he could. He had risked everything to save her: his position, his reputation. Possibly his life.

The guards jostled her as they carried her through the streets with her feet dragging behind her through the mud.

They made a considerable amount of noise, but no one emerged from the shuttered cottages. Mayhap they remained inside out of fear of what the night air might do to their health in such stricken times. Mayhap it was the bitter cold that kept them nestled in the warmth of their beds. Regardless, Leila was grateful they did not come out to bear witness to her being humiliated once more before them, for this time they might see her tears.

She said nothing as she was drawn toward the castle, as the mud at her feet became cold, unyielding cobbles. The weight of her belt was gone, and she knew without looking down that it had been stripped away when she'd been taken.

They brought her to the dank, chilly dungeon below the castle and threw her unceremoniously into a cell. What had been hope only an hour ago now faded like a curl of cold ash in her chest. What would they do with Niall? Would they kill him as they'd killed his father and then place the blame upon her?

The blood iced in her veins.

She'd had no visions of Niall drowning her since they had confessed their love. If this was how the future had changed, she did not want it. Better she die than they both did. Better he kill her than his death be laid at her feet.

She closed her eyes and begged for a vision to come to her. Of her father, who she had hoped to see once more, to confirm his survival of the pestilence. Of Niall and another moment of shared passion and love. Of any of her sisters, who she had dared hope to see again one day. But no visions clouded her vision. There was only the darkness of the dungeon cell pressing in on her. Emotion clogged the back of her throat for *everything* she had lost.

She no longer felt like a warrior. Nay, she was once again a prisoner, and she was defeated.

～

Niall had to be hauled to the solar, for he certainly did not go of his own volition. The lock clicked in the door behind him, but he still had half a mind to ram into it to see if he could break through. Despite the shackles that bound his wrists together, he would find a way to escape, to get to Leila.

What would they do to her?

"Ye're bewitched." Lord Armstrong scowled at him from the chair beside the fire. The large hearth had been carved with ornate monsters threading through one another as they reached out with clawed hands. It gave the impression of making the earl appear to be the very devil himself. And mayhap he was.

"I'm no' bewitched," Niall protested. "What ye're doing is wrong. If ye condemn her to die, ye're killing an innocent woman."

"Cease this nonsense." Lord Armstrong spoke with such vehemence that spittle erupted from his mouth and glowed in the firelight. "I've no' ever known ye to go against me. This isna ye. This isna how ye behave."

"Ye've never gone so far against morality before. Ye're wrong in this. She isna responsible for the pestilence and has only ever sought to heal those around her who are ill. She is a good woman and I willna stand by as ye defame her and kill her."

"The people need a witch." Lord Armstrong's lips curled as he pushed himself up from the large chair. "They've found one. Her hold on ye is proof enough." He considered Niall and studiously tilted his head. "I know of a way to be rid of the enchantment."

Something gleamed in his eyes and slithered like ice down Niall's spine. He shivered despite the heat from the wicked-looking hearth.

The earl approached and clapped Niall on the shoulder, the

way he used to do with camaraderie. Now, however, the gesture pinned Niall in place, leaving him fixed beneath the malicious glint of the older man's stare.

"Ye'll be the one to kill her." Lord Armstrong nodded to himself. "Aye, ye'll be the one to drown the witch."

"Nay." Even as Niall said it, chills ran over his skin. It was as Leila had envisioned. His pulse quickened.

"Oh, aye." The skin around Lord Armstrong's eyes tightened, so the murky blue within faded to narrowed slits in the candlelight. "Ye will."

"Ye canna force me to kill her." Niall's head swirled. "I'll no' do it."

Lord Armstrong finally released his grip on Niall's shoulder. "Which is exactly what a bewitched man would say. The people will see it in how much ye care for her. 'Tis why I must compel ye to do the right thing."

Niall tensed. After all, what could possibly be worse than killing Leila?

"Ye convinced yer man Brodie to help ye." The earl wagged a finger at him. "The young man thought he was helping ye, but I saw through his deception." He strode casually to the locked door and spoke loudly against it. "Did ye get her?"

"Brodie wasna part of it." Niall clenched his hand into a fist.

"Aye," a man replied from the other side.

The lock clattered and the door swung open.

"I know ye're lying," Lord Armstrong replied coolly. "I know it isna yer fault, that ye were bewitched and that Brodie is loyal."

A man shoved a girl with long black hair into the solar. She staggered and nearly tripped. She scuttled into the room and pushed her back against the wall, large blue eyes darting about wildly. She was a small thing with stick-thin wrists and ankles jutting from her chemise, a girl of no more than seven summers.

Disgust roiled through Niall.

"Do ye know who this is?" Lord Armstrong asked.

"What am I doing here?" The girl glanced between Niall and Lord Armstrong.

Niall knew exactly who the child was. He'd recognize little Bonnie anywhere, especially when Brodie doted so much on his little sister.

"What are ye doing with her?" Niall demanded. "She's a child."

"She's incentive." Lord Armstrong turned a hard gaze on Niall. "If ye dinna drown the witch, we'll drown this girl, then we'll drown yer witch. Either way, she'll be dead and ye'll be free of her spell. Once 'tis done, ye'll thank me."

"This is madness." Niall edged closer to Bonnie. Even with his wrists bound in the iron bands, he would do what he could to protect her. "Dinna hurt her."

Lord Armstrong called for his guards. "Ye'll be the one to decide if the lass gets hurt," he said as the clansmen took the wee girl away.

Though tears filled her eyes and her lower lip trembled, the brave child kept her head lifted and her back straight. It was enough to make Niall's throat go tight.

"Ye'll be locked in a chamber tonight and will make yer decision tomorrow." Lord Armstrong waved several of his men over. They took Niall by the chained arms and jerked him toward the door.

"Tomorrow?" Niall asked, incredulous.

Lord Armstrong grinned. "When the witch dies."

The guards dragged Niall through the castle to one of the smaller rooms set aside for minor guests where he was shoved inside with the door securely locked behind him.

There, in the absence of sound, totally alone, the severity of his situation crushed in on him. If he did not kill Leila, then Bonnie and Leila would both die.

His chest constricted with a pain so visceral, he had not felt its kind since the death of his father.

Leila had seen him killing her; she had known all along. And he'd been too damned foolish to listen.

He inhaled deeply and the air dragged like fire through his lungs. How could he kill her? His beautiful Leila, so strong and full of life. His love.

A rattle of keys sounded in his door, the movements slow and quiet. The lock clicked and the door creaked open. Except it was no clansman who entered, or even a servant come to bring him fare. Nay, the woman who stood before him in a fine kirtle and a fire lit in her eyes was none other than Lady Davina.

CHAPTER 19

Niall stared at Lady Davina with confusion. Before he could speak, she rushed over to him with a candle in her hand.

"Forgive me," she said softly. "I tried to see Lady Leila, but the guards wouldna allow me."

Even in the flickering candlelight he could see the healthy pink to her cheeks and the glossiness restored to her red hair. She had recovered fully from the pestilence. Because of Leila.

"How can they do this to her after what she did to save ye?" Niall asked, his rage tearing through any flimsy attempts at control.

Lady Davina's eyes filled with tears. "They are going to kill her, Niall. I tried to ask my father for mercy, but he wouldna hear it. I awoke to the sounds of Lady Leila being returned to the castle and I understood then what had happened. Especially when I heard of yer arrest as well." She scoffed in a manner very much unlike her. "They never pay any mind to the woman around them when they speak."

"Do ye know what he has ordered me to do?" Niall asked, still reeling at the horror of the demand.

The earl's daughter slowly shook her head.

"Yer da thinks me bewitched." Niall stared off at a distant wall, not seeing it or even caring to see it. "Or he believes the people will think I am. He insists I be the one to drown Leila, so that her spell on me will be broken."

"Niall, ye canna do it."

He took a pained breath. "If I dinna do it, they'll kill Brodie's wee sister."

Lady Davina put her hand to her lips. "Nay."

The weight of the situation settled across his shoulders once more, crushing him with its burden. Leila. Dead. By his own hands.

The woman he loved, snuffed out from the world. No longer in his life. By his own hands.

The fear, the suffering she would endure before she was finally gone. *By his own hands.*

"On the morrow." His voice cracked with emotion and he rested his forehead against the palm of his hand.

"I have seen someone brought back after drowning afore," Lady Davina said carefully.

Niall slowly lifted his head. "Brought back from the dead?"

She shrugged with a helpless look. "I dinna know, but he had been in the water for some time. A healer aided him, a woman who left at the onset of the pestilence, but one who was strong in the knowledge of healing."

"How?" Niall demanded.

"She pushed the water from his chest. Hard and fast." Lady Davina pushed the heels of her hands down in the air in rapid succession. "I was a girl, but I remember it well. It was a miracle, seeing a person brought back to life."

Niall rubbed his forefinger and thumb over his forehead, but the tension squeezing there did not abate. "There has to be another way." He looked toward the open door. He could walk out now, go to the dungeon, kill a dozen of his clansmen, rescue her from the cell, and battle through several dozen more men to rescue her.

Except he'd be killing his own men, and he would leave Brodie and Bonnie to face Lord Armstrong's wrath.

He hissed out a frustrated exhale.

"I want to save Bonnie," Lady Davina said. "And I want ye to save Leila."

Niall straightened, eager to start a plan, to have something in place to keep Leila and Bonnie alive. He nodded his assent. "I'll do anything."

~

Leila sat with her back against the cold cell wall. She'd been thus through the night. Alban's eyes glittered in the darkness from where he watched her through the barred window of the door. He'd entered the dungeon several minutes prior, relieving her guard and positioning himself in front of the barred window of her door. Watching her with a reptilian gaze, cold and calculating; a predator marking its prey.

Though Leila had tried to ignore it, the pierce of his stare was beginning to fray her nerves, one ragged thread at a time.

"'Tis morn," Alban said.

Leila's heartbeat thrummed harder despite her resolve to remain calm.

She didn't need to ask what he meant by his taunting. She already knew.

"With the morning comes yer death." His voice was low and icy and more terrifying than Leila wanted to admit.

"Niall?" Leila whispered. Warmth tingled along the back of her neck and hummed through her veins.

Alban smirked. "My da has something special for him."

The icy water splashed over her feet, her ankles, so frigid it burned her skin.

Leila fisted her hand. *Not now.*

"Why don't you just kill me?" Leila asked through gritted teeth.

Water washed over her shins to her knees, churning at her thighs. The shock of its chill sucked the breath from her lungs as a shadow fell over her. The Lion.

"'Tis no' my place." Alban's voice was distant, a shadow in the corner of her fear. "Ye saved Davina. It's why I've no' touched ye. But my gratitude willna go as far as to rescue ye."

Hands shoved at her shoulders, holding her down. That face she loved was no longer soft, but hard and determined as water filled her nose, her mouth, her lungs.

Shrieking hinges tore her from the vision and men filled her small cell.

"'Tis time," Alban said.

Rough hands grasped her by the arms as she was broken from the grip of her vision and yanked to standing. She was pushed hard in the lower back, forced forward, her steps awkward with a stiff gait from knees that ached in protest at the abrupt change in position.

Leila was not given a fine gown for her walk this time. Nay, she wore the same red trews and shirt she'd been arrested in as she was led up the stairs, through the castle and into the dazzling daylight. The wind was merciless with no cloak to stop its wrath as it whipped at the thin linen of her shirt.

The guards led her to the gate as she shivered with cold and fear and anticipation.

And though she knew he would kill her, that she would die this day by his hand, everything in her yearned to see him. The Lion.

Niall.

She longed for him with need that wrenched at her heart with every thundering beat. A knot of emotion tightened in her throat until she could scarcely swallow. She wanted his hazel eyes fixed on her, loving and tender. She wanted his wonderful cedar and leather scent filling her senses. She wanted his beauty and strength, to see how the sunlight played upon his golden whiskers and how his wavy hair rustled in a subtle wind.

It would be her last time to see him.

Her *only* time to see him.

The clansmen led her through the streets, though this time they were absent the angry villagers. Her feet slipped in the sucking mud. Icy wetness seeped through her leather shoes and left the soles of her feet numb and clumsy.

The guards made her walk through a small bit of forest on the outskirts of the village, where the naked winter branches and brittle brambles caught and cut as she pressed her way through. It opened up into a clearing dusted with white snow and a racing river with chunks of ice bobbing about on frothing waves.

The water roiled against itself as it swept down to the right with rapid currents, as beautiful as it was chaotic. This was a view someone looked over to welcome a new day, not end a life.

Her breath quickened, evident in the frantic puffs of white billowing in front of her mouth and nose as panic threatened to consume her. Seeing her own fear warmed her eyes with tears, but she forced them away. She had spent a lifetime terrified of this moment.

Now that it had arrived, she would be brave.

The villagers had gathered on the shore's edge in a clustered group. This time, they had the decency to at least appear somber. None seemed to have brought with them their abundant food stores to toss her way. She would take her small mercies where she could.

But the villagers did not hold her attention long.

A dais was raised beyond the people. Lord Armstrong stood proudly at its head with Alban and Lady Davina at his side. Niall's man, Brodie, was visible, as was a girl with dark hair. A guard held her in place with a hand on either shoulder.

"Leila Barrington," Lord Armstrong's voice carried through the crisp early afternoon air. "Witch. Whore. Bastard."

Leila jerked at the last word, for it struck her more deeply than the first two. She was indeed a bastard, a child who did not deserve the love she'd received. Her chest ached with a pain she wanted to curl around. She would not see Father again to tell him she loved him. Nor her sisters, or anyone.

"You have been charged and found guilty of witchcraft," Lord Armstrong continued. "And ye will die a witch's death in the Hermitage Waters." He stepped back to reveal Niall's form standing behind him, head cast down.

Lord Armstrong addressed the villagers. "The Lion will see to her death. Through him, we will clear the land of pestilence."

The villagers cried out their gratitude, their voices warbling in a pitch that bespoke of mourning and desperation. Niall did not step forward. He did, however, look up and meet her gaze. A span of distance separated them, but it didn't matter, that stare pierced her straight to her very core, giving her strength, even as it broke her down.

"Niall," she mouthed.

He winced and his mouth formed her name in return.

Lord Armstrong gestured to Niall to walk. "Let justice be served."

But Niall did not walk, not until the girl issued a quiet whimper, one Leila barely caught. Brodie stepped toward the child and halted. For his part, Niall glanced at the girl, squared his shoulders and strode forward.

Leila's stomach twisted with understanding, for the girl's

identity was apparent. That was how they intended to convince Niall to kill her; through Brodie's young sister. Did their sins know no bounds?

And yet, it served to ease the burden of what she knew was to come. Niall did not do this because his affections had shifted. He did it because he had no choice.

Leila had briefly considered shouting out the vision she had seen of Lord Armstrong before her death. Now, she realized that would be impossible. She could not have the earl retaliate with threats on the child.

Leila's death would not stop the great pestilence; it would not cure the ill or raise the dead. Her death, however, would save the life of a little girl.

Niall strode toward her, his gait slow where once it had been purposeful, hesitant where once it had been confident. Her heart clutched mid-beat as he approached. She took in every detail of him, drinking him in, memorizing him.

He did not look at her when he finally stopped before her. His hazel eyes scanned the hills in the distance, then the sky above, as his jaw locked into a hard line.

"Niall." Leila's voice caught on his name and she could say no more.

Finally, his gaze settled on hers, red-rimmed and glossy with unshed tears. "*Mo chridhe.*"

CHAPTER 20

There was nothing more Niall could say. Not with Alban following closely behind. That scant moment out of earshot had not been enough to tell her that he and Lady Davina had worked out a plan, and how desperately he hoped it would work. It wasn't enough to tell her he had a backup plan in mind as well, one that carried the risk of losing her forever.

It hadn't even been enough time to tell her he loved her. And yet he'd said what mattered most.

Mo chridhe. My heart.

For surely, she was. And that heart was about to be cut from his chest.

Her wide blue gaze slipped purposefully from his own and lingered on where Bonnie stood beneath the guard of a clansman. When her stare returned back to Niall, she gave a single nod.

In that one nod, Niall knew she understood it all. About Bonnie, that he had no choice. It didn't abate the excruciating pain squeezing him from all angles. Nothing would. Not now, not ever.

"To the river," Alban snarled. "Take yer prisoner, Lion." He drawled Niall's moniker like a sneering slur.

Niall didn't care. His name didn't matter, the way it was said didn't matter. Nothing mattered but her.

Leila.

Agony blazed a new hollowness in his chest. Together, they were forced to turn to the swiftly flowing river. It was swollen with the heavy rains they'd recently had and moved more quickly than Niall had accounted for.

He forced his gaze steadily ahead, so he did not glance back at Lady Davina. She would try to cause a distraction so that Niall might manage an escape with Leila, and while his departure drew the attention of everyone else back to him, Lady Davina would free Bonnie and Brodie. It was a risky plan. The alternative, however, was far riskier.

Snow crunched underfoot as he made his way to the riverbank. His heart ached with every thrum and finally he turned his attention to Leila.

Her chest rose and fell quickly as she looked out on the river. She had seen this fate many times. And she had always known it would be him.

He gritted his teeth to quell the scream welling in the back of his throat. How could he do this? How could he kill Leila?

The river rushed past the bank, snagging bits of twigs and leaves along with it. It moved too damn fast.

If Lady Davina couldn't distract everyone... Nay, he wouldn't think of it. He couldn't.

"Now," Alban growled. "Grab her and go in the water."

Niall reached out and took Leila's slender arm in his. She wore only her red leather trews and the white linen shirt. Her body trembled. He wanted to sweep the cloak from his back and throw it over her shoulders. Not that it would do any good when they were in the water.

He pulled the cloak off and handed it to a nearby guard.

She stiffened at Niall's touch, looked at him, then relaxed with a nod. "This is how it must be," she whispered.

He wanted to tell her of the plan with Davina, that she would be saved. But Alban was too damn close. A creak sounded behind Niall.

He glanced over his shoulder to find Alban with an arrow nocked. "I'll be watching ye the whole time. If ye canna do it, I'll kill ye and the witch with ye."

Niall tensed, but not with fear of Alban. Fear that the first plan was no longer an option. Lady Davina would never take the risk with Alban's aim and gaze locked on Niall.

Which meant it had to be the second plan, where the spectacle of Leila's drowning would distract the people enough that Lady Davina could help Brodie and Bonnie flee. Then when they were well hidden in the forest, Niall would grab Leila's body and take her to the horse strapped to the trees nearby, hidden from view. There was a cottage set up deep in the woods with everything he needed to care for her once he brought her back to life.

Even as Lady Davina had suggested it the prior evening, her words were hesitant, as though she herself did not believe it to be possible.

Niall stepped off the bank and into the frigid water. It sucked at his ankles, tugging greedily at him, as though it wanted to tear his feet out from under him and sweep him away with the bits of ice and debris. Panic welled in Niall, a wild, frenzied sensation unlike anything he'd ever experienced before. It was too fast, the currents too strong. Leila's body would be swept away.

The plan would not work.

He looked to Leila whose already fast breath had quickened further still. "I love ye," he said aloud. It mattered not who heard him. The villagers. The reivers standing by. Alban.

Leila bit her lip as her eyes filled with tears. "And I love you. Always."

"Do it now," Alban bellowed.

Niall put his arm around Leila, shielding her slender body from the wind with his body. It wouldn't warm her, not with such freezing water now rising up to their knees. Already his feet had gone numb and Leila's mouth held a tint of blue. As though she was already dead.

He shuddered.

They were mid-thigh and not even a stone's throw away when Alban called to them. "Stop there."

Nay. Not yet. Not now. Not ever.

Niall turned to Leila and took her face in his hands. An arrow whizzed past the narrow space between their chests.

"Do not risk yourself." Leila lowered herself in the water, kneeling before Niall. She blinked and gasped, her breath huffing, no doubt in shock at the chill of the water.

He shook his head.

"End your bewitchment by killing her," Alban said. "Or the girl dies as well."

A sharp child's scream came from farther up the bank. Bonnie had been dragged from the dais, along with Brodie. Lady Davina was at their side, her demeanor commanding. A ruse, of course. She would force them to the outskirts of the crowd with one of her loyal clansmen. At least Bonnie and Brodie would live.

"I am ready." Leila looked up at him with wide blue eyes. The current dragged her long, dark hair forward along either side of her like a black cape and the thin linen shirt was nearly transparent in the water. A single tear ran down her cheek. "I love you."

"I love ye." He settled his hands at her slender shoulders and tears filled his eyes. "*Mo chridhe*."

He wanted to tell her that she might be rescued yet, but the idea was laughable now. To bring her back from the dead. It was a myth and nothing more.

There would be no chance to save her. This was the last time he would see her, touch her.

His breath came in ragged gasps that fogged the frigid air around him. Bonnie's cry broke through the roaring in his ears. He had to do this.

Damn him.

He had to.

Leila leaned back into the water under his hands, making it look as though he was pushing her down. Water rushed on either side of her head, the powerful current streaming her dark hair on either side of her face like ribbons. Bonnie's sobs became louder, filled with a terror no child should have to endure.

He *had* to.

He set his face with a resolve he never wanted to feel, in a paltry effort to remove himself from what he did. His hands tightened on Leila's shoulders, ones he had caressed and kissed, and he pushed her down beneath the water.

She gazed up at him through the water sweeping over her face, her blue eyes open, her face serene. He stared down at her, unwilling to break the connection between them, wanting to hold onto any part of her that he could.

She would be gone forever. *Forever.*

The word rang in his head and echoed in the vast space carved out of his chest. Bubbles rose from her mouth and nose as she released her breath. She tensed against his hold and he braced himself.

He longed to release her, to pull her from the watery depths and allow her to raggedly suck in air. Wet heat ran down his cheeks. Tears. His tears.

He wished it was him who was dying, for surely, death would be more welcome than what he was being forced to do. Nothing had ever been so difficult in his life as holding down the woman he loved and watching her life slip away.

Nothing, at least, until she began to struggle.

∼

WATER FILLED Leila's mouth and nose. Impossibly cold, like a million needles stabbing into every part of her. Except her legs, which were blessedly numb.

Her lungs ached, desperate for air. She twitched beneath Niall's firm hold.

Don't struggle.

The thought was a shadowy whisper in the back of her mind. Her shoulders wrenched forward of their own volition, her body ignoring her command. Niall's face above was locked with a hard stare, mouth thinned. She wanted to comfort him, to let him know she understood, that she realized he had no choice.

Fire.

Her chest was on fire. Alight with the need to breathe. The need for air.

The need, the need, *the need.*

The desperation was clawing, scrambling over her resolve like a sharp taloned beast. She sucked in as though she could bring in air. Except it was not air. It was water, and it only made everything burn more brilliantly.

Her legs kicked against the bottom of the river and her lungs tried desperately to breathe. *Pain.* In her throat in her chest, in her eyes, her head. Her moving feet slipped over something and kicked again.

This time she found purchase and shoved. A barrier held her shoulders and kept her down.

Niall's face above her was no longer set in a mask of steely determination. It had crumpled with the pain she felt resonating through her. *Loss.* The only emotion more powerful than love.

Niall.

The Lion.

Was this a vision?

Confusion swirled in her mind.

Her lungs ached with an intense agony she could not bear. She needed to stand up. To breathe.

Don't struggle.

Why would she not struggle? She shoved harder, but the resistance at her shoulders did not yield. She had to breathe.

She grabbed at the pressure on her shoulders. Wrists. Hands. Someone was shoving her down. She tried to wrest the person's grip off her.

The Lion.

Panic ran like poison through her veins. She couldn't breathe. Air. She needed air.

She clawed at the arms holding her, raking her newly grown nails over tender skin. Her vision came in flashes, the sky beyond the shadow of her mind, a face visible between the thrashing of her hands and the churning water.

Golden hair. Hazel eyes. She'd know the handsome face of the Lion anywhere.

The man she would love. The man who would kill her.

Her thoughts slowed, too difficult to focus on and her limbs too tired to fight against the weight of the water. The world began to dim.

A warm tingle started at her neck and washed through her.

She fell into the familiar sensation, allowing the calm to ease through her tortured body.

Visions flashed in her eyes, the way a brilliant sun flares between leaves in a copse of trees. It was a lifetime of them: the past, the present, the future. The attack on Werrick Castle, her mother's screams, the siege, the great pestilence, all of it.

The man in a cottage who vowed to poison another. Witches. That vision lingered longer than the others. The Lion. He shoved her under the water, holding her. He carried her to the bed, loving her.

Finally, the last of the visions crawled to an end as the world began to fade. One final spark, a glimmer of a vision she had never before seen, whispered through her dying brain. One so beautiful and so precious that she tucked it against her heart as it stopped beating.

CHAPTER 21

Niall clutched Leila's shoulders long after she'd stopped struggling, reeling with the horror at what he'd done. What he'd been forced to do.

It didn't matter either way.

He had killed Leila. Snuffed the light from her eyes, held her down as she struggled against him, fighting for life. Her head was pushed forward by the rapidly flowing water, sparing him the sight of her still face. Her slack limbs were pulled forward as well, sucked by the current as it tried to pry her from his grasp.

He tightened his grip.

"Let her go," Alban said from where he stood dry and unfeeling on the shore. Close enough for Niall to throw a dagger and strike with little need to aim.

Niall did not obey immediately. He had a role to play, he knew. The bewitched man with his spell finally broken. He was to release her without consideration and walk away. As though he had never cared. As though he did not still love her.

But it wasn't true, damn it. He did love her. He did care. He always would.

Not that it mattered now. She would be gone to him forever as soon as he released her.

The river pulled harder and the silence between himself and Alban turned harsh.

"Let her go," Alban repeated, biting out each individual word.

There might still be a chance.

The thought floated in his mind. It was delicate and fragile, but something in him clung to it in his awareness, cradling that thread of hope.

He relaxed his fingers and Leila was immediately drawn from his grasp and swept away, like a bit of driftwood. His heart went with her, dragged from his body and carried off, leaving a burning, gaping hole.

"Do ye feel better?" Alban asked.

Niall was supposed to agree, to act lighter, more liberated. How could he?

Instead, he glared at Alban. "Do ye?"

The earl's son smirked. "Aye, I do."

"Ye dinna want to rape her anymore, then?" Niall should stop talking, but he couldn't resist the prod.

Alban narrowed his dark eyes. "And ye dinna love her anymore."

This was where Niall could not afford to misstep. Any hope Leila had hinged on his detachment. He couldn't see her body any longer. He steeled himself for the words he knew he must say. "I never did."

Alban's mouth spread into a wide grin beneath his red beard. "Good to have ye back."

"Mayhap now ye'll actually follow orders," Niall replied.

"No' likely." The earl's son shrugged his shoulder.

The arrogant bastard. Rage whipped through Niall's blood and fired enough energy into his body to kill the blighter in one messy strike. Niall ignored the comment and accepted Alban's proffered arm as he shoved down the temptation to pull it rather than take it.

A commotion arose from the dais, drawing both of their attention as their arms fell from one another. Not that Niall needed to see. He already knew what caused the disruption.

"Get them," Lord Armstrong's order rose above the din. The guards scrambled like ants on a demolished hill to comply with his command.

Niall rushed into action, moving with the cluster of men, losing himself among them. The fledgling hope within him had grown brighter, clearer.

If he left now, mayhap he could find her. He edged to the outskirts of the surrounding villagers as they dispersed. The spectacle was complete, and they'd seen their fill, their vengeance placated. A missing prisoner held no meaning for them.

But they would not find solace and respite in Leila's death like they thought. It might take a sennight, mayhap a fortnight, but they would see many still falling ill, many still dying.

Leila had forgiven them for their fear, but Niall hated them for it. It made them weak. Stupid.

Anger rose up in him once more as he slipped away into the surrounding forest. He eased behind a tree and waited to ensure he wasn't being followed. When no one came, that was when he ran. All the pent-up energy exploded from his limbs, carrying him along the inside of the forest's edge lining the river. As he ran, he looked out over the water, seeking a glimpse of red trews or pale skin.

All he was able to make out were bits of ice caught in the rushing water. By the time he had arrived deeper into the woods where his destrier had been tied up, the fledging hope had begun to wane. He swung up onto his horse and guided him to the bank once more. There was the risk of being seen, of course, but if someone happened upon Niall, he could say he was searching for Bonnie and Brodie.

Niall wandered farther down the riverbank, his eyes scanning the river as frustration tightened the muscles along the back of his neck. His hand clenched the reins.

River water had soaked through his clothing and trews. Nearly all of him was wet. He hadn't noticed it before when rage pumped through him. Now, with the onset of disappointment and hopelessness, it had sunk through his sodden skin and was settling into the core of his soul.

His nail beds were blue at his fingertips and his muscles ached from the intensity of his shivering. A bit of red caught his eye, peeking out from behind a large tree that had long since fallen into the river.

Hope shot through him. He jumped from his horse and ran closer to the shoreline. There it was. A bit of red, just a sliver, but enough to make him forget his drenched clothing once more.

He rushed into the water, shoving through the weight of it dragging at his legs. A foot came into view, pale as death, where it had been wedged between two branches. The current washed over it, heedless of the obstruction.

Niall cried out Leila's name and rushed to where she lay face down, her hair dragged forward like dark seaweed. Niall ran deeper into the river, to his waist now. It pulled at him, tugging, threatening him with death at the slightest shift in his balance. It wanted him, as it had wanted her. But the river would have neither this day.

Niall bent to put Leila's chest to his shoulder and gently loosened her foot as he stood, bringing her with him. She hung loose over him, unmoving. He carried her to the shore and lay her upon the gritty surface. Her eyes were closed, her face serene in death.

She'd only lost the one shoe; the other remained sodden on her foot.

He put his hands over her chest like Lady Davina had instructed and pressed down hard. Leila's body was cold, the bones of her chest unyielding. Lady Davina had said to push with the weight of his body as the healer had, to make the movements fast.

He braced his hands on her and shoved his weight down on her chest. It felt wrong, as though he were beating the body of the woman he'd been forced to kill. Which was exactly what he was doing.

But if it worked...

He repeated the action again and again, each time becoming easier than the last. Desperation drove his hands as tears burned in his eyes. He kept going until water gurgled from between Leila's lips.

Niall's pulse jumped at the sight of such a miracle, at the spark of hope.

Leila might truly live.

He grasped her by the shoulders and hauled her to a sitting position as she coughed and sputtered more of the river onto its shore.

Leila was alive.

∼

FIRE BLAZED up through Leila's chest and throat with a glowing hot intensity. Every cough, every sputter seemed to draw up more water. Her body was weak and pain shot through her. She raised herself on the bank with arms that could scarcely bear her weight and retched.

Her elbows buckled, but she remained upright, held aloft by the strong hands at her shoulders. She should care about hands on her shoulders. She should try to fight, to move away. That was what her last thoughts had been before this moment.

But how could she fight when she couldn't even support herself? She gasped in a harsh breath. It did not fill her with relief like she had expected. Nay, it only served to stoke the flames of her pain so that she sputtered and retched all the more.

Aggressive shivers overtook her body, no more able to be controlled than the choking breaths that delivered violent sips of air to her starved lungs.

"Leila," a male voice whispered brokenly in her ear. "'Tis a gift from God, *mo chridhe*."

Mo chridhe.

She went still and slowly turned her attention toward Niall to find him watching her with tears shining in his eyes.

"Forgive me." He brushed a bit of lank, wet hair from her face. "Forgive me, my love."

Niall. She opened her mouth to speak and found her throat unable to work properly. Instead, she shook her head and began to cough more. He pulled her against the solidness of his body, against the slight heat there.

She could stay there forever, melting into him until they were of the same shape and contour. Not that it stopped her shivering, as if she were completely frozen in the middle and nothing might ever warm her through again.

"I need to get ye from here." Niall kept her in his arms as he stood, removing his grasp from her only when he set her atop the horse and swept up behind her.

Leila's torso sagged toward Niall as they rode, pushed back by the speed of their travel and remaining there due to lack of strength to do anything otherwise. Icy wind rushed at them as they went deeper and deeper into the dense forest. Several times blackness claimed Leila until she awoke with her head lolling and her body firmly secured between Niall's powerful arms.

She had no idea how long they had been riding when they finally drew to a stop. A cottage was nestled in a dense thicket of trees, virtually hiding it from view. Niall leapt from the horse and carefully eased her down into his arms. She wanted to protest she didn't need to be carried, that she could walk. But if she were being entirely honest, she didn't know that she could actually walk. Indeed, she didn't even know if she could speak to say the words.

A pallet had been made up on the floor of the cottage with furs piled atop it. Niall set her in a chair before the empty hearth and immediately knelt before a pile of kindling.

She curled her arms around herself and shuddered with the cold while Niall pushed log after log into the hearth from a neat stack of dry wood. He struck a flint several times. So desperate was she for warmth that she imagined little pockets of heat emanating from those glinting sparks.

At last the fire caught and the logs erupted into hot, glowing flames. Leila stretched her shaking hands out to the heat. Her eyes closed with bliss and she had the irrational urge to put herself into the hearth to let it blister the cold away.

"We need to get ye from those wet clothes," Niall said softly. "Or ye'll get ill."

She opened her eyes to find him watching her, his forehead creased with worry.

He shook his head. "I had no choice."

She swallowed around her aching throat and nodded. "I know." The words eked their way out and emerged huskier than usual, the pain evident in her speech. "Brodie's sister?" she croaked.

"Bonnie is safe, thanks to yer bravery." Niall knelt before Leila and took her frigid hands in his. "Lady Davina is hiding her and Brodie for the day. They will join us when 'tis safe to do so."

He settled his brow to their joined hands in supplication. "I dinna know what I've done to earn the miracle of ye coming back to me, or if mayhap my da was in heaven looking out for ye. All I know is that I'm grateful ye're alive."

She touched his face to turn it up toward her once more. As she did so, she reveled in the scrape of his golden whiskers against her palm. "I love you," she said softly.

"And I ye." Niall got to his feet. "Now let us get from these sodden clothes, aye?"

Leila nodded, beginning to shiver again despite the blazing fire Niall had stacked as high as a solstice pyre. He grasped the hem of her shirt and drew it over her head. This time as she was undressed before him, she didn't blush. She couldn't spare the heat to do so.

He knelt in front of her and helped free her from her trews. She held onto his broad shoulders for support as he slid them from her legs. Her skin was damp and all the colder without any clothing. Niall straightened and carefully unbound the length of linen from her chest while she shuddered uncontrollably against the chill.

When he was done, he wrapped her in a linen he'd warmed by the fire. It was blissful against her skin, soothing and hot and wonderful. He assisted her into a fine chemise and a finer kirtle, wool dyed a soft lavender.

"Whose are these?" she asked in her strained whisper.

"Lady Armstrong's." Niall spoke from behind Leila as he finished lacing up the back. "She dinna have a happy marriage and made Lord Armstrong rather miserable toward the end of her life. Lady Davina's betrothal was a sore spot between them, an alliance Lady Armstrong had insisted on that Lord Armstrong soured on over time. Apparently, she pressed the issue often, trying to encourage the union, and Lord Armstrong did not approve."

Leila nodded. Lady Davina had spoken often of the man she loved, the man she had been so eager to finally wed.

Lady Armstrong's insistence on the marriage explained why Lord Armstrong had so readily given Leila several gowns while she was being held at Liddesdale Castle. No doubt the earl saw it as an insult to his wife's memory to let a woman he presumed to be a witch wear her clothing.

"It is rumored he had her killed." Niall came around Leila with a slight frown. "I dinna believe it before. But now..." He shook his head. "I was blinded by what I wanted to see and may have missed what was actually there."

The memory rushed back to her of what she'd seen in her vision at the cottage on the night of their failed escape. "Niall, I saw something before we were captured. I tried to tell you..."

Niall pulled her to the bed. "No' now, *mo chridhe*. Ye need to get under the covers while I make ye a tea and see to the horse."

Leila allowed him to pull her toward the pallet piled high with furs. Already, her body had ceased to shiver. "I must tell you."

"Later." Niall pulled back the furs to the inviting heat.

Leila's eyes were heavy, her mind still murky from drowning. Still, she stopped allowing him to pull her forward and instead took his hand in hers. "Now."

He nodded. "Aye, but by the hearth at least."

"Only if you put on dry clothes as I speak," she countered.

Niall's mouth thinned into a hard line, but he nodded in agreement.

Only after he had her set before the hearth with enough heat on her back that she feared she might catch on fire, did she speak. As he undressed, she watched his body move with appreciation and deeply regretted her exhausted state. She wanted nothing more than to go to him and let their chilled bodies heat up together.

She turned her mind from such lustful thoughts and instead told him of what she'd seen in the vision. She spoke of how Lord Armstrong had ordered the death of Niall's father, how he had intended to supplant the former deputy with his son, and how they used the man Niall had ransomed to their benefit, to kill both Niall's father as well as the old woman.

When she was done, Niall staggered back in his newly donned dry clothes and sat down hard in the chair.

"I tried to tell you sooner," Leila said.

Niall stared blankly into the flames. "There was no time." His fingers curled around the wood arms of the chair. "I'll kill the bastard."

He said it with such vehemence, a sliver of apprehension worked its way down Leila's spine, and she had the sudden fear that she'd made a grave mistake in telling what she'd seen.

CHAPTER 22

Niall's anger wasn't easily set aside, but he forced it from his mind. Leila needed him. Aye, she'd been saved and stood before him, breathing and glowing with the flush of life on her cheeks. But it didn't mean she was safe, especially when she had just been brought back from the dead.

Leila watched him with a concerned expression pinching her brows. "I shouldn't have told you." There was a slight strain to her voice that bespoke of a pain she did not complain of, and it tugged at his chest. "I have never learned exactly what I should and should not share of my visions."

"Nay, I needed to know." He rose from the chair and took her hand in his. Her fingers were like ice.

She gasped and touched his forearm with her free hand. The skin there was shredded with claw marks that gauged angry red wounds from where his shirt had not covered his wrists.

"I'm sorry." She looked up at him with tears in her eyes.

A familiar knot formed in his throat. Being safe in a comfortable, quiet moment brought the horror of what had happened rushing back.

"Ye were being killed, Leila." His voice broke. "I was holding ye down and ye were fighting to live. Because that's what ye do, lass. Ye're a fighter. And I..." He looked away, ashamed of his tears. "I was killing ye."

Leila touched his chin and turned his face back to her. "You saved Bonnie. They would have killed me anyway. And yet you still managed to save me. You pulled me from the water and you..." She shook her head. "I don't even know what you did, but you saved me. And now here I am, in a cottage with you."

He pulled her into his arms, reveling in the wonderful sweetness of her body against his.

She reached for his face and cradled it in her cold palms as she pressed her lips to his. "I love you," she whispered. Her mouth found his and her tongue teased between his lips.

His body responded, immediately hot and hard to reclaim the woman he had thought he'd lost. "I love ye." He pushed her gently away with a tight groan. "Which is why I'm going to tuck ye into that bed on yer own. Ye need to rest, aye?"

He took her hand and led her to the pallet where he tucked her beneath the many layers of furs. "I'll be outside tending to the horse if ye need me."

She nodded with a soft smile hovering on the corners of her lips. He'd never thought to see that expression again. He leaned over her and pressed a kiss to her hair and breathed her in. The subtle hint of rosemary still clung to her hair despite what she'd been through.

Once she was settled, he saw to his horse, placing the massive destrier in the small single stall attached to the side of the cottage. He removed the horse's bridle and paused when the sleeve of his shirt fell back to reveal his gouged forearm.

Tears prickled in his eyes again, recalling that awful moment. Leila had fought like a warrior, her hits powerful enough to have most likely left bruises on his shins and arms. It had taken a considerable amount of effort to keep her under water. To kill her.

He scrubbed a palm over his face, but he couldn't get the image out of his mind of her clawing at him, forced to such actions through the sheer will to survive. And he'd had to hold her down until that awful moment when the fight left her body. When he'd known she was dead.

Lord Armstrong had made him do that. Lord Armstrong, who had used Niall's adolescent misconduct to kill his da and then twist events to bring Niall to his side.

He balled his hand into a fist, his pain and tears transforming into an emotion he could control: anger. One of rage and vengeance. With a snarl of intent, he slammed his hand into the wall of the stable. The destrier was bred for war and did little more than flick his ears back irritably at the audible smack of Niall's fist connecting with the boards of the stall.

Lord Armstrong would pay for his crimes with his own life.

Leila was safe for now. That was all that mattered at the moment. Once Brodie and Bonnie arrived at the cottage, they would all venture to Werrick Castle where Niall hoped he could negotiate for the safekeeping of his friends.

In truth, Niall wished he could take Leila now, but the trek would be too cold on her battered body. She needed the time to rest and warm up. Once she was at Werrick, tucked securely behind the stone curtain walls of her home, then Niall would exact his revenge.

He willed his body to calm and lowered his aching hand. Vengeance would come later. Now was for finding supper and preparing a hot stew.

It was hours later when the stew was ready. It contained a bit of rabbit mixed in with some vegetables that had been brought to the cottage, along with the bedding and tinder, by one of Lady Davina's discreet servants.

Niall had continued to add logs from the abundant pile to the fire, keeping it blazing until the cottage was hot enough to force him outside on occasion to cool off. He checked on Leila periodically as she slept, to ensure her chest still rose and fell with even breathing.

It pleased him to find her cheeks and lips were a bonny shade of rosy pink, no doubt set there by the roaring fire. He gazed at her for a long moment before waking her for food, cherishing that she was alive and there with him. The firelight caught her glossy dark hair and glowed golden over her skin. She looked so peaceful, so lovely.

He reached a hand out and caressed her cheek. She was warm under his touch and he thanked God for it.

"*Mo chridhe*," he said softly.

She smiled and cupped his hand with hers, holding him to her.

"Ye feel much better," Niall said. "Are ye hungry?"

Her eyes opened and found his. "Aye, I am. And I'm finally no longer cold. Thank you."

Her voice was stronger than it had been before she fell asleep, less strained. He was grateful Lady Davina had provided the cottage. He had been anxious about it before, thinking that stopping to rest through the day and night was a dangerous idea. Now he understood the wisdom of the offer, for Leila would never have survived the ride to Werrick Castle after he'd found her in the river.

Niall served them both stew, and side-by-side, they ate it with some of the bread left for them at the small table. This was how Niall wanted it to be all their lives. The two of them together, side-by-side, in a home of their own. Mayhap with a bairn or two running about.

"What are you thinking about?" Leila asked. "You're smiling."

Niall lifted his shoulder noncommittally. "Ye."

She smiled in return. "You were thinking of me?"

He nodded and winked at her. She laughed, that sweet, husky sound that made him want to pull her into his arms and kiss her, touch her, love her. Appreciate her, relish her.

He had lost her that day.

The recollection was as stark and painful as an unexpected blow. He reached out and pulled her chair toward his until she was nestled against him.

"Ye're a miracle I'll no' ever stop being grateful for." He kissed the top of her head, then lifted her chin and lowered his mouth to hers.

"I love you," Leila whispered against his lips. She returned his kiss. Not just one, but several. And not only chaste kisses either, but ones filled with such suggestive promise that it made his loins stir.

"Leila," he groaned. "Ye need rest."

"I've rested." Her voice was throaty with desire and like a physical caress that left his skin prickling with heightened sensitivity.

He shifted away from her, despite the difficulty to do so. "Ye need to fully recover." He would not hurt her or put her at risk. Not so soon after having her back and safe. But God, how he wanted to revel in having her here once more, to love every inch of her body in full appreciation.

"My body feels very well recovered." She slipped off her seat and straddled his lap. She put her arms around the back of his neck and rolled her hips with blatant sexuality. The heat of her center pressed to him, reminding him of every way he wanted to show her the gratitude he held for her being with him.

"I know much about healing," she whispered. "And I assure you, I'm quite well."

"Are ye certain, lass?" he groaned. His hips flexed upward of their own volition, pushing against her.

Her lashes fluttered. "Very," she breathed.

He kissed her then, with the full force of his passion, slanting over her mouth to stroke her tongue with his. His hands eased up the skirt of her kirtle, skimming over silky smooth, blissfully warm skin.

She was alive. With him. And he would not waste even a single precious moment.

~

Where Leila had been cold before, she was now blazing with heat. Not only from the steady fire flickering in the hearth, but the one burning within, the one desperate for the connection with Niall.

She had not seen beyond the vision of being drowned and knew not what was ahead of them. All she knew was that she wanted to savor these moments with him before they ran out.

Death, after all, was a rapacious beast that was not easily cheated out of his winnings.

She tugged at Niall's shirt, desperate to have it off, to have his bare flesh under her fingertips for exploration. He drew the shirt off and worked at the back of her gown, even as he kissed her hungrily. His arousal strained at her center, making her pulse throb with longing.

Her hips arched against him in a show of mock intimacy while he unthreaded the back of her kirtle and nudged it down to reveal her breasts. He broke off their kiss to regard her and growled his approval. It was a guttural, primitive sound that heightened her own desire.

He bent forward and pulled one nipple into his mouth, flicking and dancing across the little nub with his tongue until

Leila was crying out. It wasn't enough. She needed him. All of him.

With shaking hands, she pulled at the ties of his trews. His prick sprang free, hard and as eager for their joining as she. She grabbed it at the root, positioned her hips and sank down on him.

He hissed out a breath of surprise. He was full and hot inside her. She rocked against him, rolling her hips against his. The movements were too subtle though, not nearly firm enough to get the friction she wanted. Needed.

Niall skimmed his hands up her naked legs and grasped her bottom in both hands. He guided her with strong palms, showing her how to stroke herself with him. She gripped his shoulders, holding tight to him, this man who impossibly had found a way to save her and bring them together once more. This man she loved.

He thrust up inside of her as her hips shifted back and forth against him, teasing the little bud at the top of her sex. Their panting breaths filled the cabin amid the moans and grunts as their bodies strained to be closer, to create more wonderful friction hum between them.

Leila's muscles tensed with the warning of her impending release. Niall growled and increased his speed, rubbing that place between her legs that made her unwind. She clutched him and let herself fall over the edge of pleasure, crying out as the waves and waves of bliss crashed over her.

Niall drove deep into her and held her against him with a powerful groan. All at once, they sagged into the chair together, clutching each other and staring into each other's eyes.

"I canna believe ye're here with me." Niall swept a length of hair from her face. "I thought I'd no' ever see ye again and yet here ye are, taking me on a chair in the middle of a cottage buried in the woods."

"Good thing 'tis a strong chair," Leila teased.

Niall's brows lifted. "Aye, 'tis. We should move to the bed though." He shifted his back and gave an exaggerated grimace that made her laugh.

Leila eased off of him. "But I'm not tired anymore."

Niall stood and stepped out of his trews. "Me neither, lass." He grinned and brushed his hand down her shoulder, nudging her kirtle to the floor. His mouth whispered over where his hands had been.

"I think Death got what he wanted, *mo chridhe*," Niall murmured against her skin.

A little chill trickled down Leila's spine. "Why do you say that?"

"Yer shoulder." He leaned back and ran his thumb over the spot where Death had left his mark. "The spots are gone."

Leila arched her shoulder forward and glanced down at it in disbelief. Niall was correct. Death's mark was gone. She ran her fingers over the area and found only warm, smooth flesh.

Had she been released then? Or would he be coming to find her still?

Mayhap she would dream of it that night, for it was evening when she had most of her visions. Most nights went by with at least one vision in her sleep. They were not always large or impactful, but they were there, nonetheless.

She frowned slightly.

"What is it?" Niall asked.

"I didn't see anything when I slept earlier."

"No visions?"

She nodded.

"Does that displease ye?" he asked.

His question took her aback. Did it displease her? She'd spent a lifetime despising her visions, hating the terror they infused her with, the cryptic delivery, and how different it made her from her sisters.

And yet, it'd been part of her entire life, as much a piece of her as her hands or her heart.

"I'm not certain," Leila said quietly.

"Mayhap it was simply because of how tired ye were," Niall suggested. "What ye'd been through."

"Mayhap." Leila nodded. But there was a strange hollowness inside her that said otherwise.

"We'd best get ye to bed then, so ye can see." The corner of Niall's lip lifted in a slow, sensual grin. "Ye'll need yer rest."

"Will I?" Her grin matched his.

"Aye, Brodie and his sister, Bonnie, will arrive on the morrow." He led her to the bed and pulled her under the covers with him. She lay on her back, looking up at him as he braced himself on his elbow and traced the line of her jaw with his fingertip. She closed her eyes against the sweet sensation of his touch gliding over her.

"Then we will all travel to Werrick Castle," he said.

Her eyes flew open. "Werrick," she whispered.

Niall winked. "Ye're going home."

"My father..."

"We've no' heard anything." His hazel eyes crinkled with sincerity. "I think if there'd been bad news, we'd have heard it by now."

Leila nodded in agreement. No doubt Alban would have waved it in her face like a banner if word carried of Lord Werrick's death. Niall was right; hearing nothing was for the best.

Home.

She would be home soon. To see her father and her family and her friends, to return to the life she had before... She looked up at Niall. Where would he fit in with her world?

"Yer da may no' forgive me for imprisoning ye." Niall lifted a shoulder apologetically, as if reading her thoughts.

"You saved my life," Leila protested.

Worry creased his brow. "What I've done is unforgivable, Leila."

She chuckled. "You haven't met my brothers-in-law." The thought of her family made tears prickle in her eyes. The family she had thought never to see again.

"What is it, lass?" Niall brushed a tear from her cheek.

"I fear sleeping and what visions it may bring." She sniffed. "I've never seen past this moment of my life and everything right now is so perfect, I dread seeing what else might come our way. And I also dread not seeing anything at all." She gave a mirthless smile at her own indecisiveness.

"Then mayhap we shall have to keep ye from sleeping." His hand ran up the side of her waist and brushed against her breast.

Desire heated between her legs with a needy thrum. She sighed in her eagerness and shifted her body closer to him. Already, his longing was becoming apparent and hard against her thigh.

And while they did eventually fall into an exhausted slumber together, their shared passion was enough to prevent Leila from fearing the future. Especially when, for the first time in her life, she had no idea what it might bring.

CHAPTER 23

The sun painted the room to a cheery golden yellow the following morn. Leila curled deeper into the comfortable bed and the man snuggled up beside her. A contented smile touched her lips. She had slept through the night without waking once. For the first time in her entire life. Or at least as long as she could remember.

Her mind was clear with having been thoroughly rested. She stiffened with awareness. There had not been any visions. Again.

Niall immediately sat up in bed, his body tense as he braced himself in front of her. "Did ye hear something?"

Leila shook her head. "Nay."

Niall did not relax but turned to regard her. "What is it?"

His reaction broke through the calm of her thoughts, a reminder they were still in danger until they reached Werrick Castle.

"The sun," Leila replied. "And then the realization that I didn't have a vision. Again."

"Are ye all right, lass?" He asked.

Leila chewed her bottom lip, unsure how to answer. Unsure how she even felt.

"We should dress," Leila replied.

Niall studied her for a moment, as if he planned to press the topic she'd purposefully navigated around. In the end, he rose from the bed, naked and beautiful in the light of day, and proceeded to wash up from water in the ewer.

They dressed not a moment too soon, for once they'd donned the last of their clothing, a knock came at the door. Niall slid his sword free and motioned for Leila to stay back.

Unarmed, she had no choice but to do as he asked, though she hated every moment of it. While she knew she could rely on her fists, she wanted her belt of daggers back.

He opened the door and his blade hissed back into its scabbard as he waved their visitors into the small, single room cottage.

Brodie strode in with Bonnie hugging his side. He blinked as he saw Leila and made the sign of the cross. "It worked."

"Aye," Niall said. "Lady Davina has saved us all."

Leila peered behind them. "Is she with you?"

"After she'd saved us, she returned back to the castle," Brodie replied.

"She dinna want her father to know what she'd done," Niall said.

"Pray God he never finds out," Leila added solemnly.

Niall pressed a kiss to her forehead. "I'll saddle my steed, then we must make haste to depart." He lifted his pack from the floor beside the table. "The sooner we are at Werrick Castle, the less we have to worry."

He was inside almost as soon as he'd left. "Riders are approaching."

Leila threw on the mantle that had been left for her and raced out of the cottage with Brodie and Bonnie beside her. A subtle rumble sounded in the distance, almost like the onset of thunder in an upcoming storm.

Niall cursed under his breath. "They're approaching swiftly."

Brodie grimaced. "They must have followed me."

"It doesna matter now," Niall said in authoritative tone. "Brodie, take my destrier. He can handle Leila and Bonnie along with ye."

Leila did not move as Brodie and Bonnie swung up onto Niall's horse.

"I can fight," Leila protested. "I would rather die at your side than be separated from you again."

"Nay." Niall's voice was commanding, as it was when he ordered his men. When he spoke again, his tone was softer, more sincere. "I canna lose ye again, *mo chridhe*."

"Then we all ride to Werrick together," Leila insisted. "We can outrun them."

He cast a regretful glance in the distance where the rumbling grew louder. "Get on the horse with Brodie and Bonnie, or we'll all die."

Niall mounted Brodie's smaller horse as Leila grudgingly climbed between Brodie and Bonnie. With a cry from Niall, they tore off through the forest, abandoning the cottage and making their way to Werrick Castle. *Home.*

The wooded area was tight with trees and the branches snapped and scratched at them as the horses raced onward. Though the sun shone bright overhead, the wind still carried an iciness to it that stung Leila's cheeks. A chill started within her, reminiscent of the day before, and rattled through her body.

Even over the sound of their own horses' hoofbeats, Leila could make out the rumble of the men behind them as the riders came closer. She chanced a glance behind her. Men on horseback raced after them. A group of mayhap twelve men, led by a man she recognized all too well.

Alban.

Niall's horse rounded abruptly. He shouted something Leila

could not make out. But then, it had not been meant for her. Brodie gave a stiff nod and hugged his arms close to her and Bonnie with determination.

"Stop," Leila gasped. "Niall is turning around."

"Nay," Brodie said sharply. "He is the only one they want. I'm to keep ye safe no matter the sacrifice."

Leila's heart caught in her throat. "Nay, please. I can help."

But it was too late. The English border loomed in the distance and not much farther would be Werrick Castle. If she flung herself from the horse, she would surely die from the impact and Bonnie may end up injured as well.

"They would stop at the English border," Leila cried over the thundering hooves.

"Alban willna care about the border," Brodie said from behind Leila.

He was right, of course, no matter how awful the truth of it was. Leila twisted in the saddle, helpless as she looked over her shoulder. Niall sat proud and tall on Brodie's horse, disappearing into the distance as he faced down their foe completely on his own.

He was a strong fighter, but against twelve men... Thirteen, including Alban.

All too soon, Niall was gone, lost in the distance. Why had she not seen this future? How could she not have known this was coming?

She choked back a cry of frustration and held tight to Bonnie's small frame as they raced even faster across the countryside. Werrick Castle rose like a beacon on the horizon, a sight that would have been welcome earlier, but was now a symbol of what she had lost.

The portcullis raised as they approached. Brodie did not slow the destrier until they were in the bailey of Werrick Castle where Peter, the Master of the Horse, ran to see to the steed.

Leila slid from her horse on weak knees, along with Brodie and Bonnie.

"We left him." The words echoed in the void within Leila's chest.

"We had to," Brodie said. "'Tis what he asked me to do."

An excited shout rose from the castle, pulling Leila's attention to her four blonde sisters rushing from the castle's arched entryway toward her, each one dexterous and graceful, one with a bow slung over her back.

A mixture of emotions flew through Leila in rapid succession: joy to see those she loved again for the first time, fear at the risk of their travel through the pestilence-laden land and hope that she might have help. That they might all be able to save Niall.

Anice reached her first, face flushed. "Leila. Thanks be to God you are safe."

Leila reached for Anice's hand. "We must go to him. Please. He'll die."

"What are you talking about, Lamb?" Anice stroked the hair from Leila's face in a motion she recalled well from her childhood. "What's happened?"

"Niall," Leila said. "The Lion."

Marin pulled Leila into her arms in an encompassing hug that smelled of lavender and comfort. "The Lion? Leila..."

"I met him," Leila said. "We have to go after him. To save him."

Ella and Catriona were both there suddenly, embracing Leila. It was then Leila noticed Brodie and Bonnie standing there.

"This is Brodie and his sister, Bonnie," Leila explained. "They helped me escape, except Niall—"

"Leila?" A frail voice came from the entryway of the castle and stopped her words as well as her heart.

She spun around to find her father bundled heavily against the cold, with Rose at his side helping him to walk with the aid of a new cane.

He was alive. Leila's spirits buoyed for a brief moment and she found herself running to him.

His face was too thin, but his eyes crinkled with the same affectionate joy they'd always held. Her sisters crowded around her as she gently embraced her father.

There would be much to explain to them and little time to do it. She only hoped she wouldn't be too late.

～

THE LION FACED the men charging toward him, and like his namesake, he lay in wait for his prey. His focus centered on Alban whose red hair shone in the overcast light. The arrogant bastard had thought Niall so easy to take down, he hadn't even bothered with a helm as protection for his head.

The cur would learn his lesson today.

A quick glance over Niall's shoulder told him the remainder of the party was traveling over the English border. Some of the tension abated from his muscles. Leila was safe, as well as Bonnie.

He winced at the twinge in his chest, at having to let Leila go. Alban and his men would have caught them all if Niall had not stopped to fight.

Alban threw a dagger as he rode closer, but Niall did not swerve from its path. He'd known the attempt to be poorly aimed. He didn't flinch as it sailed past him at a speed that would have bounced from his gambeson even if it had hit. It was a pathetic attempt. A true warrior would know better than to lose a weapon in such a careless fashion.

It would cost the younger man his life.

Niall adjusted his grip on the hilt of his sword. After a lifetime of serving someone unworthy of his loyalty, he had abandoned his previous role. He now had only two points of focus: to ensure Leila's safety and to avenge the death of his father.

Leila would be in Werrick Castle soon, leaving only the purpose of vengeance.

Niall waited until the men were nearly upon him before he charged, his blade held aloft to catch Alban just above the knee where the greaves ceased to protect his leg. Alban jerked aside at the last minute and spun about on his horse in an attempt to strike Niall.

"Stay back," Alban ordered his men, who promptly fell back.

Some of the guards with him were men Niall had commanded previously, but ones who had always paid homage to the Lord Armstrong and his son.

Alban's horse circled Niall's. Each man brandished his weapon in preparation for battle. Alban lashed out with his sword, but Niall dodged the blow and parried with one of his own. He feigned right before jabbing left, stabbing his blade hard against Alban's gambeson.

The whoreson flew backward, thrown off his horse, and landed with a solid grunt. It would be easy to kill him now; a stamp of a hoof, a dagger to the throat. But Niall wouldn't lower himself to such a level. Not like Alban would have.

Instead, Niall jumped from his steed. "Get up and fight like a man."

Alban groaned and dragged himself to his feet. He pulled his sword free and glowered at Niall. "Ye'll wish ye killed me when ye had the chance."

"I fully intend to." Niall lunged first, swinging his blade toward the cur's throat.

Alban stepped back with a cocky grin and thrust his sword at Niall, who ducked to the side.

"Did ye know about my da?" Niall gestured to the reivers that stood by as the two fought. "Do *they* know about him?"

"That he was always in the way?" Alban wielded his blade with two hands and brought it down with enough force to fell a tree.

Niall darted out of the way, then ran at Alban with his blade aimed toward the bastard's heart. Alban blocked the hit. Their swords clanged together and held for a long moment, rasping the discordant song of metal scraping metal.

"My father was killed, and an innocent woman was accused of being a witch," Niall ground out. "Same as yer da did to Leila."

Alban shoved Niall back with such force, they both staggered a step. "It was yer fault. Ye escaped with Leila, and ye took her as yer lover. Ye fool. And ye killed yer da the day ye kidnapped Lord Elliot. If ye hadna—"

"Nay," Niall roared. "Yer father killed him." He rushed at Alban and arced his sword toward the bastard. No sooner had Alban blocked one strike, Niall had another sailing toward him, then another, and yet another still. The sharp ring of weapons clashing was staccato as their blades met again and again and again.

Niall's muscles burned with aggression. If they tired, as they often did in battle, he did not feel it. The power of his need for vengeance was too great.

Niall's sword caught on Alban's arm and a bright blossom of crimson bloomed on his white shirt, visible in the parting of his cloak. The injury did not appear to slow Alban down as he continued to evade the blows. At first.

Several hits later, his movements began to slow as exhaustion worked into his muscles. And that was exactly what Niall had expected. What he needed.

"Ye'll pay for what ye did to Leila." Niall swept his sword left, then right. Too quickly for Alban to evade the hit.

Niall's blade sank into the soft side of Alban's torso. His eyes went wide with surprise. Niall pulled his weapon free and watched as his opponent staggered back in shock. Niall should walk away, mayhap use Alban as a means of escaping the other clansmen.

He could return to Werrick Castle with Leila, to live out their life. Except that Alban and Lord Armstrong would get away with all they'd done. Mayhap do it to someone else.

Niall stepped closer and let every awful memory pour over him.

When Alban had tried to rape Leila.

Another step.

How he'd terrified her to the point of mutilating herself to obtain a weapon.

Niall stopped in front of Alban. "Yer da will pay for what he made me do to Leila and what happened with my da. Ye both will."

On the final word, he shoved his sword into Alban's chest, between the plates of leather in the gambeson so the sharp sword punctured through bone and cartilage. Niall didn't stop pushing the weapon into Alban until the hilt touched the man's stained gambeson and blood flowed hot over Niall's hands.

A choked cry issued forth from Alban's mouth, along with a string of pink saliva. Niall pulled his weapon free as the first Armstrong guard crashed into him.

The attacker was too close for Niall to strike with his sword, so he slammed the pummel of his weapon into the man's back. The guard grunted in pain and released Niall. He jabbed his blade into the man's shoulder as a second man descended upon him. Then a third, and a fourth.

Sweat poured down his brow and stung his eyes. There was a

saltiness in his mouth, but he didn't know if it was from sweat as well, or blood. It had been reckless to kill Alban. He knew that. But he had to do it.

A life for a life, and he was not done yet.

Niall thrust his sword where he could, finding critical hits. He'd always been a damn good warrior, but even a damn good warrior could not take on twelve reivers and walk away unscathed.

The first blade nicked Niall on the forearm of his sword arm. The second strike was a gash to his thigh that left his leg weak and heavy. The third was a fist to the eye that sent him reeling backward. He fell to the ground, battered and bleeding.

Leila.

Her image rose in his mind, the way she'd looked at him with fear when he left her. Even without her visions, she had worried it might come to this. He'd seen it the night before, when regret creased her brow for having told him about his father's death.

A foot raised over Niall's face, preparing to come down and end his life.

"Nay," one of the guards said. "The earl will want to deal with him personally."

With that, Niall was hauled to his feet, head lolling, and put roughly on the back of a horse. Lord Armstrong would seek to claim vengeance for his son, but Niall still had his own to see to. For certes, when this war was over and done, vengeance would only be claimed by one.

CHAPTER 24

Leila gathered with her family and Brodie in the warm, familiar comfort of the solar, while Nan took Bonnie into the kitchen for some honey pastries. Rose joined them as well and remained at the earl's side, as tender and gentle in her assistance as she'd been with Leila when she was ill.

As quickly as she could, Leila shared the details of what had transpired at Liddesdale Castle, about how Niall had indeed taken her, how he had shown her kindness, how he managed to break down her defenses and they'd came to love one another. It was at this part of the story, she left out some of the more intimate details that her family, most especially her father, would be best not knowing. Regardless, Ella gave her a knowing grin, but then, she always did love a romantic tale.

Leila went on to tell them how Niall had tried to free her, about their capture, and eventually about Niall drowning her.

"He did it?" Marin gasped. "He actually did it?"

Leila looked at her a long moment and remembered all at once that final vision she'd tucked against her heart, the last one she'd seen as she was dying. It had been lost momentarily in the recesses of her dark memory when life slipped from her body.

"He had no choice," Brodie spoke up. "Leila's bravery and Niall forcing himself to do the impossible saved my sister. We left Niall fighting Lord Armstrong's son and twelve guards on his orders. I had no choice but to obey."

"Thirteen men is no mean feat," Anice said softly. There was a delicate note to her voice, one that suggested it might be too great an obstacle.

"But not impossible," Cat added brightly.

"Niall would be too great a prize," Brodie said. "They wouldna kill him on the field with over a dozen men against him. He knew that. They'll bring him to Liddesdale Castle to have him strung up before the people."

"'Tis true," Lord Werrick agreed with a somber expression. His thin chest expanded in a sigh. "We will have more than a few soldiers to contend with, my daughters."

"It matters not." Catriona fingered her bow. "We shall fight, as will our husbands when they return from their hunt."

She'd told Leila how the men went out hunting in the nearby forest opposite the village where no one else went. It helped the staff of Werrick and guaranteed everyone's strength stayed up to resist the pestilence.

"All of us will fight." Anice looked around at all the sisters, who nodded in unison. "Together."

"I wish Drake were here," their father lamented. Drake, the former Captain of the Guard, had left the earl's service to pursue his own life, and they were all glad to see him achieve the happiness he'd found. Sir Richard, who had been Captain of the Guard before Drake, had returned from retirement to serve while the earl tried to find a permanent replacement.

And while their father didn't say it, Leila and her sisters all knew this rescue would be too difficult for Sir Richard to take on at his age.

"We can do it without Sir Richard." Marin lifted her head

with the air of authority she'd always held. "Our guards spent years following me before. They can do so again now."

"Nay, let them stay here, lest it cause a war between England and Scotland." Leila got to her feet and everyone turned to look at her. "And, forgive me, Sister, but you cannot come."

Marin's face flushed. "Why would I not? Surely, you don't think *me* too old?"

Leila shook her head as she approached her sister. "I had a vision before I died."

Marin watched Leila warily.

"Marin," Leila said softly. "There is life within you."

"What did you say?" Marin blinked and a single tear fell from her eye.

Leila gently laid her hand on Marin's lower stomach. "You are with child."

A sob broke from Marin and she placed her trembling fingers over Leila's hand. "Are you certain?" She stammered. "Mayhap you saw it wrong? Surely I am too old…"

"Nay, Marin." Leila's throat went tight with emotion. "You are soon to be a mother."

Marin cradled her stomach and openly wept. She was not alone in her tears, for all the sisters, and even Lord Werrick, were wiping at their eyes. Poor Brodie, however, shifted uncomfortably amid this group of crying women and discussions of childbearing.

He rocked back on his heels. "I can join ye," he said. "Er—at Liddesdale Castle. I know it well."

The solar door opened, and four large men pushed into the room. James, the tallest of them, grinned at Leila. "She *is* safely returned."

James made his way to Anice's side and paused to ruffle Leila's hair. "Ye gave us all quite the scare, lass."

"I'm only glad Lark wasn't with you." Bronson smirked as he

mentioned his sister. "Ever since she's started training with the arrow like Cat, she's had quite the penchant for mischief."

"Where does she get that from?" Ella teased her husband. "I believe it runs in the family."

Bronson scoffed and then slid her a grin.

"The Armstrongs will be punished for what they've done to you," Geordie vowed.

"We've already planned to go after them." Cat curled an arm around her husband's and pulled him close. Geordie glanced down at her and immediately the tension drained from his body.

"Then what else is amiss?" Bran asked, approaching Marin. "Why are ye crying, my love?"

A shared look passed around the room and flew over the understanding of the husbands.

"We need to prepare." Leila made her way toward the door, knowing others would follow suit. "Time may be running out, depending on how eager Lord Armstrong is to exact his punishment."

As anticipated, the room cleared, leaving only Marin and Bran in the sunny solar. Leila caught sight of them as she strode away, their hands touching, leaning together for the intimate conversation that would change their lives forever.

She didn't need to see to know what would transpire on the other side of that door. She'd seen it already.

Their heads were close as Marin spoke words Leila could not hear. Bran raised his brows in question and tears fell from Marin's eyes. He knelt before her, cradling her lower back with his powerful arms. His gaze wandered up, finding hers as she nodded. Then, he lowered his forehead to her stomach and wept.

Leila wiped a tear from her eye at her sister's joy. Marin had been too long without a child of her own; her hope too bright to never be fulfilled. Mayhap someday, Leila would have such joy, and a life with Niall.

Her heart squeezed. First, they had to get to him in time. At least with the pestilence raging through Liddesdale, the clan's forces were dwindled. That would be to her benefit.

She made her way to the armory to get a new belt and some daggers, while the rest of her family prepared for battle. She would bring Niall home to Werrick Castle safely with her, or she would die trying.

For no longer was she afraid of Death, but she was terrified of losing the man she loved.

∽

Niall would die for the offense of killing Alban.

He wriggled his foot in his boot where he'd tucked a small dagger into the high edges. Were the leather not so fitted to his ankles, he might have lost it when the reivers attacked him.

They passed under the portcullis of Liddesdale Castle with Niall trussed up like a pig for market with his wrists bound. His head ached with every step of the horse's hooves and one of his eyes had swollen nearly shut. The pressure of it was so great that he felt it might pop from its socket if he hung over the beast's back a moment longer.

The horse riding alongside his carried the body of Alban. His arms hung limp over the steed's belly, bouncing lifelessly with each jolting step.

At least Niall was in better health than Alban, small mercy though it might now be. The horse was pulled to a stop and Niall practically groaned with relief. Every part of his body throbbed.

Someone demanded Lord Armstrong be summoned at once.

Niall felt nothing at this. Not fear, not concern, not even rage.

How could one waste energy on emotions when every damn part of them was alight with pain? But he should be feeling something, especially when he had sacrificed his life with Leila to be here.

Leila.

A twinge, sharper and deeper than anything physical, cut through his agony. Two reivers approached Alban and carefully pulled his corpse from the horse. Rough hands gripped Niall's gambeson and tugged him backward, sending him crashing to the ground.

His body slammed onto the cobblestones with a force that made his teeth clack.

"What is the meaning of this?" Lord Armstrong's voice filled the bailey and echoed off the stonework.

Every reiver in sight snapped upright. Niall pulled himself up to standing as the men all looked at one another, as though silently weighing who would be the person to deliver the news of Alban's death.

Lord Armstrong's cold gray gaze found Niall. "I see they've captured ye." He tossed an irritated glance at his men. "Ye could have just brought him into the great hall. No need for me to be out in this cold to see a mere prisoner." A fiercely cutting wind swept through the bailey and he nestled back deeper into his cloak.

"It isna merely a prisoner..." A tall man with dark red hair said. He rubbed at the back of his neck.

Lord Armstrong let his gaze slide down Niall with contempt. "I assure ye, he is."

The man winced with discomfort. "'Tis yer son, my lord."

"What has that idiot done now?" Lord Armstrong muttered irritably.

"Forgive me, my lord," the guard said. "But he's dead."

Lord Armstrong straightened, as if he no longer felt the bite of the wind he'd complained of only moments before. "What did ye say?"

The tall guard lowered his head reverently. "Alban is dead. Slain by the Lion."

Lord Armstrong looked to something Niall could not see. The stricken expression on his face suggested that "something" might be Alban. He turned slowly to Niall and stared, unspeaking, for a long moment. His mouth worked wordlessly, and he swallowed before parting his lips once more.

"Ye killed my son." His gaze shifted to Alban and then back to Niall. In that single instant, the aging earl looked older than he ever had, his skin withered and lined, his eyes hollowed. It changed in an instant, with his face reddening and lips peeling back from his teeth. "Ye killed my son," he roared, the tendons at his neck straining.

Niall widened his stance, bracing himself for whatever may come. "Ye killed my da. Ye made me hold down the woman I loved and drown her."

Lord Armstrong fisted his hands and glared with wild wrath. "Guards, arrest this man." He spoke low and even and it sent a chill trickling down Niall's spine.

Niall knelt to the ground, hunkering low and tensing, intending to make it as difficult for the guards as possible. His injured thigh blazed with pain and his head swam, but he pushed the agony away.

"My da was loyal to ye. I was loyal to ye." He slipped his fingers into the lip of his boot where the leather covered his ankle. "Was it because the people wanted someone moral? Because it made ye look good to have me in yer counsel?" He pulled the dagger free. "Except I am no' as malleable as ye thought."

Niall drew his arm back and launched the dagger at Lord Armstrong. The blade sailed through the air and sank deep into

Lord Armstrong's chest.

The earl's eyes went wide with surprise, not unlike how his son's had. He looked down to the dagger jutting out from his chest.

Niall sagged back. He would be killed, he knew, but it had been worth it to see Lord Armstrong dead.

A rumbling sounded in Lord Armstrong's chest and bellowed out. Not a death cry, or a howl of agony, but a laugh.

Niall narrowed his eyes at the old man. Had the bastard lost his mind?

Lord Armstrong opened his cloak to reveal a book clutched to his chest with his right arm. The dagger had gone through the cloak and stuck in the middle of the manuscript.

"My psalter I'd brought to chapel with me." The earl lifted the stabbed book. "God isna done with me yet, and I'm no' done with ye. Guards, take him to the dungeon, while we ready the gallows. Before the sun sets, he will die." He looked back at Alban, his mirth fading to something akin to sorrow. "And dinna be gentle when ye deliver him into his cell."

Several guards rushed forward, catching Niall by the arms and drawing him upright. Lord Armstrong's fine shoes appeared on the cobblestones in Niall's line of vision. Niall tensed, expecting the old man to take a hit at his gut. But he did not. Instead, he leaned over and said in a thin, papery voice, "I'll see ye in hell, Lion."

The dagger clattered to the ground at Niall's feet, so close, yet as unobtainable as it would be if it were on the other side of the castle.

The guards who took Niall to the dungeon were mostly men who had served under him rather than being men who had fought alongside Alban previously. They were not rough with Niall as directed. They delivered him to his cell with guilty glances before sliding away into the darkness.

One man, a guard who often served under Niall, lingered behind after the others had left. Connell. He was a good man with a wife who had recently given birth to their first bairn. The younger man stared into the cell with a pained expression pinching his face. "I canna help ye," Connell said regretfully. "There is a potion I may be able to get, to dull yer senses for the—"

Niall shook his head. "Nay. Dinna put yerself at risk."

"Forgive me, Niall." Connell scratched at his thick, dark beard. "I wish there was something I could do."

"There is one thing." Niall closed his eyes, succumbing to the vibrant pain blooming in his chest. "When all has transpired and they cease saying my name, I want ye to go to Werrick Castle…" His throat drew tight and he was forced to swallow.

"Aye?" Connell asked in a soft whisper.

Niall leaned his head back on the hard stone wall, mindful of the painful throb on his right side. "Tell Lady Leila that I will always love her."

CHAPTER 25

Leila and Brodie made their way into the village before Liddesdale Castle, disguised as Armstrong guards in gambesons and helms with heavy cloaks to further mask their identity, as well as protect them against the cold. The streets bustled with considerable activity, especially in light of such dangerous times. Certainly, not a good sign.

And then, there was the incessant banging. It rang out rhythmically, ominously. Every new alley they walked down. *Bang, bang, bang.*

Every cottage they rounded. *Bang, bang, bang.*

Leila and Brodie kept their steps confident as they followed the rush of people to the center of the village. Leila's family remained in the surrounding forest while she scouted with Brodie.

Their steps were in time; even the puffs of white air exhaling from their cold lips fell into the same steady rhythm. No one seeing them would question if they were anything but guards.

They turned the corner and drew up short.

Bang, bang, bang.

And suddenly, Leila's worst suspicion about the sounds was

confirmed. There, being built in the center of the town, was a gallows.

"Brodie, is that ye?" a male voice asked.

Leila's pulse tripled, but before she could dart away, Brodie put a hand out to stop her.

"Connell, ye'll get us all killed, saying my name like that." Brodie backed behind a cottage with Connell, dragging Leila with him.

"Are ye here to free the Lion?" Connell asked in a low voice.

Brodie nodded.

"He's to be hanged after noon," Connell provided. "Most likely as soon as the gallows are done being built." His lips pressed grimly together. "There are many of us who dinna support his death. If ye mean to attack, ye'll find our forces divided. He'd have had more men on his side had he no' killed Alban, then tried to kill Lord Armstrong."

Leila bit the inside of her cheek to keep from asking questions about what the guard said. Alban was dead? By Niall's own hand?

"Niall tried to kill Lord Armstrong?" Brodie repeated.

Connell nodded solemnly. "Aye, threw a dagger at him. Would've landed right in his heart were it no' for the psalter the earl was carrying. 'Twas quite a sight to behold."

"Brodie, ye were with the lass, aye?" Connell lowered his voice further still. "The woman Niall had to drown. The men riding with Alban said they saw her alive."

"Aye." Brodie kept his tone and his demeanor casual, as though Leila wasn't at his side.

Connell's gaze slipped toward Leila in a contemplative, studying manner. She did her best not to shrink back from him. Would he accuse her of being a witch since she survived having been drowned?

"Mayhap ye can pass on a message for her," Connell said. "Tell Lady Leila, the Lion says he will always love her."

Brodie nodded. "Thank ye, Connell. I will."

"Brodie?" Connell glanced around the corner where the gallows was being erected. "Did ye know Lord Armstrong had Niall's da killed?"

Brodie nodded grimly.

"My da was killed too." Connell sniffed, his nose red in the dismal gray daylight. "When I was a lad. He'd had a disagreement with Lord Armstrong before it happened. I wonder…"

Brodie nodded. "I dinna think Niall's da is the only one of us to fall under Lord Armstrong's blade."

"At noon then, brother." Connell clasped arms with Brodie and casually strode toward the village center once more.

Brodie said nothing but turned back to the direction they'd come and together they causally made their way back to the forest. Each step took them further from Liddesdale Castle where Niall was no doubt being held in the dungeon as he awaited his death. And all the while, the sound of hammering followed them, taunting them. *Bang, bang, bang.*

Brodie and Leila made their way through the village unnoticed. A rumble of thunder sounded overhead, and a fine sifting of wet snow filtered down on them. By the time they arrived on the outskirts where her family awaited news in the forest, they were all sodden with wet snow.

Leila shook her head as she approached. "We can't go now. The castle is too heavily guarded. They intend to kill him at noon." She swallowed. "We will attack then."

Cat came to her and embraced her, something Leila wished she had not done, for it threatened to undo the composure she was working so hard to maintain.

"When they arrive at the gallows will be the best time to attack," Cat offered with reassurance.

Geordie nodded. "Aye, and Cat will be able to snap the rope with her arrow."

Brodie took off his helm. "There will be many guards, but some are no' loyal to Armstrong anymore. Seeing what he's done to Niall, what he did to Niall's da...it's raised many concerns among the men."

"It will certainly be a number we can handle." Ella ran a thumb over the edge of her battle axe. "If we thought we'd need our own soldiers, we'd have brought them."

In the interest of preventing a war, they had decided to leave the Werrick Guards at home. Liddesdale might not care for borders, but their father was still an English earl and the West March Warden who oversaw the English side of the border. War was a very real concern. One their father was willing to overlook, but they would not allow.

"Dinna worry, Leila." James ruffled her hair. "We'll get Niall safely back to ye."

Anice looked up at her husband affectionately and slid her hand into his large one. "It won't be long; noon is only an hour away."

Leila's blood raced with such energy that she dreaded the hour she'd have to wait. Interminable though it might be, it would help them overall, for it gave them more time to plan.

~

THERE WAS no sensing the time of day in the blackness of the dungeon. Niall's joints had long gone stiff with cold, though it did little to tell him the time.

Worse than the aching of his injuries from battle or the stiffness from cold were the thoughts that circled in his mind over and over and over. Or at least one thought.

Leila.

And losing her. Again. He rested his head against the wall behind him, eyes closed as if in slumber, as he sifted through his recollections of her. They started that first day in the village outside Werrick Castle, when she'd nearly killed him with a dagger to the head. He hadn't been able to stop staring at those long legs in the red leather trews, and the glossy dark hair that spilled over her shoulders like a curtain.

On and on his memories of her surfaced. Her fearlessness when he arrested her, her strength against Alban, how the hardness of her features had begun to soften around Niall. God, he loved that woman. To the depths of his soul.

And he had let *justice* get in the way of the one good thing he had. That was the worst part of his time in the dungeon: not the pain of his injuries or the fear of death looming over him. Nay, it was regret.

"'Tis time," a familiar voice said in the dark.

Niall looked up to find Lord Armstrong's face in front of his cell. The old man's face scowled down at him. "Ye killed my son. I trusted ye, and ye killed my son."

"I trusted ye, and ye killed my da," Niall spat back in return. "Ye lied to me about his death for years. Ye made me drown Leila, though ye knew her to be innocent. Ye—"

"Do it," Lord Armstrong growled as he stepped back. A guard opened Niall's door and several more guards entered the cell to haul Niall to his feet. A filthy cloth was shoved into his mouth, one tasting of the rancid fat used in tallow candles. It pressed to his tongue, cutting at the corners of his mouth, and was tied tight behind his head.

If his hands weren't bound behind his back, if his feet weren't chained, he would have been able to fight back despite his wounds. Except that they'd left him at such a disadvantage, he was at their mercy.

He was forced through the dungeon, up the stairs and

through the castle with those heavy chains at his ankles. The villagers waited outside, just past the bailey, their expressions somber as he walked by, chains clanking. He had always been well-liked among them, just as Alban had been feared and despised.

Though they did not throw mud and food at him, he remembered Leila and how she had handled her torturous walk with pride and strength. She hadn't even faulted the people for their wrath.

A drum began, low and ominous as it reverberated down his spine and thundered through his veins. His death was rapidly approaching.

The people followed him as he made his way through the streets, past the dead who lay waiting for removal, past the many homes now vacated.

The reivers stood a distance from the villagers, keeping a good amount of space between them to reduce their exposure to the great pestilence.

Niall was stopped at the stairs to the gallows and the chains at his ankles removed. He'd noted the shortness of the rope when he approached. A short rope, removing the extra weight from his person by taking off the chains... They didn't want his neck to snap when the floor of the gallows dropped. They wanted him to slowly strangle, for it to be a long, painful death.

The wind picked up and billowed the sleeves of his shirt as he climbed the stairs. A shiver wound through him and his insides quivered: with cold, with exhaustion, with fear.

Leila.

Was this what she had gone through as she had been the focus of everyone's attention? Their rapacious bloodlust made sharp and hungry by her impending death.

"Ye killed my son," Lord Armstrong said. "And now ye will die for yer crimes. May yer soul rot in hell."

Niall tried to talk, but his words were muffled by the binding at his mouth. Damn Lord Armstrong. He'd made certain Niall couldn't accuse him publicly of what he'd done. The truth of Niall's father's death would die with Niall.

The drumbeat became louder, faster, and made his heart quicken. It was time.

He was shoved to the center of the platform where lines of a trap door were visible in the wood. There would be someone beneath to pull a beam and make the door fall.

The crowd of onlookers stared back at him. Peasants with dirty faces, their eyes wide and vacant. Leila was right. They were scared. All they wanted was a cure for their families, to make the pestilence and death stop. The drum pounded faster still and left his heart racing with a frantic beat.

Thump, thump, thump.

The noose was slipped around his neck, the rope rough where it touched his skin. An icy wind blew, and he closed his eyes to savor it as the last feeling he would have in his life. He wished instead it could be the gentle caress of Leila's hand on his jaw or the brush of her sweet lips over his.

Thump, thump, thump.

Cold wind may be his last feeling, but she would be his last thought.

Forgive me, mo chridhe.

Thump, thump, thump.

The noose was drawn tight around his neck and the drum fell silent. The platform dropped from underneath him and the noose around Niall's neck went taut.

CHAPTER 26

Leila's heart caught in her throat as Niall's body dangled from the rope. "Don't miss," she whispered.

Catriona didn't say a word as the arrow flew from her bow and zipped through the air. Leila followed its path from where they hid behind one of the cottages. No doubt everyone in their party watched from their various places through the village as they all lay in wait to attack.

For this very moment.

The arrow sailed through the air, toward the rope. It slammed into the braided twine and snapped it in half.

Leila charged forward with Cat and Geordie at her side, as the rest of their party all ran into the village center to attack. The villagers fled at once for the relative safety of their homes, in as much as the waddle and dab offered protection when the walls could be so easily shoved in. Not that it mattered: the peasants were not the subject of their attack.

Her family rushed at the reivers from all angles, holding them back from the gallows as Leila ducked under its raised platform. She crouched low and launched her dagger at the man who pulled at Niall. Her dagger slammed into the man's throat and sent him reeling backward in a spurt of blood.

Leila rushed to where Niall pushed himself to his feet. Patches of cloudy sunlight shone in, casting a gray pallor within.

She cried out his name and his head jerked toward her.

She swallowed down a whimper. *His face.* His handsome face that she had cradled in her palms and gently kissed. Now mottled in bruising, one eye swollen, his lower lip split around the dirty linen tied against his mouth.

She set to work immediately drawing away the noose on his neck, freeing the cloth from his mouth.

"I thought I'd no' ever see ye again," Niall said hoarsely.

"Never." Leila pressed a kiss to his mouth as her blade sliced through the rope binding his hands behind his back. "We must hasten our leave, my love."

Outside the sounds of battle raged on. Grunts and cries, the clanging of weapons striking.

He nodded in agreement, pulled free the fallen guard's sword and together they left the underside of the gallows. Outside, her family cut through the clansmen. Each couple fought side-by-side: Anice and James as they guarded one another's backs, swords glinting in the sun; Ella with her battle axe, her rustic weapon somehow working in sync with Bronson's stylized fighting as blows were blocked and delivered. Brodie fought with Cat and Geordie, both men guarding her with slashing blades while she nocked one white-fletched arrow at a time and sent it sailing into the melee.

She only had a glance, but it was enough to see the incredible skill of so many warriors, confident, powerful, capable. Lethal. Leila wanted to be out there with them with a dagger in either hand.

But her job was the most important of all. The horses they rode in on were hidden in an abandoned cottage nearby. She need only to get there, have Niall on the horse and they would be on their way to Werrick Castle. Safe once more.

Niall grunted and pitched forward.

Leila spun around, hands going to her belt for a blade. Lord Armstrong pulled his arm back and slammed something hard across her face. She staggered, momentarily stunned by the stars dancing before her eyes. The dagger slipped from her fingers and clattered to the cobblestone, barely heard in the din of battle. It was those sounds, of fighting and dying and screaming, that had prevented her from hearing Armstrong's approach.

She continued to walk backward while she recovered, her fingers skimming her belt until they rested on the hilt of a dagger, which she quickly plucked free.

"Witch," Armstrong hissed. "I dinna actually think ye were one until this moment with ye standing before me alive even as I saw ye die."

Now armed, Leila lunged toward the older man and slashed at him with her blade. It snagged against his arm before skimming over his gambeson. At least it was a hit. He growled and switched the club he held to his other hand.

Leila aimed her dagger to throw it when Niall slashed at the older man, catching him in the gut. Lord Armstrong roared in pain and brought his cudgel down as hard as he could on Niall's thigh. The color drained from Niall's face and he collapsed to the ground, groaning in agony.

Lord Armstrong put a hand to his bloody stomach and staggered slightly. "A mortal wound." He gave a mirthless chuckle. "But I still have time to kill ye both before I die."

Leila gripped another dagger and charged again. This time, she caught the rear of his leg with her foot and shoved his torso with her full weight. He pitched backward as intended. However, as he did so, he lashed out with his cudgel.

Had she not been knocked off-balance slightly after pushing

him, she might have easily leaned away and avoided the blow. But in her haste to see him fall, she had been careless. She had assumed he would resist the attack and had put her full weight into it, leaving her unsteady.

She tried to duck away, but the edge of the club caught her in the throat. Pain exploded like a thousand stars and she could not breathe. The panic of her drowning the day before flooded her. Unable to draw in air, heart racing, water burning in her nose, her throat. More and more water.

She gasped and clutched at her throat. She fought to drag in a breath but could only pull in a scant amount. Not enough.

Burning. Her lungs were burning. She was drowning again. Being held under, water rushing into her mouth and nose.

She pushed off her helm in an attempt to get easier access to the air, gulping in as much as she could. Still not enough.

Lord Armstrong pushed himself to his feet. She should run. But her head spun with dizziness, lack of air.

God save her, she was dying all over again.

Death would claim his victim yet.

Armstrong lifted his cudgel, eyes wild. She lunged at him with the last of her strength, crashing into his gambeson. The hardened fabric was like a wall against her shoulder and face, but he fell forward over her with a savage cry.

He landed on his side on the ground with a wet gurgle. Curious though the sound was, she could not look now. She braced herself on her knees and willed herself to calm, to carefully breathe, slow and steady.

More air entered her body this time and the panic began to ebb. The fogging of her mind cleared, and she finally looked down at where Lord Armstrong lay, not moving, eyes vacant as they stared at nothing. A line of blood dribbled from the corner of his mouth and trailed a crooked path over his grizzled jaw to the dark cobblestones below.

"That was for my da." Niall limped over, wincing with each step on his injured leg. "And for the woman I love."

A dagger jutted from behind the earl's neck, having plunged through his throat.

"Your leg," Leila said.

"Ach, it was wounded when I killed Alban and this bastard hit the exact spot of the injury." Niall nudged Lord Armstrong's corpse with the toe of his bad leg.

"What in all of England are you still doing here?" an aristocratic English voice intoned.

Leila turned to see her family coming toward them. Bronson sheathed his blade. "You should have been gone already."

"Is it over?" Leila asked, her voice hoarse from the blow she'd received from that wicked club.

Ella regarded Lord Armstrong lying dead in the mud. "I'd say it is."

"Ach, the guards went running off no' long after we were into it." James grinned.

"Why are you still here?" Anice pressed. "Come, Lamb, we must leave this place."

Leila did not need to be asked twice. She gripped Niall's hand and together, they hastened to the horses. Within minutes, they were mounted and fleeing the town of Liddesdale, hopefully to never see it again, as they rode once more to Werrick Castle. With the man she loved.

⁓

THE RIDE to Werrick Castle was far more painful than Niall wanted to admit. His face ached a bit, aye, as well as the blow to his back by Armstrong's damn club.

It was his leg that burned like the fires of hell, though. The wound had been sore well before Armstrong hit it again. He kept his face impassive, however, not wanting Leila to see.

And she would have seen had he shown it, as she continued to pass glances in his direction through the duration of their trek over the English border. At long last, they came to the castle and were quickly escorted into the bailey by a troop of servants.

Niall leapt from his horse and couldn't still the grunt of pain as he landed. Leila cast him a suspicious glance.

"I'd like to take you to Isla," Leila said. "And I won't hear any argument about it."

"Is this the one who uses piss in all her remedies?" Niall asked. While he'd never met Isla, he felt as though he knew her from the stories Leila had told him in the conversations that they had shared over suppers together in her tower chamber prison.

Leila grinned and pulled him with her. "I'll make sure she doesn't use any in yours."

"I'm fine, lass," he reassured her.

"Then why are you limping?" She lifted her brows.

After such an observation, there was hardly any protest he could offer, especially since he lacked the ability to not limp. He knew. He'd tried it. Damn leg.

He was led into Werrick Castle and saw it exactly as she'd described it. Fresh rushes lent a sweet scent to the air, even in winter. Gold and silver gilt tapestries lined the walls and took the edge off the chill. Servants bustled about this way and that.

Being here, where she had lived her life, seeing what she had described to him in such perfect detail, gave him the feeling as if it was not just her who had come home, but that he had finally too. It was an odd sensation and not an unpleasant one, especially as he realized he had not felt like he had a home since his father's death.

She led him through a complicated maze of halls to where

the healer of the castle kept a neat room at the ready. Small vials were neatly lined up on top of a cabinet with many drawers. The room smelled clean and of dried herbs. Like Leila.

The comfort of that thought relaxed him, even as a withered old woman with white-gray hair approached him. Isla crinkled her amber eyes at him, studying his face. "If this is yer Lion, I hope he's bonny under all that bruising. Especially since he's caused ye a lifetime of trouble." She jerked her head to the side. "Get on the pallet."

Leila indicated a raised pallet next to a table full of bottles and Niall obediently climbed onto it. His head ached and his leg thrummed with pain, but at least he knew he'd live. Somehow, some way, he'd figure out a life with Leila where he could support her.

"I'd like to stay." Leila folded her hand into Niall's. "To help."

Isla appeared over Niall. Her lips pulled back in a grimace as she looked over him, revealing her brilliantly white, perfect teeth. "Ach, look at this leg."

She prodded at him with her bony fingers and brilliant pain seared through his wound. He ground his teeth against one another rather than cry out.

Isla tsked. "'Tis filthy and angry and will need to be cleaned before I can stitch it."

Leila tightened her grip on Niall's hand. "You know I'm strong enough to stay."

"Ye give him some of the resting tonic," Isla said. "Then be on yer way so I can see to him properly. I'll no' have ye fretting about around me."

"Resting tonic?" Niall asked.

Leila left for a moment then returned and pushed a small cup into his hand. "It'll put you out of your senses, so you don't feel all the pain. Isla recently concocted it and it appears to be quite effective."

Niall sniffed it and wished he hadn't. "What's in it?"

Isla set her fingertips to the underside of the cup and tipped it upward. "A bit o' this, a bit o' that."

He held his breath and tossed it back. It was a bitter brew indeed. The terrible taste clung to his tongue and stung his eyes. He choked, his body wincing with each flex of his muscles. Dear God, his back ached. "What was in that?" he gasped.

Leila took the cup from him, looked in it and nodded at Isla.

"Fine," Isla conceded. "Hemlock, opium, vinegar and a bit of heifer's piss."

Niall sputtered.

"I made this last bottle last month," Leila whispered. "Without the heifer's piss."

"Bah! Ye dinna appreciate the benefits of a fine blending of piss in a tonic." Isla waved dismissively, clearly having overheard. "Off with ye now. Ye know how nasty tending to a hot wound can be."

Leila rested a hand gently on his shoulder. "Please, Isla."

"I'm no' giving ye a choice." Isla pointed to Niall. "Look at him, he doesna care a whit anyway."

Leila and Isla both peered at him. Odd that they would do so together like that. Foolish, really. Almost comical. He'd laugh if he had the energy, but he suddenly found he didn't possess even the amount to lift his lips. Not that it mattered.

The air rushed into and out of his lungs, a strange sensation when one focused on it. Especially when one was so tired.

"Off with ye now," Isla said from the distance. "I'll summon ye when it's done." She approached him and pulled open an eyelid with her cool fingers. Belatedly, he realized it was his bad eye, the one which was nearly swollen shut. "Heifer's piss would've made it work better," she muttered indignantly. With that, she took a pair of shears and cut away his trews.

He should stop the old woman. He didn't have another pair

of trews with him. But it was more than that. The space beside him was empty without Leila.

"Dinna worry, lad, she'll be there when ye wake." Isla nodded her head at him. "Close yer eyes now." She glanced down at his leg. "Ye dinna want to be awake for this."

His eyes slipped closed, and he imagined Leila sitting at his side as sleep took him away.

However, when he opened his eyes, it was not Leila sitting beside him, but Lord Werrick. A quick glance around the room confirmed they were alone.

Niall shifted on the small pallet and a twinge of discomfort pinched at his thigh. He looked down to find a swath of linen bound over it.

"I heard it was pretty bad," Lord Werrick said. "Isla is a strong healer. I am certain you will recover without issue."

"Did she wash it out with heifer's piss?" Niall asked.

To his surprise, Lord Werrick laughed. "I don't think Leila would have allowed that, but it wouldn't surprise me if she'd wanted to."

Niall flicked an uneasy glance at the Earl of Werrick, the West March Warden of the English side of the border—a powerful man whose daughter Niall had killed. Even more than that, the father of the woman he loved.

"I love her," Niall said.

Lord Werrick's eyes crinkled into a smile. "Aye, I know."

"I dinna have a choice in killing her." Niall drew in a pained breath. "I would have rather it had been me that day in the river."

Lord Werrick's expression became more somber. "Aye, I know. But you saved her. What's more, you brought her home." The earl glanced toward the door. "She'll be back soon. You slept longer than expected and Marin demanded she take a reprieve for some food."

Niall's chest lightened with the thought of seeing Leila again. Now that Lord Armstrong and Alban were dead. Now that they were safely back at Werrick Castle.

A flicker of nervousness fluttered through Niall's veins. "Before she comes back, my lord, I'd like to ask ye something."

Lord Werrick leaned forward with his elbows on his knees, his face expectant, as if he already knew the question. And mayhap he did. If so, Niall hoped it would be to his benefit.

"I'm in love with yer daughter," Niall said. "As I've said."

Lord Werrick nodded.

Niall cleared his throat. "I'd like to wed her. With yer permission." He tensed for the earl's reply, expecting questions about Leila's safety, about how Niall anticipated making a living now that he'd killed his employer, about what sort of alliance Niall might bring with him.

Lord Werrick straightened and answered without hesitation, "Aye, you have it. But I've a question for you."

Niall couldn't help the grin pulling at his lips. "Aye?"

"How do you plan to support my daughter?" Lord Werrick arched a brow.

Niall's smile wilted. He'd considered that on the painful ride back to Werrick. The question had been a burr in the back of his brain, digging in with spiny thorns. And he had no good answer to offer Lord Werrick.

"I will manage something. But I dinna yet have a plan," Niall said honestly. ". I can promise ye I'll do anything to ensure she is well cared for."

"Anything?" Lord Werrick folded his long, slender hands together. "Including considering a position as Captain of the Guard for Werrick Castle?"

Niall blinked in surprise. "Ye'd hire me as yer Captain of the Guard? And still allow me to wed yer daughter?"

The earl nodded. "Your reputation is well-known. You're a

good man, Lion. I would be honored to have you lead my men. And regarding your station and your ability to still wed my daughter...Marin taught me a long time ago that love does not see wealth or position. I want my daughters to be happy above all else." He leaned forward and patted Niall's shoulder. "I've never seen Leila light up at anything the way she lights up when she speaks of you."

Niall's chest went warm at such words, to hear from another's lips how much Leila truly did love him. "Aye," he replied. "I'm honored to be yer Captain of the Guard."

"I'm pleased to hear it." Lord Werrick squeezed his shoulder and released him. "Then I'll show you to your chamber, so you can freshen up a bit and then ask my daughter for her hand in marriage."

"I'd like that verra much," Niall said gratefully and got to his feet, eager for the moment he could see Leila again. And ask her to be his wife.

CHAPTER 27

Leila swiped clean the last bite of stew with a bit of bread and popped it into her mouth.

"Doesn't that feel better?" Nan asked with a proud smile on her face.

"Aye," Leila agreed. "This is some of the best food I've eaten since my capture."

"Ach, don't speak of it." Nan's eyes went glossy and she dabbed at them with the corner of her apron. "I couldn't bear to think of you trapped there with such terrible food and horrible conditions." She rushed over and wrapped her large arms around Leila. "I was so worried about you."

"I'm fine now," Leila said when Nan released her. "More than fine now that Niall is here."

"I'm so happy for you, child." Nan ran an affectionate hand down Leila's clean hair.

She was glad she'd taken Marin's advice and bathed while she was waiting for Isla to finish with Niall. But now after cleaning up and eating food, she wanted nothing more than to be with him again, to ensure he didn't have pain after being stitched up. More than anything, she just wanted to see him again and revel in the timbre of his warm voice.

"Off with you now." Nan shooed Leila from the kitchen. "Go see to your man."

Leila didn't need to be told twice and rushed to the healing room. Except when she opened the door, she found the pallet empty and Isla sorting through a stack of dried herbs.

She looked up as Leila entered the room. "That man of yers did fine and is already in his own chamber getting ready to see ye." She winked. "Are ye well, lass? Do ye have any injuries I need to see to?"

"Nay," Leila answered readily, but hesitated to leave. "Or rather, my body is fine." She looked down at her hands. "I think...mayhap I have lost the sight."

Isla considered, her thoughtful forehead furrowed into a map of crinkles. "Sometimes such things work in curious ways," Isla said carefully. "Ye had visions long enough to save yer family from the pestilence. And ye fulfilled yer own destiny when ye met the Lion."

Leila nodded slowly as she processed what Isla had said. She had been able to save her family. Of that, she was grateful. The more she'd thought on it though, the stranger it seemed to not have visions, especially when it had been part of her for so long.

"Do you think they will come back?" she asked.

Isla smiled sadly. "I dinna know, lass."

Leila chewed her lip. "I don't even know if I want them back."

"'Tis been yer burden to bear for yer entire life." Isla approached and took Leila's hand in her cool, dry one. "Ye'll just have to live life like the rest of us, no' knowing what will come next."

"I like the sound of that," Leila said. And she did. To not be plagued by terrible dreams of the past or see terrible things in the future she feared telling others about. To live a normal life.

"Go on to yer man." Isla winked at her. "I imagine he's waiting on ye."

Leila hugged Isla, then made her way to the chamber set aside for Niall and rapped softly on the door.

"Aye?" Niall called out.

"'Tis Leila."

The door swung open immediately and there he was: the Lion. His gold hair hung in damp waves and he wore only a linen shirt over a pair of trews that appeared to be too short and ill-fitted.

"Leila." He gave her a lopsided grin and opened the door wider to allow her to come in. He closed the door behind her. "I suppose this isna proper." Leila rose on her tiptoes to kiss him. "I don't care about proper."

He lowered his head and caught her in his arms, kissing her bottom lip, then her top lip, then her whole mouth, as if he was savoring her. Her moan hummed between them.

"I need to ask ye something." Niall straightened.

There was a seriousness to his expression that made Leila tense with concern. "Is everything all right?"

Niall took her hands in his and gazed down at her. "I canna imagine ye no' being in my life. I want to build a home with ye here and have bairns of our own together. I dinna ever want to be separated from ye again." His brows knit together with sincerity. "Leila, *mo chridhe,* will ye marry me?"

Her heart caught midbeat. Words failed her as she stared up at the man that she loved more than life itself. In the time they had known one another, she had hated him and loved him, she had feared she'd lost him several times over and he had killed her and saved her.

And now, there was this new moment, as he asked for her hand in marriage.

"I'll be yer da's new Captain of the Guard," Niall said. "We'll be able to stay at Werrick Castle where ye can help Isla and the people of the village. If that's what ye want."

"Aye," she said finally.

He grinned. "Then we'll stay in Werrick Castle."

"I mean, 'aye', as in I'll marry you." Leila laughed with joy.

He beamed at her and pulled his lower lip into his mouth where it had been split, as if the act of smiling so broadly hurt. "Ye've made me the happiest man in all of Christendom."

"Thank you for making me overcome my fear of you." Leila gazed at Niall. "For letting me see how wonderful you are, so that I could love you."

She kissed his mouth, careful of his cut lip. She ran a finger over it. "I think I have some heifer's piss that might help with this."

"Nay, thank ye." He chuckled and pressed a kiss to her lips. "I love ye."

"And I love you." She stroked a hand down his face, reveling in the way his golden whiskers rasped against her palm.

His lips moved over hers again, deepening the kiss with the sweep of his tongue. Leila moaned again and leaned her body against his.

Remembering his wounds, she arched back. "I don't want to hurt you."

He pulled her to him once more with his strong arms. "If I have to suffer a moment longer without ye, it'll hurt me far more than this damned leg."

She melted into his embrace and allowed him to lead her to the large bed set against the back wall of the chamber. This would be the first day of their future together. A future Leila found she was glad she couldn't see. She wanted to relish each day as it came, like a wrapped parcel to be opened and discovered and enjoyed. Together.

～

THE WEDDING TOOK LESS than a fortnight to prepare. With all her sisters and their husbands already assembled at Werrick Castle, the preparations were quickly done.

They had all wisely left their children safely at home, despite taking their own risks in traveling to Werrick Castle, risks Leila appreciated but did not condone. While the sisters enjoyed being with one another, all of them were eager to get back to their families.

The day of the wedding, all the sisters gathered in the room they had grown up sharing. The room that had once seemed large enough to house them all, and which had even seemed cavernous when Leila had been left alone, was now cramped with kirtles and ribbons as well as chatter and laughter. They had dressed Leila in a violet silk gown with silver thread flowers stitched along the generous skirt and down the sleeves, all by Marin's own hand.

Once they had finished plucking at and combing and smoothing her, they all stepped back to regard her, tears glistening in their eyes. "You look lovely," Marin said in a choked voice. Her palm rested tenderly over her stomach, where it often remained, protectively cradling her babe every moment her hands were free.

"I'm so pleased to have you all here with me," Leila said around the tightness in her throat. "It was so dangerous for you to travel to Werrick in such treacherous times. Too dangerous. But I..." She swallowed down her emotion. "I cannot imagine this day without all of you with me."

A flurry of hugging and well-wishes ensued, and they were

nearly ready to make their way to the chapel. Before they left, Marin awkwardly paused and put a hand to Leila's shoulder. "Leila, dear, do you need to be..." Her cheeks flushed pink. "...instructed on the wedding night?"

Leila's own face went hot at the question and she brusquely shook her head.

The tension drained from Marin's face. "Thanks be to God. Your sister made the discussion quite a task for me before." She gave Anice a pointed stare. "I didn't relish the idea of going through that again."

"You were wrong on the battle axe bit though." Anice grinned.

Marin's mouth fell open. "You are so wicked." She laughed and hurtled a pillow at Anice, which Anice plucked from the air.

"What's this talk of battle axes?" Ella perked up.

"Nothing," Anice and Marin said at once as they shared a smile.

"I think it might be better not to know." Cat gave an exaggerated grimace and they all laughed again.

Anice ran a hand down Leila's hair, smoothing it one final time. "'Tis time, Lamb. Are you ready?"

Leila lifted her chin and beamed at her sisters with all the excitement glowing inside her. "I've been ready my whole life."

She followed her sisters out of the room, and then hesitated in the doorway before turning back to look at their shared room one last time. She had felt alone so often in there when she'd been younger, even as she was surrounded by her sisters.

Now, however, she knew that loneliness to be of her own making, her own guilt for something she could not control.

A warm hand slipped into hers and Leila looked up to find Cat grinning down at her. "Come on, or you'll be late for your own wedding." She caught Leila in a great, exuberant hug, the kind only Cat could give, and the two ran off toward their sisters.

Together, they all made their way down to Werrick Castle's chapel.

For the first time, Leila realized she truly did belong with them and that she always had.

~

NIALL WAITED at the front of the chapel, beside the twitchy priest who had heard his confession prior to the wedding. The very same priest that had pissed himself during questioning when Niall was initially seeking out Leila for charges of witchcraft. That had been a lifetime ago, or so it felt. And though Bernard cast furtive little glances at Niall in nervousness, the priest had absolved Niall of his sins.

The pews were full of Werrick Castle's inhabitants. Nan sat beside Edmund, the butcher, and his son, already mopping at tears. The Master of the Horse, Peter, and his wife, Freya, and their children were there as well.

On and on, Niall could name and share at least something personal about each one. He'd spent the last fortnight learning all the various servants who lived at Werrick Castle and had realized Leila's family was not limited only to her father and sisters, but all the people within the castle.

Isla was one of the last people to enter. She nodded to Bernard as she took her seat and he nodded to her in return, their greeting one of old friends. From what Leila had told him, their amicable relationship was new and had been a direct result of her care of the priest after Niall's questioning. So, at least there had been something positive to arise from it.

The doors swung open and Leila's golden-haired sisters swept into the room and took their seats next to their husbands, opting to sit below with everyone else rather than on the raised platform at the rear. Her family occupied the front pews, along with Brodie and Bonnie.

Niall's heartbeat quickened.

And there she was. Leila in a lovely purple gown with her dark hair unbound and flowing around her shoulders. Bits of heather had been woven together and set upon her head, and a smile lit her face.

Pride swelled in Niall's chest. This woman would be his wife.

She strode slowly to the altar, graceful and lovely. More women joined Nan in crying, and someone gave a honking blow to her nose. Most likely Nan, but Niall wasn't looking at Werrick's cook, or anyone else—not with Leila joining him in front of the chapel.

"Nervous?" he asked.

She grinned and shook her head. "You?"

"Nay." He took her hand in his and Bernard proceeded with the wedding. Through it all, Niall kept his fingers linked with Leila's, speaking every word of his vows with the whole of his heart and soul until at last, they were declared man and wife.

He drew her into his arms and lowered his mouth to hers in a tender kiss that elicited cheers from the congregation.

Lord Werrick and Rose approached them first, all smiles and joy, with the two children that Rose had rescued, Joan and John, hovering close behind them. The remainder of the family quickly joined them, followed by the rest of Werrick Castle's occupants.

Once felicitations had been given, they all made their way to the great hall to celebrate. Leila leaned close to Niall. "I'm glad I never saw our wedding in my future," she whispered.

He raised a brow.

"I got to experience it for the first time this moment." Tears sparkled in her eyes. "And it was beautiful. I'm so happy."

Happy.

It was a word he had not considered being part of his own future. He had success with what he did; he had a comfortable life. But happy?

Nay. Not like this, not with that tickle of joy that warmed his chest every time he looked at Leila. Every time he thought of her.

"The future surprised us both," he replied. "And I'm just as glad as ye are for it."

He pulled his new wife close, caressed the softness of her cheek, the line of her jaw, then gently, tenderly kissed her. He released her and took her hand. A soft flush stole over her face as she smiled up at him. "I'm looking forward to learning each new, unexpected day with you."

"As am I," Niall replied. For they had a lifetime of kisses to look forward to, and new days and everything each one would bring. They would experience it all together.

EPILOGUE
MARCH 1350, BRAMPTON, ENGLAND

Good news was always best when it came in threes. And so it was at Werrick Castle. Leila rushed about, making the final preparations for the wedding to take place later on that afternoon.

After all, it was not every day one's father finally remarried.

A touch of nausea teased at Leila's awareness, but she set it aside, not having time to bother with it. A pack of children rushed toward her with Gavin at the front, Anice's twelve-year-old son, who already was showing the authoritative leadership of his father as he led his band of miscreants.

"To the kitchens," Gavin called to his cousins behind him.

Ella's daughter, Blanche, followed quickly behind him, her green eyes alight with excitement. "I could smell the pastries this morning. I know she has some."

"Pastries?" Little Eversham piped up. Cat's youngest rubbed his hands together and grinned. "Oh, I like pastries very much."

"So do we," cried Joan and John together in unison. They had plumped up with good health from the thin, ill children Leila had first seen in the village when she feared they would die from the great pestilence.

An elegant girl with curling brown hair walked swiftly to keep after them, obviously attempting to keep from running indoors as her cousins did. Cat's eldest, Evelyn, tutted. "We mustn't get in the way."

Leila caught Gavin by the arm and spun him playfully about as he passed. "The kitchens, you say?"

His blue eyes sparkled. "Aye, Nan promised us a treat."

Even little Bonnie grinned excitedly at this. She and Brodie had settled easily into life at Werrick Castle.

"If you go, you must stay out of the way," Leila cautioned. "In to get them and straight back out again."

They all nodded solemnly at her.

"If we're good at the wedding, will you show us how to throw knives?" Blanche asked.

Leila made a show of considering their request.

Blanche fluttered her long lashes and gave a smile so endearing, it nearly crumbled Leila's resolve. "Please, Aunt Leila."

"I'll speak to your mothers about it." It was as good an answer as Leila could muster under such endearing persuasion.

"Off with you now, and mind you stay out of the way." Leila tilted her head down the hall.

They all ran off toward the kitchens for their promised pastries. Even Evelyn, though she did pause to tuck Eversham's little hand into hers first.

"We'll have one of those soon." Niall's warm voice pulled Leila's attention behind her. "Did the herbs Isla gave ye help at all?"

"Aye, they did." In fact, they'd minimized the nausea so well that Leila had asked her what was in it. Fortunately, it was absent any heifer's piss. But then, Leila had sniffed it beforehand as a precaution. After so many years of working with Isla, Leila would have known the distinctly sharp odor at once.

She grinned at him as Niall pulled her into his arms. "Do you think we'll have a boy or a girl?"

Niall set his hand to the small bump of Leila's lower stomach and looked pensive. "Feels like..."

Leila raised her brows in expectation. The babe had been an unexpected and wonderful surprise. She knew children were a possibility when they wed, of course. But after having spent her life thinking she would be slain early in life, never once had she considered she might have a child of her own. Now though, the idea was seeded deeply in her heart and she thanked God every day for the child growing in her womb.

"Feels like a wee babe growing." He shrugged. "I wasna ever good at knowing the future."

Leila laughed and kissed her husband. "Nor am I anymore." She'd grown used to no longer having visions. Her sleep was deep and uninterrupted and the constant worry that had shrouded most of her life had finally lifted.

"All of Werrick's soldiers are prepared for the wedding celebration of a lifetime." Niall winked. "Any attack would be thwarted immediately without any of us being the wiser."

She beamed up at her husband. He had excelled at his role as Captain of the Guard. Every one of his men respected him, first by his reputation and then by his treatment of them. He did not expect his men to do what he would not do himself.

His experience with reivers in the chaotic world of Liddesdale brought an edge to fighting that Werrick's soldiers had never implemented before. It made them all better, stronger, more confident. Aye, Werrick Castle was in good hands for such a grand wedding feast, especially with Brodie in charge of the men in Niall's absence.

"I remember our own wedding." Niall nuzzled Leila's face with his, his face scraped smooth. "And our wedding night." His mouth found hers. "I love ye, *mo chridhe*."

"And I love you." Leila kissed him again. And again. And again. "Nay." She put a hand to his chest. "We don't have time."

"But we will later." He grinned.

She kissed him once more and strode away. "I have to see to my father."

Niall winked at her and headed in the opposite direction to finalize his own preparations.

Leila found her father walking out of Rose's chamber, of all places. He opened his arms when he saw Leila.

"Father, you aren't supposed to see your bride before the ceremony." She went into his arms and embraced him.

He released her with a shrug. "I'm too old for convention, Daughter. And she sent a maid for me to come and offer my opinion on her hair. Who am I to deny the woman soon to be my bride?"

"I'm so glad you've found such happiness," Leila said earnestly. It had been a sweet thing to watch the love blossom between her father and Rose. What had come from Rose's aid while she helped heal him had developed into a beautiful bond that left Rose's cheeks flushed and her eyes sparkling every time Lord Werrick was near.

And likewise, Leila had not seen her father smile so readily in many, many years. One day she noted the sadness that lined his eyes had lightened and she knew it was all Rose's doing.

"Have you seen Joan and John?" Father asked. "The rapscallions have disappeared."

"Running about with your wild grandchildren and Bonnie in search of pastries," Leila replied.

Lord Werrick nodded and chuckled affectionately. "Aye, that sounds like them."

"Leila," Cat cried out from down the hall. "Papa! Come quickly! She's here!"

Leila's heart gave a leap of excitement. "Marin's here," she whispered eagerly. She had delivered a healthy baby boy nearly seven months ago. They'd all kept their distance as the last of the great pestilence died out for fear of bringing danger to their doorstep. After the years Marin and Bran had waited for their miracle, no one wanted to offer the least bit of risk.

Now she was at Werrick Castle and they would meet the babe. Finally.

Leila and her father made their way swiftly to the great hall to find Bran and Marin standing together, gazing down at a bundled babe sleeping in her arms. Anice, Ella and Cat were already there, quietly observing the baby.

Marin had a soft smile on her lips, her attention fixed on her child. The contented joy of Leila's eldest sister seemed to glow and fill the entire room.

Tears immediately warmed Leila's eyes.

Marin looked up with the most beautiful smile Leila had ever seen. "Leila, this is your nephew, Nicholas."

The child in Marin's arms was perfect. Chubby rosy cheeks, a mouth that puckered in mock nursing even as he slept and a fuzz of downy blond hair on his perfectly round head.

"Oh, Marin," Leila breathed. "He's beautiful."

"I love him so much." Marin's voice broke and her eyes misted with tears of her own. "I am so grateful for him every day."

"I know." Leila gently squeezed her sister's shoulders.

A black cat slinked from the shadows and trotted over to Bran to wind between his feet.

"Ach, there ye are, Bixby." Bran lifted the cat into his arms and a low vibrating purr filled the air. "I missed ye too, ye wee beast."

Bixby simply lifted his chin and squinted his eyes shut in pleasure.

Niall entered the great hall and made his way toward them.

"Ach, what a sweet wee bairn." He gazed tenderly down at Marin's new son and cast a secret glance in Leila's direction.

They were waiting to tell everyone their own good news until after the wedding. Today was for Marin to introduce her son, and for Rose and Father to celebrate their union.

"I think all is ready," Niall said. "Or at least, so says Bernard." He turned his attention to Bran. "Yer timing is perfect. The servants can tend to yer things while we're at the chapel."

"We would have arrived sooner, but *someone* made us stop every few moments." Marin cast a teasing glance up at Bran.

"I might be a bit of a worrier when it comes to my family." He gave a roguish grin. "But I'll kick the arse of any man that dares call me that."

Marin chuckled and shook her head at her husband.

Nan appeared in the doorway and put her hands to her mouth. "Ach, Lady Marin." She rushed over to her, cooing over the sleeping Nicholas. "I was told to summon everyone to the chapel and look here at what I find."

Niall gallantly offered Leila his arm. "Can I walk ye to the chapel, my beautiful wife?"

She accepted his offer and slipped her hand against the strong warmth of his arm. He led her to the chapel, where the pews quickly filled with family and friends close enough to be family themselves.

Rose was beautiful in a pale pink gown with her red hair hanging in glossy waves down her back. Lord Werrick looked regal as he made his way down the aisle in a new doublet with gilt edging and a sparkle in his eyes that warmed Leila's heart.

And as they listened to the vows being spoken, Leila's heart swelled to near-bursting. The border between Scotland and England was seldom one of joy or security and yet her family had found both. Even as their lives had been shadowed by sorrow for so many years, now happiness shone down upon them.

The dangerous lands made for precarious living, and yet through it all, love found each and every one of them. And they would all, as Ella put it in her stories, live happily ever after.

ALSO BY MADELINE MARTIN

Wedding a Wallflower

The Earl's Hoyden

The Borderland Ladies

Ena's Surrender

Marin's Promise

Anice's Bargain

Ella's Desire

Catriona's Secret

Leila's Legacy

The Borderland Rebels

The Highlander's Lady Knight

Faye's Sacrifice

Kinsey's Defiance

Clara's Vow

Drake's Honor

Highland Passions

The Highlander's Challenge

A Ghostly Tale of Forbidden Love

The Madam's Highlander

Her Highland Destiny

The Highlander's Untamed Lady

Matchmaker of Mayfair

Discovering the Duke

Unmasking the Earl

Mesmerizing the Marquis

Earl of Benton

Earl of Oakhurst

Earl of Kendal

Heart of the Highlands

Deception of a Highlander

Possession of a Highlander

Enchantment of a Highlander

Standalones

Her Highland Beast

ABOUT THE AUTHOR

Madeline Martin is a *New York Times, USA Today,* and International Bestselling author of historical fiction and historical romance with books that have been translated into over twenty different languages.

She lives in sunny Florida with her two daughters (known collectively as the minions), two incredibly spoiled cats and a man so wonderful he's been dubbed Mr. Awesome. She is a die-hard history lover who will happily lose herself in research any day. When she's not writing, researching or 'moming', you can find her spending time with her family at Disney or sneaking a couple spoonfuls of Nutella while laughing over cat videos. She also loves research and travel, attributing her fascination with history to having spent most of her childhood as an Army brat in Germany.

Check out her website for book club visits, reader guides for her historical fiction, upcoming events, book news and more: https://madelinemartin.com